R ... ..ie *New York Times* best...
th...... ...al Spyness Series, Molly Murphy Mysten.
Constable Evans. She is a recipient of the Agatha Best Novel
Award and an Edgar Best Novel nominee.

Praise for Rhys Bowen

'The latest addition to Molly's case files offers a charming combination of history, mystery, and romance.' *Kirkus
Reviews* on *Hush Now, Don't You Cry*

'Engaging . . . Molly's compassion and pluck should attract
more readers to this consistently solid historical series.'
Publishers Weekly on *Bless the Bride*

'Winning . . . The gutsy Molly, who's no prim Edwardian
miss, will appeal to fans of contemporary female detectives.'
Publishers Weekly on *The Last Illusion*

'This historical mystery delivers a top-notch, detail-rich
story full of intriguing characters. Fans of the 1920s private
detective Maisie Dobbs should give this series a try.' *Booklist*
on *The Last Illusion*

'Details of Molly's new cases are knit together with the
accoutrements of 1918 New York City life. . . . Don't miss
this great period puzzler reminiscent of Dame Agatha's mys-
teries and Gillian Linscott's Nell Bray series.' *Booklist* on *In
a Gilded Cage*

Queen of Hearts
Malice at the Palace

Time of Fog and Fire

Rhys Bowen

Constable • London

CONSTABLE

First published in the USA in 2016 by Minotaur Books,
an imprint of St Martin's Press, New York

This edition published in the UK in 2016 by Constable

1 3 5 7 9 10 8 6 4 2

Copyright © Rhys Bowen, 2016

1 3 5 7 9 10 8 6 4 2

The moral right of the author has been asserted.

A CIP catalogue record for this book
is available from the British Library.

ISBN 978-1-47211-891-2 (paperback)
ISBN: 978-1-47212-052-6 (ebook)

Typeset in Berthold Baskerville by TW Type, Cornwall
Printed and bound in Great Britain by Clays Ltd, St Ives plc
Papers used by Constable are from well-managed forests and other responsible sources

Constable
is an imprint of
Little, Brown Book Group
Carmelite House
50 Victoria Embankment
London EC4Y 0DZ

An Hachette UK Company
www.hachette.co.uk

www.littlebrown.co.uk

This book is dedicated to my friend, touring partner, and writer extraordinaire Cara Black. Thank you for turning book tours into fun adventures.

Also as always a big thank-you to my agents, Meg and Christina, and my team at Minotaur, Kelley, Sarah, and Elizabeth. And to John for being my first (and most critical) editor as well as my chauffeur, bodyguard, and travel companion.

❧ Prologue ❧

North Texas, Spring 1895

A fierce wind swept down from the north across the desolate landscape with nothing to stop it except for the barbed wire fence that had trapped the tumbleweed. He turned his back on it, shielding his eyes from the harsh light as he stared out across flat nothingness.

"Are you sure this is the right spot?" he asked.

"I'm sure." The other was a man of few words, talking through clenched teeth to keep out the grit and dust in the wind. They stood together, the prospector and the city slicker, saying nothing for a while. Staring together at featureless scrub with not a tree or bush in sight.

"And there is nothing? You're sure there's nothing?"

The other shook his head. "Not a trace. Sorry."

"Then I've been hoodwinked." The first man spat out the words.

"You and a lot of others, pal."

"He won't get away with this, you know."

"I'd like to bet you he will. Ain't got your big-city law out here, pal.

That guy is long gone and I bet he's spending your sweet cash right this minute."

"Not all of it," the man said. "I wasn't a complete fool. I have ways of finding him and when I've hunted him down, I'm going to kill him."

"Good luck," the other said. "You're going to need it."

The Texan turned and started to walk away, his cowboy boots leaving neat and distinct prints on the dry crust.

❧ One ❧

New York City, March 1906

It had been an unsettled spring, both in the weather and in my life. We had experienced an early warm spell that encouraged blossoms and narcissus to appear, birds to chirp loudly in mating calls, and New Yorkers to cast off layers of clothing and emerge from hibernation. Even the beggars and crossing sweepers managed a smile and a cheeky reply for the odd coin. Then no sooner than March had come in like a lamb it turned into a lion, blasting us with frigid winds that stripped blossom from trees and then with snow that sent us all scuttling indoors again.

My own life had been just as unpredictable and unsettled as the weather. We had started the year with Daniel still recovering from a bullet wound, shot as he tried to stop a new and keen recruit from taking on that dreadful new Italian gang called the Cosa Nostra. Daniel had survived but it had cost the young recruit his life. To make things worse the current police commissioner did not like Daniel. He and his cronies at Tammany Hall found Daniel too straight for them, not willing to toe the party line, and not open to the occasional bribe. So I suspect they'd been looking for a way to get rid of him, which wasn't easy as he was one of New York's most respected police captains. But while he was out recovering from a bullet in his shoulder dark forces had been at work, trying to besmirch his name when he was not around to defend himself. Some unknown source had spread the rumor that Daniel had ordered the young recruit to go and arrest the boss of the Cosa Nostra—a foolhardy move, as he surrounded himself with more bodyguards than the emperor of China. The truth had been quite the opposite. Daniel had found out what the young man planned to do and rushed after him. Unfortunately Daniel couldn't stop him in time and he had been shot and killed. Daniel had taken the second bullet himself, but survived. But now half the police force believed Daniel was to blame. My husband, as responsible and brave a man as you could ever meet, was desperately unhappy about this and unable to set things straight. Now, for the first time, he talked about resigning, about becoming a lawyer or going into politics as his mother had been suggesting. I hated to see him silent and brooding, picking at his meals, hardly noticing his young son. It had almost reached a stage when I was tempted to go down to that police headquarters myself and give them a piece of my mind.

Luckily it didn't come to that because John Wilkie came back into our lives. As the wife of a police captain, I suppose I should have learned not to be surprised by any unexpected twists of fate. But opening the front door and finding John Wilkie on the doorstep certainly caused my jaw to drop. For one thing it's not every day that the head of the U.S. Secret Service comes to visit, and for another, we had not parted on the best of terms the last time I had encountered him. When I found out he had used me as bait to catch my brother, who had come to America trying to raise money for the Irish Republican Brotherhood, I had not been able to contain my anger. The result had been my brother's death, for which I blamed John Wilkie.

Mr. Wilkie seemed to have forgotten this unpleasant episode as I opened my front door onto our quiet little backwater called Patchin Place to see him standing there on a blustery March evening. Snowflakes swirled around him and it took me a second or two to recognize him, muffled as he was in a big red scarf.

"Good evening, Mrs. Sullivan," he said, extending a gloved hand. "It's good to see you again."

"Mr. Wilkie," I replied, not returning his smile. "This is an unexpected pleasure."

"I hope I don't call at an inopportune moment," he said.

"Not at all. I take it this is not a social call on such a cold and miserable New York evening?"

He smiled then. His mouth was still hidden under the scarf but I saw his eyes smile. "I hoped for a quiet word with your husband. Is he home?"

"He is just finishing his dinner," I said. "Won't you come in and I'll go and tell him you're here."

I had just closed the front door behind him when Daniel came out of the kitchen, wiping the corners of his mouth with his napkin. It had been Irish stew for dinner, Daniel's favorite.

"Who was that at the front door, Molly?" he asked, then I saw his eyes register surprise. "Mr. Wilkie. This is an unexpected honor, sir. Let me help you off with your overcoat. And Molly, would you be good enough to take Mr. Wilkie's gloves, hat, and scarf?"

We divested Mr. Wilkie of his outer garments.

"I'm afraid we've no fire in the front parlor so it will have to be the back parlor, which also serves as my study these days, now that all the bedrooms are occupied," Daniel said as he led Mr. Wilkie down the hall.

John Wilkie smiled. "Of course. You need a nursery now, don't you? You've had a child since I saw you last. Boy or girl?"

"A boy," I said. "He's eighteen months old now. We called him Liam, after my dead brother."

I saw Daniel shoot me a warning look, but Mr. Wilkie seemed unaffected by my comment. Perhaps he had already forgotten how my brother died. Perhaps he didn't care.

"Congratulations," he said. "A fine son to start your family."

"Can we offer you something to drink, Mr. Wilkie?" Daniel said as he paused to turn up the gaslight in the back parlor. "I believe I've still got decent whiskey left, or I'm sure Molly would be happy to make you coffee or tea."

"I wouldn't say no to the whiskey."

"Then please take a seat near the fire and I'll see what we can do," Daniel said. He looked at me again. "Molly, could you bring us two glasses?"

That was indeed making it clear that I was not to be included in the conversation, especially since Mr. Wilkie said nothing as he pulled up a chair to the fire. Fair enough, I thought. The further I kept away from John Wilkie's kind of business, the better. I went back to the kitchen, where Liam was protesting about sitting in his high chair when there was clearly company in the house, and Bridie, the young girl I had brought across from Ireland all those years ago, was starting to clear the table. She was currently living with us so that she could go to school in the city, and was proving to be a grand little helper.

"Leave those for now, Bridie love," I said. "Could you take Liam out of his chair and get him ready for bed? Captain Sullivan has a visitor."

She put down the plates she was stacking. "Come on, Liam," she said. "We're going to get you ready for bed."

Liam let out a wail. "Mama," he cried.

"Bedtime, young man," I said firmly. "And if you're good Bridie will tell you the Three Bears story and then Dada will come up to tuck you in."

Bridie carried him upstairs, still protesting. But then she whispered something in his ear and he smiled at her. She was becoming quite the little mother, I thought. So grown-up. Ready to blossom into womanhood. I took two of our good glasses from the cupboard, wiped them clean, added a dish of cheese straws I'd baked the day before, and carried them through on a tray.

As I opened the door Daniel was saying, "I admit you're not wrong about what your spies tell you and I think I might be wise to look for . . ."

Conversation was broken off as I came in. I placed the tray on Daniel's desk. "Is there anything else I can get you before I go to put Liam to bed?" I asked.

"No, thank you. It's very kind of you, Mrs. Sullivan," Mr. Wilkie said.

"I'll leave you then." I went out and closed the door behind me. In the past Mr. Wilkie had told me I was a fine detective and wanted to recruit me to work for him, but clearly this time I was to be excluded from whatever they were discussing. Unfortunately I could hear nothing through the door although I confess that I did try pressing my ear to the wood. My mother always told me that my curiosity would get me into trouble one day. So I was forced to go back to wifely duties and wash up the dishes.

I had cleaned up the kitchen and still they were closeted in that room. I went up to check on Liam only to find he had already fallen asleep. Bridie was sitting beside him, reading a book in the dim gaslight.

"You don't have to stay up here, my darling," I said. "Come down and keep me company in the kitchen. It's nice and warm in there."

"All right." She followed me down the stairs.

"What are you reading?"

"*Little Women*," she said. "My teacher lent it to me. She knows I like to read."

"You're turning into quite a student," I said. "Your mother would be so proud of you."

"And my father?" She looked up at me wistfully. "He was never much for books and reading. I think he must be dead too, don't you?"

Bridie's father and brother had taken a boat to Panama to work on the new canal and we'd not heard any news from them for a year or more. Having heard rumors of the horrendous conditions down in that hellhole, I thought it was quite possible that Seamus was dead, but I put an arm around Bridie's shoulder. "Not at all. I think he might be in a place far from any communication. There aren't any roads or post offices, you know. And as you say, he was never one for writing much. Perhaps it never crosses his mind that you're worried about him. Men are different that way. They don't think that we women worry."

She managed a brave smile then. "He won't know me when he comes back," she said. "I hope I can still stay with you or with Captain Sullivan's mother out in the country."

"We'll cross that bridge when we come to it . . ." I said, and broke off as I heard a door opening and voices.

"You'll think about it then?" John Wilkie's voice. "What will I tell President Roosevelt?"

"I'll give you my answer by the end of the week," Daniel said. "It's a big step. I can't decide lightly."

"I'm sure I can smooth it over with the commissioner, especially if the request comes straight from the president," Mr. Wilkie said. He stood in the hall as Daniel helped him into his overcoat and then handed him his scarf, hat, and gloves.

"So good to see you again, Mrs. Sullivan." Mr. Wilkie turned to me. "Many thanks for the cheese straws. They were delicious."

I nodded politely as Daniel ushered him out the front door. The second the door was closed I demanded, "What was all that about? Mr. Wilkie wants you to work for him?"

"I'm afraid I can't talk about it," Daniel said. "But yes, that's the gist of it."

"You'd leave the police force?"

"If Wilkie can work it out properly, I'd be seconded to him, on assignment."

"And the request would come direct from President Roosevelt?"

"It would."

"So you'd be working for the president himself?"

"Indirectly."

"You are infuriating, Daniel Sullivan," I said in exasperation. "How can you not tell your wife what you'll be doing? Surely any decision in your life concerns me."

"I haven't decided yet," he said. "I need to weigh the pros and cons. This assignment is not exactly straightforward. It involves an element of subterfuge."

"And danger?"

"Possibly that too. But I live with danger every day in my current job, as you know only too well. I've already taken one bullet recently."

I put a hand on his arm. "Then do what your mother wants. Go into politics."

He laughed then. "Can you actually see me in Albany as a congressman? Or worse still, in Washington? If I've fallen foul of the police commissioner because I won't take bribes and turn a blind eye to corruption, how much worse do you think it would be in politics? I'd be beholden to those who elected me. I'd have to toe the party line and go against my conscience."

"Is this assignment from John Wilkie in New York?" I asked. "Can you tell me that much?"

"No, I don't think it would be in New York."

"We'd have to move?"

"No. It would only involve a brief trip away from home, I hope. A month or so at the most."

"And I would stay here?"

"You'd stay here," he said. "Much better all around. Bridie has her school. You have your friends to keep an eye on you. And I'd be free to do—what I have to."

I wrapped my arms around his neck. "I don't want you to do anything dangerous, Daniel."

"Don't be silly." He kissed me on the forehead. "I know how to take care of myself. I won't take any stupid risks. It will be fine."

"You sound as if you've already made up your mind."

"I think I have," he said. "I'd rather be out and doing something than hanging on here, watching my colleagues get handed the juicy investigations, waiting for my enemies to find the next nail to hammer into my coffin."

"Don't speak of coffins, please." I looked up into his face.

❧ TWO ❧

Two days later Daniel told me that he had decided to accept Mr. Wilkie's assignment. It would be a good challenge for him, he said. And a chance to sound out other opportunities. If he got on well with the president, if the president came to value him, who knew where that might lead.

I looked up from the potatoes I was peeling at that moment. "I'd love the folks in my village in Ireland to see me now," I said. "Molly Murphy, from the tumbledown cottage with the drunken father, now married to a man who has been personally summoned by the president of the United States for a special assignment."

Daniel grinned. "You make it sound more important than it really is," he said.

"You could at least give me a hint about what you'll be doing." I glared at him. "Will you be chasing criminals, catching spies? I don't exactly know what the Secret Service does."

"Neither do I," Daniel replied. "Neither do they, I think." He laughed. "The service was started to prevent the counterfeiting of money and to protect the president. But John Wilkie is an ambitious man and I'm sure he seeks to expand its role."

"So you'll be protecting the president?" I asked innocently.

"No. My task is humbler than that, I can assure you."

"Is it espionage then?" I asked. "Anarchists?"

"No anarchists, I promise you." He smiled. "And you're making much more of this than it really is, Molly. I don't think it will amount to much more than a simple case of fraud."

I felt a small spark of relief that at least he wouldn't be battling dangerous foreigners. "So why is Mr. Wilkie coming to you? Doesn't he have agents of his own to do his dirty work?"

"Of course. But I rather think he wants me because I'm not one of them. I'm an outsider. Unknown."

I stood there, a half-peeled potato in my hand, staring at him, willing him to speak. "Daniel, won't you at least tell me where you're going?"

"As to that I can't tell you because I don't rightly know. I'll be meeting with the president in Washington, D.C. After that . . ."

"After that? I'm your wife. Don't I have a right to know where you'll be? What if Liam was taken deadly sick, God forbid? Or your mother?"

"John Wilkie will know where I am. In case of dire emergency, you can contact him."

"So what sort of clothes should I be packing for you?" I asked. "Will it be your winter long johns or your summer blazer?"

He laughed then and slipped his arms around my waist. "I'm not going to fall for your subtle attempts to get a confession out of me, Molly Sullivan. I'll pack my own bag when I'm ready to leave."

I sighed and went back to my potatoes.

The next few days passed too quickly. Daniel received telegrams and presumably sent replies. I made sure all his clothing was clean. He packed what seemed to be a ridiculously small bag. At least this cheered me up a little. He could not be expecting a long absence if he was taking so little clothing. When I'd gone to Paris I'd taken a trunk. So maybe I was worrying too much over nothing. It might be no more than a brief consultation with the president and then he'd be home.

Daniel himself seemed in the best of humor when he said goodbye to us on a brisk March morning. Wind whipped at his scarf as he paused halfway down Patchin Place and turned back to wave and blow Liam a kiss. Then he was gone. I blinked back stupid tears. I was being unnecessarily emotional. He wasn't being sent abroad to be a spy. He was doing a simple job for the president. No more dangerous than his normal work in New York.

The door across Patchin Place opened and my neighbor Gus Walcott came out.

"He's off then?" she said as Daniel's back disappeared around the corner onto busy Greenwich Avenue.

I nodded.

"Cheer up. He'll be back before you know it." She gave me an encouraging smile. "And they do say that absence makes the heart grow fonder. I'm going to the French bakery to pick up croissants. Come over in half an hour and have coffee with us. We'll plan some exciting things to do while Daniel is away."

I tried to seem more cheerful when I was ushered into their warm kitchen later that morning. The good smells of brewing coffee and warm breads filled the air. Gus's companion, Sid Goldfarb, was standing at the stove, stirring a bubbling pot, looking like a rather glamorous witch in her emerald green velvet jacket and black silk trousers. I suppose I should explain that Sid and Gus were nicknames for two women officially called Augusta and Elena. They had enough private money to live a Bohemian lifestyle, completely ignoring the rules of polite society. They were always trying new things, painting, writing, traveling, and enjoying themselves. They were also passionate suffragists. While I supported their cause I had to tread carefully as Daniel did not approve of women making spectacles of themselves (nor of women getting the vote, I suspect). And since he was well respected in New York society, I couldn't do anything that might jeopardize his position. However it occurred to me as I put Liam down to toddle around that I'd have more freedom to be involved while he was gone.

Sid and Gus must have been thinking along the same lines because Sid looked up from the pot she was stirring. "So the cat's away and the mice are going to have tremendous fun playing, eh, Molly?" she said with a mischievous smile. "We were just talking about you last night and how it's up to us to keep you entertained. We have art galleries you have to visit and we'll invite all our disreputable artist friends your husband so disapproves of. Also we're planning a spring suffragist campaign and we'd love you to be part of it. We're even talking of marching in the Easter Parade again with our banners."

"Is that a good idea?" I asked as Gus put a cup of coffee in front of me. "It wasn't too successful last time, was it? And Daniel was furious that he had to rescue me from a jail cell."

"That was several years ago now," Gus said. "I think more women are coming around to our way of thinking. And we can't give up because of a few petty setbacks." She took a croissant from the basket on the table and handed it to Liam, who promptly sat down on the rug and began to suck on one corner.

"At least you'll come to our meetings, won't you?" Sid asked. She put down the spoon and came to sit beside me at the table.

"Of course I will."

"We have to keep you occupied so that you won't pine," she said. "It's worked for us. You see how busy we've kept ourselves since the children went to live with their grandfather."

"You still miss them?" I said. Sid and Gus had taken in two street orphans who had now been happily reunited with their family. (Thanks to a spot of my detective work, I should add.)

"Of course we do. But we are to see them soon. Their grandfather wrote to us last week. It seems their family owns a cabin in the Adirondacks and we are to take the children up to the snow as the old man is not up to that kind of travel yet."

"Oh, that should be marvelous fun," I said. "I'm glad for you."

"I've been meaning to improve my skiing technique for ages," Sid said. "I tried it once in college but never quite got the hang of it. My German instructor kept telling me to 'bend zee knees.' I bent them but I still couldn't control where those darned skis were taking me."

Gus exchanged a glance with me. "I think I'm going to prefer the hot cocoa by a roaring fire with mountain views through a window," she said. "I may even take my paints and capture the scenery."

"You'll want to play in the snow with the children, I know you will," Sid said. "Think what fun we'll have sledding and making snowmen. And even . . ." She leaped up again as the pot on the stove began to bubble furiously.

"What are you cooking? It smells interesting," I said.

"It's a mulligatawny soup from that Indian cookbook you gave us. We're getting quite proficient at Indian cookery, aren't we, Gus? We're planning an Indian banquet soon. We'll dress up in saris and put dots on our foreheads and invite someone to play the sitar."

"Sid was talking about seeing if we could borrow an elephant from the Bronx Zoo to transport our guests along Patchin Place," Gus said.

"I don't see what's so odd about that," Sid retorted as Gus and I started to laugh.

"And how would you bring the elephant from the zoo? Certainly not aboard the tram or the subway."

"Details. Mere details." Sid waved a dismissive hand. "We are determined that our next big adventure will be to go to India, Molly. You know how much we've been longing to. But of course we won't go anywhere until Daniel is safely back and you can do without us."

"You lead such exciting lives," I said. "Mine seems so humdrum compared to yours."

"It wasn't humdrum when you ran that detective agency, was it?"

"No. It certainly wasn't."

"A little too exciting at times, I'd say," Gus added as she scooped Liam up from the floor before he disappeared into the pantry. "We feared for your safety, Molly. We're glad you've given up such adventures."

"I suppose so."

Sid looked up from her coffee. "Do you still miss it? The excitement? The satisfaction of solving a case?"

"As if she's really given it up," Gus said. "Who used her detective skills to find out the truth about the children last Christmas? Or solved the mystery of that poor girl's dreams?"

"I suppose I have had to put my skills to the test occasionally," I admitted. "And I confess that I'm rather annoyed that Daniel will tell me nothing of this latest assignment. I don't know where he's going or what he will be doing."

"It must be something rather hush-hush," Sid said. "I bet he's going to be a spy. How exciting for him. I'd love to be a spy, wouldn't you, Gus?"

"He's not going to be a spy," I said rapidly. "He promised me he wasn't going abroad."

"Perhaps he can't tell you," Sid said, giving Gus a knowing look.

I wished she hadn't said that. Now I'd have more to worry about—Daniel secretly in Russia or Japan or Germany. . . . I couldn't bear to think about it.

So I was relieved to get a postcard from Daniel a few days later with a picture of the White House in Washington. On the back he had written, *All going well here. Sending a kiss to my wife and son.*

He was in Washington, only a few miles away. And if he had time to buy and write a postcard then he couldn't be in any imminent danger, I told myself. Maybe he was telling the truth when he said he was handling a simple case of fraud. I resolved to enjoy my time while he was away. Sid and Gus were true to their word. They took me to an exhibition at the Tenth Street Studio—a huge warehouse-like place where poor local artists could rent a studio to work for a very small rent. The rent, unfortunately, did not include heating. The exhibition was under the central dome and even though the setting was quite grand, it still felt chilly and inhospitable. I was glad that I had my fur muff with me and even more glad when I was offered a glass of mulled wine, cradling my hands around it and feeling the warmth flowing back into my fingers.

Also I have to confess that I was not impressed with the latest trends in art. I had found the paintings of the Impressionist school to be beautiful and serene. These post-Impressionists, Cubists, Fauvists, or whatever they liked to call themselves, were not producing pictures I should care to hang on my walls—all distorted figures, garish colors, and nightmare designs. Still, I suppose they represented the new century we lived in with its mechanical progress, political upheaval, and new scientific ideas. I was naturally polite when Sid and Gus enthused over various canvases and compared them to Gus's own work (which I found equally unappealing, although of course I had never said so).

I did meet one young man whose work I liked. His name was Feininger and he painted elongated figures in pleasing colors, rather like stained glass windows. I was just chatting with him when Gus came up to me in great excitement and dragged me away.

"You'll never guess who we've just met, Molly. Mr. Samuel Clemens." When she saw my puzzled face she went on, "You know, Mark Twain himself. He's taken a house here again and we're invited to a soiree on Saturday. Do come over and meet him."

Of course. Mark Twain. I flushed at my own ignorance. I had actually heard him speak once before when he was visiting Greenwich Village so I was not unprepared for the shock of white hair and impressive white mustache. He shook my hand when we were introduced.

"This is what I need around me now," he said, looking at the audience who had gathered around him. "A bevy of beautiful women. Young and beautiful women. Ever since my dear wife and daughter died the world has seemed extremely bleak and forlorn." He squeezed my hand. "You'll come to my little gathering, won't you, my dear Mrs. Sullivan?"

"Of course. I'll be glad to," I said.

"How about that," I said as we walked back down Fifth Avenue, our arms linked, striding out over the lingering fragments of snow. "Not only does my husband receive a summons from the president, but

I am invited to hobnob with Mark Twain. If only Sister Mary Patrick could see me now. Or my mother. They both told me that I'd come to a bad end if I didn't reform my ways."

We were still laughing as we turned into Patchin Place. I believe it was the last time I laughed for a long while.

❧ Three ❧

On Saturday night we dressed in our finery to attend Mr. Twain's gathering. I had been given some rather lovely silk gowns by a generous young society lady after our house had burned down. I had had little occasion to wear them during the normal course of my life, but was pleased to find them in my wardrobe now. I chose the dark blue with a matching lace fichu and affixed a blue flower to my hair. I was feeling quite glamorous when I bade good-bye to Bridie.

"You'll be all right here alone for a little while, won't you?" I asked. "I don't plan to stay out late and I'm only a block away on Fifth Avenue if you really need me."

"I'll be fine," she said. "I am almost twelve years old, you know. And Liam's already asleep."

I hugged her. "You're such a big help to me. I'm so glad you're here."

She beamed at me, but then her face became wistful. "I don't really remember my real mother very much. You're more like my mother now. I only hope . . ." She broke off.

"And you're my big daughter," I said quickly, knowing that she worried as much about having to go back to live with her father in squalor as she did about finding he had died. "Between myself and Daniel's mother we're going to make sure you have every chance in life, and you'll always have a home."

She nodded then, her eyes very bright. I have to confess I did have misgivings as I closed the door. I had left her alone with Liam before, but during the daytime and on occasions when Sid and Gus were just across the alleyway. But I told myself not to be silly. I had checked Liam and the house. All was well. I should go out and enjoy myself without worrying.

However, I have to confess that I was relieved when I tapped on Sid and Gus's front door only to learn that Gus had a headache and did not feel like going to a noisy party.

"Then we don't have to go," I said immediately.

"That's what I told her," Sid said. "But she insists that you and I go and enjoy ourselves."

"Then I'll just pop back and tell Bridie that Miss Walcott is home, should she need her," I said. I did so then Sid and I set off. The parlor at Mr. Twain's house on Fifth Avenue was already full of noisy company by the time we arrived. More women than men, I noticed, and most of them stylishly dressed.

"How good of you to come." Mr. Twain took my hands in his. "Another radiant beauty to light up my small and dreary life."

"As if anything about your life could ever be small, Mr. Twain," the man beside him said. "You've been a giant in American society since you were a boy."

"I hope you're not going to write such exaggerated twaddle now that I've given you permission to write my biography, Albert," he said. He turned to us. "This is Mr. Albert Paine, who has been pestering me about writing my autobiography. Or failing that, to let him be my biographer. Clearly he thinks I don't have much time left on this earth, but I've always sworn that I plan to go out with Halley's Comet so I've a few more years yet. I came in with it and I'll go out with it."

"It would be a grand notion if we could all arrange the day of our deaths in advance," Mr. Paine said. "So much tidier."

More newcomers arrived and Sid and I were swept into the crowd. Sid seemed to know some of them. I felt rather shy as I found myself chatting with writers, artists, and members of the Four Hundred. I was glad I had been to Paris the year before as the conversation seemed to revert back to that city and to London.

"I wouldn't dream of having my clothes made anywhere else these days, would you?" a woman was saying. She was dressed in the height of fashion in a mauve dress with the new bolero waist and generous lace trim all over, a jaunty mauve turban on her head, plus a little too-obvious coloring on her lips and cheeks.

I caught the eye of an older woman standing behind her, soberly dressed, and we exchanged a grin. At least there are others here who think like me, I decided and was glad when she came across to speak to me.

"I'm feeling a little like a fish out of water here, I have to confess," she said to me. "I don't know why I came but my dear friend Irma Reimer told me it was time I came back into society more and dragged me from the house. Do you know Irma Reimer? She is very thick with the Vanderbilts and the Astors."

"I'm afraid not," I said. "I don't move much in society these days. I've a young baby."

"How fortunate you are," she said. "Mr. Endicott and I were not blessed with children. It has been a thorn in the side for both of us." She extended her hand. "I'm Rose Endicott."

"Molly Sullivan." We shook hands. "Are you a widow now?" I asked, noting her dark gray dress and that her friend had told her it was high time she came back into society.

"Oh, no," she replied. "But my husband is away so much. He is in the import and export business. His company has an office in London and one in Havana. He is sometimes gone for months at a time."

"Oh, that must be hard for you," I said. "Can he not take you with him when he travels?"

She looked away from me then. "I'm afraid I have a delicate constitution. I do not travel well. I get seasick and Wilbur gets impatient with me. So it is easier this way, although I find the loneliness hard to bear."

"My husband is also away at the moment," I said. "I hate to be parted from him, so I understand your feelings."

She took my hand. "Do you? I'm so glad I met you this evening. May I be so bold as to invite you to visit me while your husband is away? I don't live too far from here. Just on Eighth Avenue."

"I live close by too," I said. "On Patchin Place, just off Greenwich Avenue. And I'd be delighted to come and visit."

"You'll bring your child?"

"I'm afraid he's eighteen months old and into everything at the moment," I said.

"Oh, but it always cheers me to have a lively youngster about the place. Do say you'll bring him—for tea, maybe?"

"Very well," I said.

Sid came over to join us then. "This is my dear friend Molly Sullivan I was telling you about," she said and I noticed she had a young man beside her. He was less fashionably dressed than most of the company and looked rather skinny and undernourished. More like the students who frequented Washington Square near my home, in fact. "Molly, this is Richard Graves, who edits a magazine I sometimes write articles for. His magazine is a great champion of the suffrage movement. He is doing a piece on women in a man's world and I told him that you had run a successful detective agency."

"I don't know about successful," I said. "I managed to solve cases without getting myself killed."

We laughed.

"I'd be most interested in interviewing you, Mrs. Sullivan," Mr. Graves said. "I am anxious to show the world that real women are not little wallflowers and violets who must be cosseted, but can handle almost any job as well as a man."

"Not quite as well always," I said. "You try chasing a suspect in tight skirts and pointed little shoes. We are severely hampered both in prejudice and clothing."

"Absolutely right!" Sid interjected. "But clothing is designed by men, is it not, to keep up the illusion that women are delicate flowers, and thus to keep them in their place."

"Although some like yourself refuse to accept such conditions and conventions," Mr. Graves said, smiling at Sid, who was wearing a man's smoking jacket and trousers this evening.

"Of course. I have never been one to be bound by the rules," Sid said. "All the more reason I admire someone like Molly, who is the devoted wife and mother and still manages such impressive feats."

"Oh really, Sid." I blushed with embarrassment. "I worked because I had to keep my head above water. Had I been blessed with money I doubt that I should have chosen a career as a detective."

Sid smiled. "I can't picture you ever being content to sit at home and hold tea parties."

"Maybe not."

Mr. Graves touched my arm lightly. "So may I count on you, Mrs. Sullivan? You could come to my office or I could come to your residence. Whichever is more convenient for you."

I was tempted. I suppose I was flattered. But a small warning voice was going off in my head. If Daniel's bosses were looking for excuses to get rid of him might they not jump on an article like this in which Daniel's wife his portrayed as a great detective? At the very least he'd take a ribbing that I had been solving his cases for him, and at worst his superiors could claim that he had been improperly involving me in police work.

"This might not be a good idea," I said. "You see my husband is a police officer. If there was any suggestion that I had helped him with his cases you can see what embarrassment I could cause him."

"I understand," he said. "You don't still run this detective agency, do you?"

"No, I gave it up when I married."

"As do all women, I regret to say," Sid interrupted. "What husband can tolerate a wife who has a successful career?"

"Other than Nellie Bly," Mr. Graves said. "I gather her marriage is a happy one and look what exploits she gets up to."

"We both know Miss Bly, don't we, Molly?" Sid said.

"Isn't she wonderful? And yet most women see her as a freak rather than a shining example of what a female can accomplish," Mr. Graves said earnestly. "We need to educate women and make them realize that all things are possible for them. And you can help. If you grant me the interview, Mrs. Sullivan, I promise you may vet my copy and we'll make sure it is clear that your adventures were in the past."

I was still torn, conscious of the crowd around me and people eyeing me with curiosity. I suppose a lady detective is a rarity, even in the company of the likes of Mark Twain. "I'll think about it and make my decision when I know how long my husband will be away," I said.

"Your husband is away?" Mr. Graves gave me an almost impudent grin. "Then what could be better? He will not be able to object. The interview will be over and complete by the time he returns."

Sid touched my arm. "Say yes, Molly. Think of all the good you can do for our poor housebound and dominated sisters."

"I'd still like to have time to think it over," I said. "I do have Daniel's career to consider and I can't afford to put a foot wrong when there are those at the police department who would love to see his downfall." I turned to Mr. Graves. "If you will give me your card, I promise I will contact you in a few days with my answer."

He fished in a pocket. "Very well," he said. "Here you are. I look forward to hearing from you. You are the neighbor of Miss Goldfarb, are you not? I trust she will work her persuasive magic and make you see what an asset you are to the women's rights movement."

He forced his way back through the crowd. Sid gave me an encouraging smile before she followed him, leaving me alone with Mrs. Endicott.

"I'd no idea I was chatting with a celebrity," she said. "Now I am all the more excited to entertain you at my house. Can we say next Tuesday? How about luncheon instead of tea? My cook is really quite good."

"Thank you," I said. "I look forward to it."

"And you'll bring the little man with you? It will be such a treat for me."

"All right. Although I do warn you that he has reached the inquisitive stage."

"I should add that my cook does make the most wonderful cakes and pastries. What child can resist them?"

When she laughed she looked suddenly younger and I got a hint of former prettiness that the severe hairstyle and worry lines had masked until now. I had two children within my care, friends just across the street, and now, it seemed, a newspaperman waiting to interview me, and yet I knew I'd still be worrying about my husband every day. I could see all too clearly how those worry lines had taken over what used to be a pretty face.

❄️ **Four** ❄️

On Tuesday I dressed Liam in his best sailor suit, packed a bag of his favorite toys, and set off pushing the buggy to Mrs. Endicott's house. It was a tall, solid brownstone on Fourteenth Street. The epitome of middle-class New York respectability. The maid who admitted me to a warm entrance hall was dressed in a smart uniform. She took our coats and scarves and told me that madam was expecting me in the sitting room.

"Meeting you has been a godsend, Mrs. Sullivan," Mrs. Endicott said after she had made a fuss over Liam and settled us in an armchair beside a roaring fire.

"How is that, Mrs. Endicott?" I asked.

"You have been an inspiration. Here you are, also abandoned by your husband, and yet you do not let it get you down. You are determined to live your life, to make the most of it. You are a brave woman and I've made a resolution to become braver. I will get out more. I will take up new hobbies and make a life for myself while Mr. Endicott is away."

We went through to the dining room and enjoyed a really good meal of roast chicken and crisp potatoes. Liam was surprisingly good, sitting propped up on pillows at the table and eating mashed vegetables.

"He's a little angel, Mrs. Sullivan," Mrs. Endicott exclaimed.

I smiled. "I think he also approves of your cook, Mrs. Endicott. He is not normally so angelic."

The main course was followed by meringues and cream, of which Liam also approved. When we parted after dessert and coffee she invited me to visit her again soon.

"Oh, no," I said and watched her eager face fall. "You must come to me," I added hurriedly. "Remember you promised to get out more. Come to luncheon at my house later this week and I'll invite my lively neighbors from across the street. They are so witty and have great stories to tell."

Her face grew troubled. "One of them wasn't the strange woman at Mr. Twain's, was it? The one with mannish hair, wearing trousers?"

"Yes, that was Miss Goldfarb."

The frown grew. "And I was told that she resides with another woman of similar tastes?"

"That's also correct."

She hesitated. "I'm afraid . . . Mr. Endicott might not approve of such acquaintanceship, Mrs. Sullivan. He is rather rigid in his ways and beliefs."

"But he's not here, Mrs. Endicott," I said. "How would he ever know unless you tell him? Do you have to write to him with your movements every day?"

She wavered then. "I never know where to write to. And he is always too busy to write back. Sometimes I don't hear from him for a month on end."

"Well then. Come and meet my neighbors. I can guarantee you'll find them kind, charming, witty. The very best conversation you've ever had."

She managed a tentative smile. "Very well. I will come. This is all part of spreading my wings, is it not?"

"And if you're not careful my friends will persuade you to join them in the women's suffrage movement."

"Oh, dear." Her face fell again. "Mr. Endicott would not like that. Is it wise to want the vote, do you think?"

"Is it wise for a nation to be governed by only half its inhabitants?" I asked. "Are women not blessed with equal powers of reasoning? Why should our menfolk decide what is best for us? When it comes to bills about women's health and child labor, should they be decided only by men?"

She hesitated. "I suppose not. But Mr. Endicott would say . . ."

"Mr. Endicott is not here, is he?" I gave her a sweet smile.

We parted, agreeing that she should come to luncheon later in the week, as soon as I had found out when Sid and Gus were free.

"My my. What excitement I seem to be having," she said as she stood at the front door, her face flushed with pleasure. "My friend Irma Reimer wants me to go to the moving pictures with her tomorrow. I had said no, but now I'm thinking that I should go. Although I always find them a little alarming, don't you? Did you see the one where the wave breaks right at the screen? My dear. I thought I'd be washed away. So did half the audience. There was much screaming, I could tell you."

"I saw that movie with the wave," I said. "People tried to rush out of the theater when I was there."

I pushed Liam home with Mrs. Endicott on my mind. I couldn't help feeling sorry for her—a lonely woman under the thumb of a dominating husband. How would I cope if Daniel were gone for long periods of time? No mention had been made about how long he might be away this time. I had endured a summer without him in Paris. But I had my friends with me and a young baby to take care of. I found myself wondering if Mrs. Endicott had had a child would her husband have stayed away so much. Does it not take a child to cement a marriage?

The next day I had just put Liam down for his nap after lunch and was deciding whether the lace curtains needed to come down and be washed when there came a tap at my front door. I expected to see either Sid or Gus standing there, coming to invite me to join them for coffee, but instead I saw a strange young man. Rather unkempt and windswept looking, wearing a jacket patched at the elbows.

"Mrs. Sullivan," he said, raising a cap to me, "I am sorry to spring myself upon you unannounced, but I decided to strike while the iron was hot, so to speak."

As he spoke I remembered why he looked vaguely familiar and before I could say anything he held out his hand and added, "Richard Graves. We met at Mr. Clemens's house and I told you how keen I was to interview you for my periodical. May I come in?"

"Oh, Mr. Graves." I stood there in indecision. "I really don't think the time or place are appropriate. I am, as you can see from my apron, in the middle of housework and the house is not fit to receive a guest."

He smiled then. He had a very pleasant smile. "I care little about the state of your house, Mrs. Sullivan. I myself live in a most untidy bachelor apartment but always welcome a visit from friends. And since you seemed a little reluctant the other night, I thought that an impromptu visit might persuade you."

We were standing facing each other at my front door, and I was still trying to make up my mind whether to invite him in. I took a deep breath and said, "As I told you, Mr. Graves, my husband is a police captain. Surely any mention of my former work as a detective would bring scorn and derision on him. Maybe put his whole career in jeopardy."

"How so, Mrs. Sullivan?" he asked.

"Might not his enemies mock him for having a wife who is a detective? Might they not say that he had needed my help to solve his investigations?"

"Then we will make it quite clear in the article that you gave up your profession when you married and your policeman made a pact never to discuss his work at home. And think of the good an article like this can do, Mrs. Sullivan. Showing young women that a woman can hold her own in a man's world. Not only hold her own, but suc-ceed. Nellie Bly fired up young women when she showed them what one woman can achieve. She went around the world, didn't she? She broke all rules and conventions. Now you can reinforce that vision."

I gave a nervous laugh. "I assure you I am no Nellie Bly. I have had moderate success as a detective."

"You are being too modest," Mr. Graves said. "Your friend Miss Goldfarb tells me you have confronted murderers. Faced mortal dangers."

"If women read my story, most of them would decide I have been imprudent and reckless. As indeed I have been on occasion."

"I can tell you are only trying to stall me, Mrs. Sullivan. I tell you what—I'll make you a proposition: let me interview you. I will write the article. You shall see it and have the last word over whether it can be published. Surely you can't say no to that?" When I still hesitated he added, "For the betterment of the status of women everywhere."

"Very well," I said, still hesitant. "I suppose I have to agree that is fair. Come inside then. We'll have to talk in the kitchen as the rest of the house has no fire lit at the moment."

We went through to the kitchen and I offered him a cup of coffee. He was a skilled interviewer and I rather think I told him more than I intended to. We were just winding up with the story of the orphan children I found on the streets at Christmas when the front door burst open and Bridie came running in. "Molly, I got an A in English," she called as she came down the hall. "Mrs. Slopes said it was a fine paper and showed great creativity and that I should think about going to college someday."

"That's wonderful, my dear," I said as she stopped short in astonishment, seeing a strange man in the kitchen. "This is Mr. Graves. He is also a writer. He has been interviewing me."

Mr. Graves had stood up. "Your daughter, Mrs. Sullivan?" he asked.

"My ward, Bridie. I have a one-year-old son who is mercifully napping. Otherwise we should have had no conversation at all."

As if on cue we heard a wail coming from upstairs.

"I'll go up to him," Bridie said.

"And I should take my leave." Mr. Graves stood up. "I will return when I have finished the article and you shall be the judge. But I sincerely hope you will agree to its publication. For the advancement of women."

I laughed then. "I think you must be Irish, Mr. Graves. You certainly have a touch of the blarney."

He laughed too as I escorted him down the hall. As I opened the front door I was startled to find someone standing there, hand poised as if about to knock.

"Mrs. Endicott!" I exclaimed. My first thought was that the house was in no fit state to receive a visitor of her quality. Surely we had parted without setting a date for our luncheon? "I didn't think we had set a date for your visit and I'm afraid . . ." I began. But then I saw that her hand was on her bosom and she was breathing hard as if she had run a race. "Whatever is the matter?" I asked.

"I saw him," she gasped. It did cross my mind to wonder whether she might be a little touched and I had somehow gotten myself mixed up with an unstable woman. "It was he, I swear it."

I put a hand on her arm as she was still gasping for breath. "Calm yourself, do," I said, "and please come inside. I've just made coffee."

"I'll take my leave then, Mrs. Sullivan," Mr. Graves said. "I'll be contacting you as soon as the article is written in a few days."

"Yes. Well, good-bye then," I said, rather more curtly than I had intended.

He put on his hat, tipped it to us ladies, and set off down Patchin Place.

"Your husband returned home?" she asked.

"No, that was a reporter, wanting to write an article about me for a magazine," I said. "Come in, do."

"Such an interesting life you lead." She followed me down the hall and took the cup that I offered her. She took several sips before she looked up.

"I'm sorry. I don't know what you must think of me," she said. "I ran all the way from Broadway."

"You saw a man who frightened you?" I asked.

She shook her head violently. "No, I saw Wilbur. I saw my husband."

"Here in the city?"

Again the shake of the head. "No. In California."

I really did then think that she was deranged until she added, "I went to the movie theater, as I told you, and they were showing a piece on San Francisco and there he was. My Wilbur. In San Francisco. Large as life."

"But that must have been a pleasant surprise for you, wasn't it? To see your husband."

"Mrs. Sullivan," she said firmly. "As far as I know my husband's business has never taken him to the West Coast. I expected him to be in London or Charleston, South Carolina, or maybe even Havana. But never San Francisco."

"Maybe you were mistaken," I said. "The quality of the images is not that good and you saw someone who resembled your husband."

She reached out and took my arm. "Come with me," she said. "There will be another showing at four thirty. Come with me then and let me prove to you that I'm not going mad."

I glanced across the table. Bridie had brought down Liam from his crib and had sat him in his high chair, ready to feed him some bread and jam. "I have to prepare supper for the children . . ." I began.

"We don't have to stay for the whole show," she said. "It is but a brief segment."

"Can I come?" Bridie asked suddenly. "I've never seen a moving picture."

"I suppose I could leave Liam with Miss Walcott for a little while," I said.

Mrs. Endicott gripped my hand. "Oh, thank you. I have to make sure I was not wrong."

I took Liam across the street to his adoring aunts, and off we went. Bridie was excited and almost dragged me forward.

"So many of the girls at school have seen moving pictures," she said. "One of them even went over to New Jersey to Mr. Edison's studio and saw him making a moving picture. It was so exciting, she said, with people chasing each other and cops blowing whistles."

I smiled at her animated little face. Now for the first time she was able to live as a normal girl with school and friends.

We reached the theater on Broadway where the movies were being shown.

The latest innovations in moving picture technology, said the poster. *Prepare to be astounded, touched, amused. News. Comedy. Drama.* Mrs. Endicott brought out her purse and paid for us, leading us into a half-dark theater in which an organ was playing. Even though the program had already been shown several times that day the house was quite full and we had to take seats near the screen, now concealed behind red velvet curtains. After a few minutes the lights dimmed. There came an expectant murmur from the audience. The organ music became louder and grander and those velvet curtains were pulled back to reveal the screen on which flickered the words: *Welcome to the World of Wonder.*

The first feature was a comedy in which some clumsy and hapless policemen chased a clever thief. The audience laughed and clapped. Beside me Bridie howled with laughter. Then came a scene shot at Niagara Falls. The cameraman must have been very daring because sometimes it looked as if we were about to fall over the edge and the audience gave a collective gasp.

Then the organ music changed to something more dramatic and the screen announced: *News from Around the World. Caruso comes to California. San Francisco awaits the arrival of the world's greatest singer.* Then we were looking down from a hill at a city perched beside a great bay. We saw funny little trolley cars going up impossibly steep hills. Then we were passing mansions.

The most prosperous city in the West waits with anticipation for the arrival of Enrico Caruso, the famous Italian tenor, said the words on the screen. *He will perform at the Grand Opera House on April 17.* The image changed to

33

show an impressive building. *And he will be staying at the world-renowned Palace Hotel.* Now we entered a magnificent hotel with an opulent foyer. We moved to a dining room where elegantly dressed people were dining amid palm trees. A waiter crossed the screen, carrying a bucket of champagne.

Mrs. Endicott grabbed my arm. "There," she hissed in a whisper. "See that table in the corner. That man with the long side-whiskers lifting a glass to his lips. That is Mr. Endicott."

The picture was quite clear.

"It is definitely my husband," she said. "No doubt about it."

"Shhh!" someone behind us warned, tapping Mrs. Endicott on the shoulder.

I took in the big, powerful man, well dressed and looking rather pleased with himself as he said something to his table companions.

"That's all I wanted to show you," Mrs. Endicott said. She started to stand up. "We can go now. The scene will change in a moment."

I was about to follow her and slip out of my seat without too much disruption when Bridie tugged my sleeve. "Look," she exclaimed. "There's Captain Sullivan."

The camera had now moved from the dining room back to a rotunda area with a domed roof. Through glass doors we could see carriages and automobiles pulling up in a forecourt, disgorging smartly dressed people in evening attire.

Will Mr. Caruso be surprised to see the sophistication and elegance that is now San Francisco? said the words across the bottom of the screen. *Here money is no object and champagne flows like water.* The foyer was already crowded and many people were holding up champagne glasses in a toast. Then through a gap in the crowd I caught a glimpse of him. He was standing at the bar, seemingly enjoying himself, but his eyes scanned the new arrivals. A second later the crowd closed in again and he was gone. Then the organist switched to music for the can-can dance and we were now not in California but in Paris and looking at scenes from the Moulin Rouge cabaret. As the rest of the audience leaned forward in their seats to better see the scantily clad girls kicking up their legs we made our way out of the theater.

My heart was still thumping in my chest. I had only been given the briefest of glimpses of my husband, but like Mrs. Endicott, I was absolutely sure it was he.

❦ Five ❦

Y ou see. I was right, Mrs. Sullivan," Mrs. Endicott said as we came out into red rays of a setting sun that painted the lingering snow pink. "It was Mr. Endicott. I'd swear to it. So the big question is what is he doing in California of all places do you think?"

When I didn't answer right away she looked at me. "Mrs. Sullivan, are you all right?" she said. "Are you going to faint? You look as white as a sheet."

"You are not the only one who has had a shock," I said. "I just saw my own husband in the Palace Hotel."

"Mercy me. And you didn't know he'd be in California either? Well, that's a remarkable coincidence, isn't it?"

"Indeed it is a remarkable coincidence," I agreed. "I knew he was being sent on an assignment," I said, "but California was never mentioned. I rather thought he would be closer to home, in Washington. That's where he was when he last sent me a postcard."

"You're lucky to get a postcard," Mrs. Endicott said. "My husband never bothers. Sometimes I don't get a letter for weeks on end."

"That must be very hard for you."

She turned away, staring up Broadway where a trolley was now passing, its bell clanging loudly to scatter pedestrians. "I'm used to it by now. But yes, it is still hard." Then she grabbed my sleeve. "You could go to California for me. Your excuse could be that you are missing your husband and wanted to surprise him, but while you are there you could seek out Mr. Endicott for me and let me know what he's doing so far away."

I shook my head firmly. "Oh, no. I couldn't do that. For one thing I have children here who need to be looked after. And for another my husband is on some sort of clandestine assignment. The last thing he'd want is his wife arriving to spoil things for him."

"That's a pity," she said. "Because you are a lady detective and I'd dearly like to know what Mr. Endicott is doing. I'd pay your way, you know. I'm a wealthy woman. You'd know how to stay hidden and could spy on both of them."

I had to laugh at the absurdity of this. "I certainly couldn't spy on my own husband," I said. "If you want to spy on yours, then you take the trip to California."

"I couldn't do that," she said. "The train would be too much for me. And Mr. Endicott would be furious with me. He's rather alarming when he's angry."

"I'm sorry I can't help," I said, "but I'm sure he'll be home soon and then you can tell him you spotted him dining at the Palace Hotel in San Francisco. Maybe he is like the rest of the world—curious to see the great Caruso in person."

"Would you cross a continent to see a singer?" she demanded.

"I suppose not," I agreed. "But what if your husband had business on the West Coast?"

"I've never heard of him going to the West Coast before. Why would he ever need to go there when he imports French wines and Cuban cigars?"

"I hear they are growing grapes for wine in California now," I said. "Maybe he is looking into expanding his markets."

"Yes. That might be it. You might have hit the nail on the head," she said, sounding more cheerful. "That's exactly the kind of thing he'd do. He has a great head for business, has Mr. Endicott."

We walked on in silence while I considered the things that had not been said. I sensed that she was fearful that there was another reason for his trip to California. Maybe she worried that he might have a mistress out there.

"Why did we have to leave so quickly?" Bridie asked, taking my hand. "I didn't get to see Paris. And there was supposed to be a movie about men going to the moon."

"Mrs. Endicott wanted to leave," I whispered back to her. "So we had to come out with her. You and I will try to go together another time so that you can see the men going to the moon."

She nodded with satisfaction, slipping her hand into mine. "I was clever to spot Captain Sullivan, wasn't I?" she went on. "What do you think he is doing in California?"

"I've no idea," I said. In truth I wished she hadn't spotted him. I'd rather not have known that he was so far away and in a place like San Francisco. It might have mansions and elegant hotels like the Palace but it also had areas like the Barbary Coast with a reputation for wild living and for danger.

We walked Mrs. Endicott back to her house, but then refused her invitation to come in for a cup of tea with the excuse that I could not leave Liam for too long with my friends. I retrieved him from Gus and Sid and we were about to go back across the street when Bridie blurted out, "We saw Captain Sullivan in a moving picture!"

I wished, of course, that I had warned her to say nothing, because then I had to tell Sid and Gus the whole story.

"Did you know he was going to California, Molly?" Gus asked me.

"I had no idea," I replied.

"San Francisco," Sid said, giving Gus a knowing look. "Yes, that would be the sort of place you'd send someone as a spy, wouldn't it? Chinese opium dens and Japanese traders and Russians."

I told them about Mrs. Endicott begging me to go out to California and spy on her husband. I expected them to laugh but instead Gus said, "What a perfect idea. We've been dying to see San Francisco, haven't we, dearest? We could make a real trip of it."

"Absolutely not," I said. "If Daniel is doing something dangerous, we'd be the last people he'd want to see. We might even put his life in jeopardy."

Gus sighed. "I suppose you're right. Ah, well, we'll sit tight and wait for the next missive from the elusive husband."

"And you forget, dearest," Sid said. "We will not be sitting tight. On Saturday we go up to the Adirondacks with Tig and Emmy. We must start sorting out our skiing clothes." She paused. "Do we have any clothes suitable for skiing? We need stout wool trousers and waterproof jerseys, don't we? And gloves and hats. We've a lot of shopping to do."

And so they were off on another madcap adventure, fully engrossed in the procuring of ski clothing. Their shopping expeditions kept them fully occupied all week, as they returned to show me Tyrolean sweaters and padded gloves. On Saturday morning they came to say good-bye before they went to Grand Central Terminal and embarked on the train trip up the Hudson.

"They say this weekend is going to be positively springlike," Gus said. "I hope we won't roast in our Swiss wool sweaters."

"And I hope the snow won't decide to melt before I've had a chance to ski. It will be quite unfair if it turns to slush," Sid added.

I noticed that the breeze was quite balmy. The last traces of snow were going to melt quickly in the city. We stood outside to wave them off in a hansom cab piled high with a ridiculous amount of luggage. After they had departed I took the children out to Washington Square. I suggested that Bridie take her hoop with her but she decided that someone who was almost twelve was far too old to play in public. So she sat on the bench beside me while we watched boys play Kick the Can and tag. Some of them recognized Bridie from school and called out to her. But she kept her eyes demurely down. It won't be long before she has boys interested in her, I thought with a jolt. It was strange to think of her growing up. She had always been the little girl I had to protect.

Liam was thrilled to watch the big boys' games, and equally delighted to watch the sparrows bathing themselves in the fountain. We stopped on the way home and I treated the children to liquorice bootlaces, Bridie's favorite. Saturday ended with still no message from Daniel. On Sunday I took the children to church. I wasn't exactly the most devoted Catholic but I felt that I needed to pray that Daniel would stay safe. It hardly seemed worth making our usual Sunday roast for just myself and two children so we settled for pork chops.

Then on Monday morning I heard the clatter of the letter box and the thump as something landed on the doormat. I rushed to find it was a letter from Daniel at last. I tore it open and sat at the kitchen table reading it.

My dear little wife, it began. *I sit on a hilltop, surrounded by a sea of white fog and my thoughts race across the continent to you. How I wish you were here beside me so that I could share this moment with you. I know you would be astounded by such beauty and magnificence. I know the green hills and sparkling ocean would remind you of your Irish home. I only regret I could not have brought you with me, but of course we both knew you were too frail to undertake such a long trip, especially with a baby to look after.*

How I miss you, my darling girl. I miss your sweet soft voice, your gentle touch, your kind ministrations, and devotion to your loving husband. But rest assured that I am being well cared for here. Mrs. Rodriguez, at whose home, or rather mansion, I am staying attends to my every need. And in case you are feeling jealous at my mention of another woman, let me assure you that she is a widow of mature years and great fortune, an absolute pillar of the San Francisco community. She and her friends have taken it upon themselves to show me all that the city has to offer and I am never lost for entertainment or company. Have you heard that the Italian opera singer Caruso is expected in town within the month? Already the place is buzzing with excitement and my hostess is planning parties to welcome the great man. I anticipate that my work will keep me here until he arrives so look forward to seeing him for myself. I shall duly report on the momentous oc-

casion for you—I know you will be sad that I will attend the opera for once without you and we shall not be able to enjoy our earnest discussions on the quality of the singing after the performance as we always do at home.

And so, my darling girl, I send a kiss winging its way to you, wishing that so many miles were not between us. A kiss too to my darling son. How is your embroidery progressing? I expect the cushion cover to be finished by the time of my return.

I remain forever your loving and devoted husband,
Danny.

I stared at the letter with my mouth open and the blood hot on my cheeks. "Jesus, Mary, and Joseph!" I muttered. How dare he! The absolute rudeness of him to write such a patronizing, mocking letter. I presumed he had those San Francisco society women sitting beside him as he wrote and thus wanted to create an impression of his wife and his marriage that was quite untrue. My embroidery! My soft, gentle voice and touch! And too frail to travel! He had created a picture of a simpering idiot, of the kind of woman I despised so much. And what was that nonsense about our opera discussions? Daniel had never attended the opera in his life, at least not with me.

I slammed the letter onto the table and paced around. Liam watched my mutterings with big, worried eyes until I realized that I was scaring him. I went over and picked him up.

"Your daddy is an idiot sometimes," I said. I jogged him on my hip and spun him around, making him laugh and beg for more, and by the time I had put him down again I was in a better mood. I stared at that letter, lying on my kitchen table. It went against everything I knew of Daniel. He was not cruel or insulting. Neither did he ever pretend to be what he was not. He would not have written such a letter to impress a society hostess, and he could easily have written to me in the privacy of his own room so that nobody saw what he was writing—unless . . . unless he feared that his correspondence would be seen by other eyes.

I paced again, more warily now. What possible reason could he have had for writing such a letter? To make me laugh? In which case he had not succeeded. To tell me something? And most puzzling of all—why had he signed it Danny? He had always been Daniel to me, ever since we met. Never the shortened Dan or Danny. None of it made any sense.

❧ Six ❧

I couldn't wait for Sid and Gus to arrive home that afternoon. I needed to show the letter to someone because I was growing more and more uneasy as the day wore on. Daniel never did anything flippantly or without consideration. That letter had to have been written for a reason.

I fed Liam. Put him down for his nap. Bridie returned home from school and still I went into the front parlor, pulling back the lace curtains to see if my friends had returned.

"They said they'd be back by midday," Bridie said, coming up behind me. "Perhaps something is wrong. Perhaps there was a sudden snowstorm in the mountains and they are snowed in. Perhaps Tig or Emmy hurt themselves skiing. Or they took them back to Long Island and were invited to stay for dinner."

I felt a knot of worry in my stomach. What if my friends were forced to stay at the cabin in the mountains and didn't come back for days? In the end I was forced to start cooking our supper and was startled when there came a knock on our front door. I went to it to see Gus standing there.

"We have returned, as you can see," she said, "but I could use a little help, if you don't mind."

"Of course," I said. "What's wrong?"

"The cab driver wouldn't come any further up the street, saying he couldn't turn his horse around in such close quarters. He abandoned us here, horrible man. But he got no tip, I can assure you."

I followed Gus's glance down Patchin Place and saw a pile of baggage and propped against it was Sid, her leg encased in white plaster.

"She attempted the most difficult slope," Gus said, giving me a look of pure exasperation. "I told her she needed more practice first but she never listens to me. Now she's laid up with a broken leg and who knows how long it will be before we can resume our normal activities."

"I'm so sorry," I said. I hurried down to Sid. "Here, put your arm around my neck and we'll half carry you to the house." I looked back at our front door. "Bridie," I called. "Come and help with Miss Goldfarb's bags."

Between us, Gus and I managed to carry Sid into the house and settled her on the sofa, propped up with pillows.

"Tomorrow morning I'll go out and find you crutches," Gus said. "Knowing you, you will not be content to lounge on a sofa until you are healed."

"I feel so stupid," Sid said. "The hill didn't look that steep to begin with and when a young man came and asked me if I was sure I was up to such a challenging run, I wasn't about to give up. And then lo and behold the hill suddenly started plunging straight downward and I tumbled head over heels."

"I was watching from the cabin window and saw the whole thing," Gus said. "She bounced down it like a pebble. Quite alarming, I can tell you."

Bridie stood in the doorway, her arms laden with bags. "Where should I put these?" she asked.

"Oh, just leave them in the hall," Gus said. "Thank you so much, Bridie dear."

"I'd better go back," I said. "I've dinner cooking and Liam in there alone. But when you're settled I have something I have to show you." Then I added, "I'm making a big hot pot. I'll bring some over when it's done, so that you don't have to worry about cooking."

"How kind of you, Molly." Sid held out her hand to me. "I can tell you I'm not going to find it easy being an invalid. But this leg hurts like billy-o when I try to move. A compound fracture, the doctor called it. So rest is really the only cure."

"Don't worry. We'll take good care of you," Gus said, putting her hand on Sid's shoulder.

I went back across the street and finished preparing the meal. Then I fed the children, swallowing back my impatience, and it was only when I finally carried over a bowl of the hot pot for Sid and Gus that I brought the letter with me.

"You said you have something to show us?" Sid said, holding out her hand for the piece of paper I held. "Something good?"

"A letter from Daniel. But it can wait. You should eat while the food's still hot."

"Of course not," Sid said. "I can see that you're dying to show us this letter. Good news, I hope?"

"I'm not sure," I said. I handed it to Sid, and Gus came to perch on the arm of the sofa to read it over her shoulder. I saw their expressions change as they read it.

"Well!" Sid looked up as she finished reading. "I am quite lost for words. One can only conclude that your husband has lost his mind."

"Or that he was very drunk at the time?" Gus suggested. "How insulting, Molly. Why would Daniel say those things?"

"I've been thinking about it all day," I said. "At first I was angry. I thought he'd written such a letter because he wanted to somehow impress the company he was with to demonstrate that he was the man

45

of the house and I was just the little wife. But then I decided that was not like Daniel one bit."

"No, I have to admit that Daniel has always treated you with more respect than most husbands would," Sid said. "He didn't even forbid you to continue with your detective work, although he did try to persuade you to stop."

"So what does it mean?" I asked. "None of it makes sense. Daniel is not one for writing long, flowery letters, for one thing. Even when I was away in Paris and he was worried about me he only wrote a few lines. 'All is well here. Please give Liam a kiss from me.' That's about it."

"And that sentence about the opera," Gus said. "You have never been to the opera together, have you?"

"Never," I said.

"And the embroidery," Sid said with indignation. "When have you ever done embroidery?"

"Exactly," I said. "I have come to the conclusion that he must have written all those ridiculous things for a reason. Either he was being watched as he wrote or he thought there was a danger of his letter being read so he wanted to convey a false impression for some reason."

"Or?" Sid looked up at me.

"Or he thought he was being funny, maybe?" I suggested. "He thought his ridiculous statements would make me laugh?"

"But they didn't. They made you annoyed," Gus said.

"That's true."

We stared at the sheet of paper in silence.

"I suppose it really is Daniel's handwriting?" Gus said at last. "Someone else didn't write the letter to give the false impression that Daniel was in California?"

"I'm sure it's his handwriting," I said. "It's neater and less of a scrawl than usual because he's always in a hurry. But I think I'd swear that he wrote it."

"Then he wrote it for a reason," Sid said.

"That's what I've been thinking. Daniel never does things impulsively. He thinks them through. So I'm wondering if he's trying to tell me something—some kind of hidden message."

"Much of what he says is the exact opposite of the truth." Sid was frowning now as she stared at the letter. "The opera. The embroidery. Even your sweet and gentle nature. All lies."

"I can be sweet and gentle if I put my mind to it," I said hotly.

They exchanged a knowing smile. "But it wouldn't be the usual description of your temperament, would it?" Gus asked.

I paused, staring at the sheet of paper. "Do you think he's trying to tell me that he's in some kind of danger?" I asked. "If so, why not write a note in secret and slip out to mail it?"

"Unless he's being watched or even guarded," Gus said.

I shuddered. "A prisoner, you mean?"

Another silence followed while the three of us digested this thought.

"I think." Sid cleared her throat. "I think that he wants you to go out to California."

"Go out to California? How do you interpret the letter that way?" I asked.

"He stresses how much he misses you, how you would enjoy the scenery. Then he says what a pity it is that you can't travel because you are too frail. We all know that you are not too frail and could easily travel. And to emphasize the point he goes on about the opera and embroidery, both of which are the opposite of the truth. Ergo— he knows you are not too frail to travel and wants you there."

"Holy Mother of God," I exclaimed. "You really think that?"

"Don't you?" Sid looked up at me.

"I suppose it's possible." I stared at the letter again, willing its message to come clear to me.

"You know Daniel. You said yourself that if he wrote anything it would be for a good reason," Sid went on, warming to her subject now. "He says he's been well looked after, entertained. Is that meaning that he can't get away to have time on his own or even that he's being watched every minute?"

"But what could I do if I went out to him?" I was trying to stay calm but it was hard to get the words out. The thought that buzzed around inside my head was that my husband might be in terrible danger and it might be up to me to rescue him, which was absurd.

"You'll find out when you get there, presumably," Sid said.

"But if he's in danger, why not simply leave, or write to Mr. Wilkie to send out reinforcements?"

"If he's virtually a prisoner, how could he write to Mr. Wilkie?" Gus said. "And presumably if he's on some kind of spy mission he won't be using his true name or credentials."

"Oh, dear," I said. "So you really think I should go out to him? All the way to California?"

Sid nodded. "I really think so. Don't you, Gus?"

Gus looked more hesitant. "If Daniel is currently in danger, why would he want to subject Molly to the same risks? If anything, he'd want to make sure she was safe. I think he's giving her the details of where he is and who he is staying with so that if anything happens to him, at least Molly will know."

"Don't say that, please," I said. "Do you think he wants me to contact Mr. Wilkie for him? Should I send on the letter to Mr. Wilkie so that he can come to the rescue?"

"I still think he wants you there," Sid said firmly. "I know it's a frightfully long journey but why else would he have said that he's sorry you were too frail to travel with him? He'd have had no need to say such a thing if he just wanted you to know he was in San Francisco. In fact he could have stopped after the first paragraph. He goes on to tell you things that aren't true, Molly, so that you'll see that all his statements are the reverse of what he says. That means you are strong enough to travel and he wants you there."

"I just wish I knew," I said. "I need to think."

"Of course you do," Gus said gently. "Go home and sleep on it. We may all have more insights in the morning."

I nodded. "Yes. That's what I'll do. Maybe Daniel will come to me in a dream tonight and then I'll know."

But he didn't. I hardly slept at all that night. I tossed and turned. I sat up and stared out of the window at the dark street, listening to the distant noises of the city. I ran my hand over the cold spot on the bed where Daniel usually slept. Now that Sid had spoken the words out loud I realized that she was voicing my deeply hidden fears— that Daniel was in danger. That for some reason he could not tell me the truth in a letter. And that he wanted me to go to him.

In the morning I awoke from troubled slumber, bleary-eyed, and with my head throbbing and in truth no clearer as to what my decision should be. Should I send a telegram to Mr. Wilkie? But if Daniel wanted me to do that, why hadn't he hinted at it in the letter? He could have made some veiled comment about our dear friend John and how I must give him my best regards when I speak to him. I would surely have picked up on that. But then so might Daniel's neb-ulous captors, whoever they might be.

That was the trouble. I did not know the nature of his assignment. Was he dealing with foreign spies? Anarchists? Criminals? All I knew was that he was staying with a Mrs. Rodriguez who was a doyenne of San Francisco society in a mansion above a sea of fog. It all sounded eminently respectable. Maybe he was really having a good time and we were completely misinterpreting the nature of this letter.

But if he wasn't? a small voice whispered in my head. Why had he regretted I was too frail to travel? Sid had to be right. Daniel wanted me out there with him. I picked up the letter that lay on my bedside table. I even held it up to the early morning light. All I noticed was that Daniel had written the name "Caruso" extra forcefully. Even underlined it. Well, of course that made sense. Caruso's arrival was big news. The preparations had even been shown here in a movie theater. Then I noticed that he had also highlighted the word "opera" in a similar way. And the word "myself." And "embroidery." There was nothing really out of the ordinary about this. Daniel often wrote in the same forceful manner with which he spoke. He did sometimes underline words. I went downstairs to Daniel's desk and wrote down the four words. "Caruso." "Opera." "Myself." "Embroidery."

"Holy Mother of God," I said out loud. The first letters spelled out the word "COME."

❦ Seven ❧

I packed Bridie off to school and waited with impatience to share what I had discovered with Sid and Gus. Was I reading too much into those four words? But then why hadn't Daniel emphasized other, equally important words? Why would he have stressed the word "embroidery"? But for that matter why would he ever have mentioned embroidery? It had always been one of our jokes that he had not married a quiet little miss who sat at home with her embroidery. A private joke. So he was saying, "You and I both know that you never do embroidery. So I want you to take everything I say in this letter as the opposite."

And as Sid had pointed out: you are not too frail to travel. Therefore you should travel.

I believe my hand shook a little as I held the letter. A journey to California was a huge undertaking. Several days on the train with a lively toddler. Clearly I couldn't leave him behind. And what about Bridie? Should I take her with me to help with Liam? But it would not be fair for her to miss her schooling and certainly not fair if I was heading into danger. And then there was the money. We had a small amount put away in savings. We were not destitute. Daniel would inherit a property in the country from his mother one day. But a trip to California and who knows how long a stay in a hotel would certainly eat into those savings.

I just wished Daniel's message had been clearer. If he had written to say, "My dear wife, I miss you. Please take the next train out to be with me," I would have known what was expected of me. Now I worried that I'd arrive in California only to have Daniel say, "What in God's name possessed you to come out here when I'm in the middle of an assignment? You could be putting my work in jeopardy. Please take the next train home."

I was relieved when Gus tapped on my front door to say she'd just returned from the bakery and I should come to have coffee with them. I picked up Liam and carried him across the street, noticing how heavy he had become lately. How would I manage with such a lively youngster on a train and in a strange city?

Sid was sitting propped up on the sofa again. She looked rather hollow-eyed and held out a languid hand to me. "Molly, how are you? You look about as tired as I feel. I hardly slept a wink all night with the pain in this wretched leg, and I'm sure you didn't sleep much either."

"You're right," I replied. "I was awake and worrying most of the night. But I think I might have discovered something that confirms everything you said, Sid."

I came over to her and handed her the letter. Gus came over to join us, peering over Sid's shoulder. "Notice there are four words that are heavily written and even underlined?"

"I see that 'Caruso' is emphasized," Sid said. "Well, that makes sense. Obviously Daniel is impressed that Caruso is to visit San Francisco. Oh, and the word 'opera' is also stressed. And 'myself'. And 'embroidery.'"

"Look at their first letters," I said.

"They spell 'come,'" Sid said, her voice no louder than a whisper. She looked up first at Gus and then at me. "How clever of you, Molly. And now you know that I was right. He does want you with him."

"I'm afraid I have to agree now," I said. "But what a huge undertaking. Obviously I can't leave Liam behind."

"We would look after him for you," Sid said.

"Oh, no, I couldn't ask that of you," I replied. "He's into everything these days as you know very well. A real handful. And you need looking after yourself."

"How stupidly inconsiderate of me," Sid said. "If I hadn't had that ridiculous fall, then we could have taken the train to California with you. You heard us say that we were longing to visit the West Coast. We would have had a wonderful adventure together. But as it is . . ."

"As it is you can't travel," I finished for her. "But you know, I was wondering whether Bridie could stay with you? I would hate to take her out of school when she's doing so well and enjoying it so much, even though I'm sure she'd be a big help to me on the train. And you know she's no trouble. She can help around the house and run errands for you."

"Of course she can stay with us," Gus said. "And you're quite right. You should not interrupt her schooling. I've been so impressed at how quickly she's making progress."

"Like a little sponge," Sid agreed. "Loves to read. She can work her way through our library."

I sighed. It seemed that every obstacle was being removed from my path. I was going to have to go to California whether I liked it or not.

It was only when I had taken down my valise from the top of the wardrobe and was thinking about what to pack that I remembered Mrs. Endicott. If I was now really going to San Francisco, perhaps I could undertake to find her husband and report back on him. Perhaps I could even persuade her to come with me. I would dearly appreciate company on that long train journey. I bundled Liam into his buggy and set off for her house. I was shown into her back parlor, where she was lying on the chaise longue, a rug over her, and clearly still in her night attire.

She held out a hand to me. "My dear Mrs. Sullivan. How good of you to call. And dear little Liam too."

"You are unwell?" I asked as I pulled up a chair to sit beside her, holding Liam firmly on my lap as he squirmed to be put down.

"Just a little tired," she said. "I have been overdoing it recently and with my delicate constitution I have to recuperate from time to time. I am thinking of going up to Saratoga to take the waters. That always seems to revive me. Have you visited that delightful town? The waters are truly curative and there is such a variety of wonderful entertainment too. Concerts and plays and all kinds of soirees."

"I haven't had the chance to go there yet," I said.

"Then you must come with me. I'd welcome the company and I will pay your way. We shall take the waters together."

"I'm sorry, but I came to tell you that I am about to undertake quite another journey," I said. "I am going to California. My husband has written to say that he wants me to come out to him."

"But that is wonderful." Her face broke into a smile, making her look much younger. "I'm sure you will love it. They say the scenery is incredibly beautiful and San Francisco has become such a fashionable city. And Caruso. You will be there for the arrival of Caruso."

"I came to see if you would not come with me," I said. "Would you not like to surprise your husband with a visit? I would be on the train with you to help you with baggage and things. You could get a sleeper car. It would not be too strenuous."

She held up her hands. "How you do tempt me, Mrs. Sullivan. I would dearly love to see Mr. Endicott again, but I fear I have to reject your kind offer. I know my limitations. You see for yourself that after a few small excursions in the city I am thoroughly exhausted. And I travel so poorly. I should be prostrate with travel sickness within half an hour of leaving New York. And in addition Mr. Endicott might not be glad to see me."

"What husband would not be glad to see his wife?" I asked, mindful that the same doubt had entered my own head.

"You do not know Mr. Endicott. He is a very masterful man. He likes to arrange everything, to be in control of everything. He might well be furious that I had undertaken such a journey without his permission at a time that might not be convenient for him."

She sat up and leaned toward me, resting her hand on my sleeve. "But you, Mrs. Sullivan. You can go on my behalf. You can seek out my husband for me. You can report back on him. I will naturally pay you for your time and effort. I will make it worth your while to find Mr. Endicott for me."

"I'm not sure how much free time I will have, but I will certainly do my best for you," I said. "I am only sad that you will not come yourself."

"So am I, my dear. So am I. But I do know my limitations. I hope you understand them."

"Of course," I said. "Let's hope I can report back to you with good news in a week or so."

She rang the bell and had her maid bring down albums with various photographs of Mr. Endicott in them. I could see from the expression in his photographs that he was indeed a masterful man, one rather pleased with himself. In any pictures of them together she appeared a mere shadow beside him, looking out fearfully at the world. I selected a couple of pictures to take with me and promised I would send a telegram as soon as I had any news.

I took my leave then, turning down her invitation to stay for luncheon. I had much to do and wanted to be under way as soon as possible. I had once been as far as Albany by train and I knew that the route continued on to Chicago. I wasn't quite sure how one proceeded from there. My mother-in-law had taken the train to Minneapolis and had complained how wild and primitive it was. Even Sid and Gus had not made the trip across the whole continent. And yet I, Molly Murphy from a peasant's cottage in Ireland, was expected to undertake the trip with my young son. I felt sympathy with Mrs. Endicott when she said that travel was too much for her. At this moment it seemed an enormous undertaking for me. It was true I had crossed the Atlantic, but Liam had been a small baby then, easier to handle than a rambunctious toddler. And several days on several trains would undoubtedly be more of a challenge than a pleasant cabin on a boat.

As I pushed the buggy back home worrying thoughts were flying around inside my head. Why did Daniel want me to come? He was not an impulsive man. Presumably he needed me for a very good reason. And that reason could only be that he was in danger. But if a trained police captain was in danger, what could I, a mere woman hampered by a small child, do to help him? And how exactly did he expect me to help him? It was extremely puzzling. If he needed help, surely there were other policemen he could call upon in a big city like San Francisco. Or he could telegraph Mr. Wilkie and have another agent sent to him. The more these worried thoughts flew around inside my head, the more I questioned whether I had misinterpreted the letter and would be making a stupid mistake by going out West. There had been upheavals in my life. I had been in danger myself and undertaken great journeys, but I don't think I had ever felt as sick or as scared as at that moment.

❧ Eight ❧

There was no sense in putting it off. I started to pack the valise. I had no idea what the weather was like in San Francisco. If Daniel was in a sea of fog, it could well be cold. So I made sure I included a shawl for myself and a warm jacket and hat for Liam. Daniel's letter said he was staying in a mansion. I stood with my wardrobe door open, staring at the dresses hanging there. Two of them were evening gowns. Would I need such a dress if I were to fit in with fashionable San Francisco society? But that would necessitate bringing a bigger suitcase with me. Maybe even my cabin trunk. And if I was only there a few days, that that would seem to be superfluous. Then I reasoned that Daniel had written that letter from a mansion. If he were staying there, then I too would be invited to stay. And I didn't want to let my husband down by appearing dowdy and poorly dressed. And small children needed frequent changes of clothes.

So I sighed, went up to the attic, and dragged down the cabin trunk I had taken when we went to Paris. Then I packed the evening gown and the rose silk day dress in tissue paper, as well as my evening cape. For travel I would wear something more sturdy—the dark-blue two-piece costume I had had made in Paris last year, and my over-coat in case the weather was cold along the way. The trunk was then filled with Liam's clothes and diapers. I was glad that potty training was well under way as it would mean less accidents and less laundry. But who knew whether he would go back to more babyish ways when he was far from home on a long journey?

After I closed the trunk and dragged it down the stairs I packed a carpetbag for the train. I expected the trunk would travel in the luggage van and I wouldn't be able to get at it until we arrived in San Francisco. To our nightclothes and toiletries I added his favorite toys—some blocks, a little wooden train, as well as the stuffed bear he slept with. Then I stood looking at the pile of luggage and couldn't bring myself to move. Should I try to catch this evening's train, or wait one more day, just in case?

Just in case what? I demanded of myself. *Don't put it off. If you're going, go.*

I waited expectantly for the mailman, just in case another letter arrived saying: *Forget everything I told you yesterday. All is now well.* Or something along those lines. But the mailman passed by without putting anything into my letter box. When Bridie came home from school I told her the plan. She looked at me with big eyes, obviously scared by this sudden turn of events.

"How long will you be gone?" she asked.

"I really don't know, my darling girl. Not long, I hope. But Miss Walcott and Miss Goldfarb will take good care of you. You know that."

She nodded. "I know they will. But I was thinking about you. How will you manage with Liam on your own? You know he likes me to sing him to sleep. And I make him laugh when he's in a bad mood. I could come with you if you like."

"I know you're a marvel with him," I said. "But your schooling is more important right now. I don't want you to miss your lessons. So you stay here and study hard and the ladies have said you can read the books in their library . . . and you know how many books they have?"

She managed a brave little smile then and I realized that it was being separated from me that worried her. She'd had enough upheavals in her young life. She'd been taken from Ireland as a small child. She'd lost a mother, then a father. No wonder she didn't want to let go of me.

"I'll write to you every day. I'll send you picture postcards of the places I visit and I'll be back before you know it," I said, sounding a lot more cheerful than I felt.

Then I walked her across the street to my neighbors. They greeted her warmly. Gus took her up to show her the room they had prepared for her. She had even chosen a few books she thought Bridie would like and put them on the bedside table.

"And while you're with us we'll teach you to cook all kinds of interesting food, so that you can cook for Molly and Captain Sullivan when they come home," she added.

We went down to the front parlor to say good-bye to Sid. She made a big fuss of Liam and then hugged me. Since Sid wasn't normally the effusive one this made me all the more uneasy, realizing that she believed I was going into unknown perils.

"Take care of yourself, please," she said, holding both my hands and looking up at me. "Don't do anything too risky. Send us a telegram if you need to. Tell us to get in touch with Mr. Wilkie and we'll have help sent to you in a jiffy."

"Hardly a jiffy," I said. "It takes at least four days to cross the country."

"The government does have troops stationed out West, you know. I'm sure they could be mobilized into action on your behalf if necessary."

I had to laugh at the thought of the army rushing to save me. I held on to her hands tightly. "Let's hope it won't come to that. But please do say some prayers for me. I'm not quite sure who you both pray to, but I'm sure any prayers will get to the right place."

Gus walked with me to the front door.

"Godspeed, Molly. Come back to us safe and sound." Then she

handed me an envelope. "Just a little something to make you think of us," she said.

It was their emotional farewell, more than anything, that made me realize how far away I was going. Bridie was wiping away tears, and Liam, sensing the heightened emotion, burst into tears himself, holding out his arms to go to Bridie, as the front door closed between us.

With such drama I set off for Grand Central Terminal. At the booking office I found that travel across the country was not as simple as buying a ticket. There were too many choices. Did I want to travel on the Chicago, Burlington and Quincy Railroad to Denver, then westward on the Denver and Rio Grande Western Railroad to Salt Lake City and the final stretch on the Western Pacific? Or maybe I'd want to take the Chicago and Northwestern to Omaha and then the Southern Pacific via Ogden, Utah? And did I want a first-class Pullman? A second-class Pullman? A tourist ticket? A regular ticket?

When I said the quickest and cheapest way possible the clerk shook his head. "If you don't mind my saying so, ma'am, you don't want the cheapest way if you can afford better. If I sell you a third-class ticket you'll be sitting on a wooden bench. Awful hard and nowhere for the child to sleep. And your car could be attached to a freight train, shunted off into sidings. It could take you up to ten days."

"Ten days!" I exclaimed. "So what do you recommend?"

"I'd take the *Overland Limited*," he said. "Pay for a second-class Pullman out of Chicago but it will get you there in just four days. And you'll just change the once in Chicago. If you want to save some money buy your food at stations and skip the dining car."

"Thank you," I said. "I'll have to do it."

"So when do you want to travel, ma'am?" he asked. When I said today's train he burst out laughing. "Sorry, but the *Overland Limited* is booked up for weeks in advance. Everyone wants to go by the fastest and most comfortable route. I could probably get you out on the Western Pacific, Denver Rio Grande and Western routes, but it would mean changes and layovers."

"Would you take a look and see if you have any seats for today?" I said. "I've been summoned to my husband in California as quickly as possible." Having plucked up all of my courage to undertake this foolhardy journey I didn't think I could face going back home again for another night and then repeating the good-byes all over again.

He flicked through the pages of a ledger. "Very well, but I can assure you that—" He stopped. "Well, blow me down. Would you look at that?" he said. I tried to see what he was pointing at but couldn't read upside down. He looked up at me, as pleased with himself as if he'd produced a rabbit out of a hat. "There's been a cancellation. You're in luck. I've no sleeping berth between here and Chicago, but it would mean just sitting up the one night. But the cancellation is for a second-class berth between Chicago and San Francisco. That will be sixty-five dollars, please."

My heart was in my mouth as I counted out the bills and handed over the sixty-five dollars. What would Daniel say to this extravagant purchase? Was I really doing the right thing?

❧ Nine ❧

My anxiety turned to anger as I came away with my ticket and followed the porter with our luggage across the station to the waiting train. The air was heavy with smoke as massive locomotives hissed and puffed. Whistles and shouts competed with the sound of running feet. I hurried to keep up with the porter. Why couldn't Daniel have told me clearly what he wanted of me? Why did he have to put me through this?

Liam wriggled and squirmed in my arms and I wished there had been a way to bring his buggy with us. I'd have to try and rent or borrow one when I arrived in San Francisco because I certainly couldn't carry him around until we found Daniel.

My bags were safely stowed in the baggage car. My seat was located for me—certainly not a wooden bench but a comfortable plush seat in a long car. The porter put my bag on the rack above my head and I settled down. Liam had been fascinated by the trains and was happy to stand on the seat beside me, looking out of the window. When I opened my purse to find my handkerchief I pulled out Gus's envelope, which I had quite forgotten. I opened it, expecting to find a funny card or letter and was overwhelmed to see instead five twenty-dollar bills.

For emergencies, was written on the note with them.

My eyes misted over at their kindness. Who knew what emergencies I might encounter before I was reunited with my husband?

The platform became a hive of activity. Porters wheeled mounds of luggage past our window. Smartly dressed couples headed for the first-class section of the train. For the first time I felt a small thrill of excitement. I was, after all, going across a vast country. I'd be seeing things I'd only dreamed of. And at the end of it I'd be with my husband, whether he actually wanted me there or not.

A whistle blew. A shout of "All aboard!" There were running feet. Then almost imperceptibly slowly we started to move forward. Then a little faster. At the end of the platform we plunged into the darkness of a tunnel. The air in the railcar became smoky and I tasted soot on my lips. Liam had been standing up, looking at the trains with fascination, but flung himself back into my lap with a wail as we went into the tunnel.

"It's all right," I said. "We'll soon be out again."

And we came back out into daylight. We were moving fast now and the streets of Manhattan soon gave way to the jumble of new rows of houses, old shacks, and market gardens that made up the northernmost reaches of the city. Then we crossed water on a bridge and were soon traveling along the edge of the Hudson River. Twilight was falling and the snow-clad hills were tinged with pink. The river glistened as it opened up to that lake, the Tappan Zee. Lights twinkled from small riverside towns, but we didn't stop. We passed them one by one—Irvington, Tarrytown, Peekskill. I had had adventures in these towns, in my days as a working detective. I remembered the dangers I had encountered and felt a shiver of fear go through me. I was now a married woman with a child. Surely my life was now supposed to be safe and secure, and yet here I was setting off once again into the unknown.

Night fell completely as the river narrowed and we were in the wild, rocky country of the Catskills. Liam, exhausted by the emotions of the day and the new experiences, fell asleep. I continued to stare out of the window, as more old memories stirred. The mansion where I had stayed with Senator Flynn. And then the barn where Daniel and I had first made love. I remembered that all too clearly. I should never have let it happen. He was engaged to marry another woman at the time and I thought there was no hope for our future. But if I had pushed him away then, would I be sitting here now with a ring on my finger and a fine son lying in my lap? *What strange twists and turns there are to our lives?* I thought. One small decision can change the course of our histories. I paused, considering this. Would this small decision change the course of mine?

I had brought some food with me, not knowing if any would be available on the train. When Liam woke up again I fed him some hard-boiled egg and mashed vegetables. In a way I wished he were still nursing, as that would have solved the food problem, but then again it would have been hard with such lack of privacy. We'd both have to make do for a few days. I had a cold beef sandwich for myself, and then we shared some cake I had baked. I changed Liam for the night, glad that there was a lavatory close by, and he fell asleep easily enough, lulled by the rocking of the train. I didn't find it so easy to sleep. It was hot in the car with some kind of forced-air heat in operation and Liam's heavy body against me made me feel clammy and rather sick. The cold beef lay heavy on my stomach. I had never thought of myself as a poor traveler before and I sympathized with Mrs. Endicott when she had said that she would have been travel sick within the first hour. This thought made me question what I was doing yet again. Had Daniel been writing the truth and really meant that this journey was too difficult for me? How could sitting in a comfortable chair for several days be too demanding? I longed for a drink of water and wished I had brought some.

When we stopped in Albany around ten o'clock at night I lugged the sleeping Liam with me and found the station restaurant. There we both had a drink of milk and I bought cheese rolls for the morning. The milk calmed my stomach and we both slept as the train moved through the night. Morning dawned over a rural landscape still tinged with snow—neat farms and red barns making splashes of color against snowy fields. Liam awoke ready to play. I walked him up and down between the seats, pausing when older ladies wanted to make a fuss of him. Then he sat on the floor at my feet and played with his blocks. He was being amazingly good, I thought, and decided I had worried too much. Let us both enjoy this trip.

We pulled into Chicago's Union Station at midday. I found a porter without too much trouble and my bags were taken to the ladies' waiting room as the *Overland Limited* did not leave until four o'clock in the afternoon. That gave Liam plenty of time to run around and we both ate a good meal at the station restaurant of pot roast and vegetables followed by rice pudding. I bought several postcards and wrote the first one to Bridie, as I had promised to do, mailing it in the box at the station. I also bought food for the journey, hoping I could buy more plus milk for Liam at the various stops along the way.

Then at three thirty a porter took us and our luggage to board the *Overland Limited*. I found I was given what looked like a normal seat, until the porter explained to me that at night he would fold out the upper berth and turn the seat below into a bed. The porter was an older Negro man and Liam looked at him fearfully, having seen few colored people in his life. But when the man smiled at him and said, "Well, hello, big fellah, are you taking good care of your mama?" in his deep rumbly voice Liam smiled shyly back.

I had just taken my place and stood Liam beside me to watch the trains when I was joined by a young man.

"Here's your berthmate, ma'am," the porter said. "Mr. Paxton. This is Mrs. Sullivan, sir. And I'm Roberts. You just call on me if you want or need anything."

It hadn't crossed my mind before that men and women might be required to share sleeping quarters on a train. It obviously hadn't occurred to him either. He looked quite flustered and said, "Mrs. Sullivan. . . . I hadn't realized . . . I thought . . ."

"So did I, Mr. Paxton," I said. "But I only got this berth because there was a cancellation, so I suppose the original occupant was a male. I hope you will not find it too disagreeable to be faced with a young child for several days. He's usually quite well behaved."

He gave me his best smile then. "Not at all. I'll welcome the company. It's the first time I've made such a journey myself and I've left my own wife and baby behind."

I examined him with interest. He had a pleasant, open face, sandy hair and a freckled face that made him look very young.

"Do you come from Chicago?" I asked.

"No, from New York. I work for the Metropolitan Opera Company."

I could not have been more surprised. He was certainly too slender for an opera singer and his attire would have made me think more along the lines of bank clerk. "Oh, my," I exclaimed. "You're an opera singer? Or a musician?"

He grinned. "Nothing so grand, I'm afraid. I'm assistant to the administrator and I've been sent out in advance to make sure everything is in order when the majority of the company arrives in San Francisco. Perhaps you have heard that they are to perform with Enrico Caruso?"

"I knew Caruso was to sing, but I hadn't realized that the Metropolitan Opera was to perform with him."

"Señor Caruso doesn't think that local talent would be up to his standards and requested our company instead. He performed with us recently so he is comfortable reprising familiar roles with us. And so we're taking the whole production to join him in San Francisco. Costumes. Scenery. The whole shebang. And I can tell you, it's taken a lot of organization to ship everything across the country."

"I'm sure it has, Mr. Paxton," I said.

We both looked up as the train gave a sudden jerk, and then started to move.

"Looks like we're off," Mr. Paxton said. "Three days of sitting ahead of us, but I've heard there is glorious scenery ahead."

We chuffed out of the city and soon were moving very fast, passing through unremarkable countryside, snow-streaked fields, lonely farms, patches of woodland with bare branches, and no sign of the spring that must be right around the corner. Night fell. Mr. Paxton went to find the dining car, while I retrieved the food I had brought with us. We had eaten a good lunch and neither Liam nor myself felt like anything more than a snack. We had just finished when Mr. Paxton returned, having brought with him an orange and some cookies.

"I sneaked out a treat for you," he said, handing Liam a cookie.

Our porter came to make up the beds. I changed Liam into his nightclothes but didn't think it was proper for me to change. Neither did Mr. Paxton apparently, although he did hang up his jacket. I lay on the bed with Liam beside me and sang to him softly until he fell asleep, then I tried to sleep myself. I was tired but sleep wouldn't come. I had hoped that the rhythmic rocking would help me, but instead it made me feel rather queasy, as one does on a ship at sea. I ate one of the cookies and that helped a little. Eventually I nodded off and awoke to hear whistles and voices. We were not moving. It seemed we had arrived at Council Bluffs, Iowa, and dawn was just breaking.

I left Liam sleeping, asking Mr. Paxton to keep an eye on him, and disembarked to find food. I had a cup of strong black coffee, much stronger than I liked to drink it, but at that moment I was grateful for any warm liquid. I still felt a little queasy and it seemed too early to feel like breakfast, even though other passengers were tucking into hotcakes and sausage. I brought back a couple of sausages for later, plus some toast for Liam before we set off again, crossing the mighty Mississippi River into the Wild West. One could see the change in the landscape immediately. Instead of the neat fields of the day before there was now just grassland, brown and dry after the winter, with patches of snow clinging to hollows where the sun didn't shine. Sometimes we saw cattle grazing. Sometimes just empty land. We stopped for an hour in Omaha and this time I took Liam for a proper breakfast and a good wash in the ladies' facility. I washed as much of myself as I could reach too.

Then we set off again. Roberts appeared and suggested we might like to adjourn to the lounge car while he made up the beds. I hadn't known such a thing as a lounge car existed and followed Mr. Paxton through the train to a comfortable carriage with big windows and easy chairs. I was even able to put Liam down and let him play with his blocks on the carpeted floor. Coffee was served. It was all very civilized just as the country became even wilder. No sign of human habitation for miles except for a lone horseman. And then, to my delight, several Indian braves on horseback appeared on the crest of a hill. It wasn't until we had passed them that I wondered whether Indians still attacked white settlers but concluded we were safe on a train thundering through the landscape at many miles an hour. But their presence reinforced the feeling of being in an untamed part of the country, and far from home. I kept a lookout for buffalo but spotted none. We were climbing steadily. When we opened a window the air felt fresh and bracing. Wyoming slipped past us with yellow bluffs and snow-covered mountains in the distance and at the end of the day we pulled into Ogden, Utah. It was bitterly cold against a backdrop of snow-clad mountains. The wind whipped off a great lake to the west of us. I put on my overcoat and bundled Liam up before taking him to the station restaurant, where I fed us both a thick bean and barley soup. I followed mine with a piece of apple pie and returned to my seat quite satisfied.

When we set out again I turned my chair toward the window and watched as we skirted the edge of that lake. The water glowed pink in the setting sun. A flight of seagulls wheeled overhead, strange to see so far from an ocean. It was beautiful, dramatic, and so very remote. Mr. Paxton returned from the dining car as night fell and we started chatting with the forced familiarity that travel brings. He showed me snapshots of his wife and daughter. And before I knew it I was telling him about going to meet Daniel. He was a good listener and I found myself saying more than I meant to, sharing my misgivings about undertaking the journey and whether I was doing the right thing. Eventually I opened my purse and showed him the letter. He read it, then looked up at me, puzzled.

"It's hard to know," he said. "So your husband was not the sort to write long, flowery letters?"

I had to laugh at this. "I was lucky if I got three lines from him when we were apart. He is a very matter-of-fact sort of person, Mr. Paxton. And he has never called me his 'little wife' in his life."

"So he wrote the letter for a reason—either to amuse you, or to alert you."

I nodded. "I don't think he would believe that such words would amuse me. More likely to anger me. He knows I hate being patronized."

"So he was alerting you," he said. "To what?"

"My friends suggested that since everything he said was the opposite of the truth, when he wrote that he was sorry I was too frail to travel, he meant that I should travel. That I should go to him. And see—he has underlined four words whose first letters spell 'come.'"

He looked even more puzzled then. "But you have no knowledge of what sort of mission took your husband to the West Coast? Whether he was likely to be in danger and what sort of danger that could be?"

"My husband had often faced danger as a policeman," I said. "But this was a different sort of assignment, a secret assignment that he couldn't share with me. I don't know whether it was chasing criminals, rounding up anarchists, catching spies. All I have as a clue is in that letter. That he was being well looked after by Mrs. Rodriguez, a rich society matron. But then that too might prove to be the opposite of the truth."

"But you'll know everything as soon as you arrive and find him at Mrs. Rodriguez's house, won't you?" he asked.

"That's the trouble," I said. "I really can't make up my mind what to do when I get there. If Daniel wrote such a letter because his every move is being watched, or worse still, he's being kept a prisoner, then would I be walking into the same trap if I showed up on Mrs. Rodriguez's doorstep? I feel that I should tread cautiously. Find a simple hotel for the first night and then ask questions of the right people. See who might know about my husband and whom he might have met."

Mr. Paxton nodded again but he looked troubled. "Mrs. Sullivan, is it possible you are making too much of this? What if your husband wrote you a tongue-in-cheek letter and is looking forward to your arrival?"

"Then I'll find him and all will be well. I'd like nothing better. But I know my husband, Mr. Paxton. He never does anything lightly or without weighing it carefully. I have to believe that he's in some kind of danger. So to whom should I go? If he were on police business, then protocol would demand that he presented himself first to the local chief of police. But this isn't exactly police business. It's some kind of hush-hush operation. He may not even have given his real name. Tell me, is San Francisco small enough that word of a stranger in their midst would have spread around?"

He had to laugh at this. "My dear Mrs. Sullivan. I'm afraid you are in for a rude shock. It is a city of half a million people and almost all of them are strangers. It is the place to which people come to make a fortune, and when they have made it, to spend it. It is the main port of commerce with the Orient, for one thing. I'm told the harbor is at all times full of ships bringing exotic goods to our shores. The railroad barons live on Nob Hill. And it's said to be a city rife with crime and intrigue. There are parts of the town where sensible people don't go. The Barbary Coast waterfront with its saloons and houses of ill repute. Chinatown with its tongs and opium dens. I'm afraid it is the kind of place likely to shock those from the more sober and orderly East Coast."

"I've lived in New York for some time now, Mr. Paxton," I said. "Such things don't unduly alarm me." I didn't add that I'd been a detective and that one of my cases had actually taken me into the heart of New York's Chinatown.

Mr. Paxton was frowning now. "Mrs. Sullivan," he said in a low voice, "if your husband suspected he was in some kind of danger, why on earth would he ever want to bring you into such an environment? If I were in trouble, I'd want my wife to be far away and safe."

This was indeed a good question. In normal circumstance that was exactly what Daniel would have thought. So he wanted me there because there were things I could do but he couldn't. Or, as I had thought many times before, I had made a stupid mistake and he didn't want me there at all.

❧ Ten ❧

We fell silent. The question remained unanswered. I didn't feel I could tell him that I had also been a detective and that Daniel might be relying on my skill and intuition to help him. This also was hard to believe. How many times had he refused my help in the past, and then accepted it finally, but grudgingly? He had admitted at times that I was not a bad detective, but as for involving me in his cases . . . that had hardly ever happened.

Liam tired of playing with blocks and took off down the car at a run, making me leap up to go after him. I carried him back complaining. Mr. Paxton took him onto his knee and played horsey with him, making Liam shriek with laughter. I looked around with concern. The other occupants of the lounge car were mostly sedate older people who might not welcome the noise of a child.

"Perhaps I should take him back to our berth," I suggested.

"He's having fun," Mr. Paxton replied. "It's good to laugh. You were also smiling for a while there and that's about the only time I've seen you smile since we left Chicago."

I sighed. "I've been weighed down with worry," I said. "I keep telling myself that everything will be all right, but I can't believe it."

"Only one more day to go and you'll be with your husband," he said. "And all will be well, I'm sure."

"I wish I were sure too," I replied.

I carried Liam back to our berth and made him ready for the night. But he had become bored with trains and being cooped up in such a confined space. Probably he was picking up his mother's misgivings. Anyway he cried and refused to be held or comforted until at last he fell into an exhausted sleep. I was sweaty and frustrated myself by this time and left him sleeping to go to the small washroom and splash water on any parts of me I could reach.

A real bath and a change of clothes by tomorrow night, I told myself and pushed other thoughts aside. I returned to Liam and lay beside him. The light was too poor to read the magazine I had bought at the Chicago station. I was too wound up to sleep, so I lay there, being rocked from side to side by the train and feeling that bean soup heavy on my stomach. Lamps were dimmed and I lay in the unreal world of half darkness. From further down the car came the sound of heavy snoring. Outside the window was total darkness—no light, except for the stars that hung, unnaturally brilliant and so close overhead. I dozed, woke again, unable to find a comfortable position, dozed again, and was relieved when I spotted the first streaks of dawn in the sky.

Before the sun had fully risen I opened my eyes to find that the train wasn't moving. I must have dozed off again for a moment. I sat up, trying not to disturb Liam, who was lying on his back with his thumb in his mouth, looking like a little angel. Then I lifted one corner of the blind and looked out. Around us was nothing but desert— rocky scrub with mountains rising in the distance. I wondered why we had stopped until I saw a wooden sign nailed to a post. *Reno,* it said. I raised the blind completely and lowered the window to look out. Yes, we were definitely at a station of sorts. There was a crude wooden platform with a hut beside it, but no sign of a town. A few more huts further off dotted the scrub and that was all. It looked like a place of utter desolation—the ends of the earth. Other passengers were alighting from the train and going into that hut. The train was taking on water. I eased myself past Liam and threw my shawl around my shoulders as I stepped down onto the platform and made for the hut with everyone else. They were offering coffee so strong it nearly took the roof off my mouth, and biscuits and gravy. I ate some—it wasn't as bad as it looked—then dipped a biscuit in gravy and carried it back for Liam. There was no milk to be had. I'd have to ask Mr. Paxton to get some for me in the dining car.

I hoped this would be the last meal I'd be taking at a godforsaken station and hoisted myself back onto the train. Liam still slept but Mr. Paxton was now standing beside his bunk.

"We're taking on water for the long climb over the Sierra mountains," he said. "The hardest part of our journey, so I'm told."

I nodded to him. He looked down at the sorry-looking biscuit in my hand. "Is that the best they could do?"

I nodded.

"Then why don't you allow me to treat you to a decent meal in the dining car?"

I shook my head. "I couldn't possibly. Besides, we'll be in San Francisco later today."

"The little guy needs his nourishment," he said. "And besides"— he gave me a cheeky grin—"the opera company is paying."

I didn't refuse this time and when Liam awoke and was washed and dressed to the best of my limited ability we followed Mr. Paxton to the dining car, where we feasted on scrambled eggs, sausages, and hotcakes. As we ate, the train moved out of Reno station. Other passengers were muttering about the rumor of a late-season snowstorm ahead and the possibility that the track would need to be cleared.

"How long might that take?" a woman down the car asked.

The dining car attendant shrugged. "Could be a while. Could be days, depending on the depth of the snow."

Days? To be held up when the end should have been in sight almost reduced me to tears of frustration. But I had to put on a brave face for my son. If only Sid and Gus could have come with me, I thought. Then the journey would have been a splendid adventure. We'd have laughed at the men wolfing down their pancakes. We'd have talked late into the night and they'd have helped me to find Daniel when we arrived in San Francisco.

But they weren't here. I was alone and I'd have to make the best of it. "Only one more day," I muttered as I carried Liam back to our seats. Roberts was making up the berths so we continued on to the lounge car. It seemed that most other passengers had the same idea as the car was quite full.

"They say the ride over the Sierra is spectacular," a woman behind me said. A man stood up to offer me a seat. The track was beginning to climb across a bleak valley with a river rushing beside us. Then we were hugging the side of a mountain. Streamlets spurted out from under the track to cascade down to the river. It felt as if we were suspended in space and could crash down at any moment. Higher and higher we climbed, crawling at a snail's pace until we came to the little settlement called Truckee, looking like something from a Christmas card scene. We didn't stop here but climbed even higher, with snow-clad peaks all around us and the same peaks reflected in a long blue lake below us. I watched in awe as the train again seemed to cling to the side of a cliff, disappearing into tunnels and reappearing again. Indeed a remarkable feat of engineering. At the summit we came to an abrupt halt and we could hear the engine hissing as if with exhaustion. Presumably this was where the track had been blocked by snow. It was still snowing up here—great flakes fluttering down around us—and the tall pine trees were still draped in white mantels of snow. We heard shouts up ahead and fortunately the wait wasn't long until the train gave a mighty jerk and we set off again. Snow swirled around us as we moved past banks of snow, passing men with shovels, crawling at a snail's pace through a snow-covered landscape dotted with white-coated pine trees. Then we were descending and suddenly the snow was left behind and we were passing through a pine forest with a brilliant blue sky overhead.

Lower and lower we descended, as if the train sensed its destination was near and was anxious to be done. Pines became oaks among green grass dotted with orange poppies and purple lupines. The mountains turned to rolling hills. We passed through small townships and around midday we stopped at the state capital of Sacramento beside a wide river. This time we didn't stop for long and we were off again, crossing a broad plain on which fruit trees were already coming into blossom. More green hills followed, interspersed with stretches of bright water. I thought it was a lake but Mr. Paxton told me it was the delta of a great river. Flocks of waterbirds rose at the sound of the train. And overhead seagulls wheeled, letting me know that we were close to journey's end and the Pacific Ocean.

"There it is. That's San Francisco," someone exclaimed, further down the car. We stood up and looked out of the window. We were skirting the side of a great bay, which was liberally dotted with the masts of many ships. And on the other side a city rose, its buildings clinging to the sides of steep hills. There was no sign of that fog that Daniel had written about, but the backdrop of the city was a brilliant blue sky.

"Does the train have to go around this bay to reach the city?" I asked Roberts, who had appeared to help take down bags.

"No, ma'am. We come into Oakland, not San Francisco. You have to take the ferry across the Bay."

"Oh, I see," I said. At the end of such a long journey to be faced with one more complication was almost too much to bear. I was immediately disgusted at my weakness. Perhaps Daniel had been right and I was too frail to travel.

Roberts must have noticed my face. "No problem, ma'am. There will be plenty of porters waiting to help you with the bags. You just stay put and I'll find one for you. You'll be over in the city in no time at all."

I smiled. "Thank you."

"My pleasure, ma'am," he said, touching his hand to his cap. I wished I had a bigger tip to give him, but he seemed to understand my modest amount.

He was as good as his word, returning with a sturdy fellow who located my trunk, which was already sitting on the platform, and bade me follow him to the ferry. We went up the gangway and the porter found a seat for me on deck, setting my bags beside me. It seemed Mr. Paxton had followed me, keeping an eye on me, which was kind of him. He came to sit beside me, having just the one small suitcase.

"You travel light, Mr. Paxton," I said.

He smiled. "I am only here until the company arrives and are settled into their hotels. Then I'm to return to New York."

"Where are you staying?"

"At the Palace Hotel," he said. "Our leading lights will be staying there, so they've kindly granted me a room for a few days to make sure everything is to their liking."

"Is the Palace the leading hotel in town?"

"It is. I've heard it is almost as impressive as a real palace. The lesser lights of the company are booked into not-so-grand hotels and the musicians into boardinghouses."

"Do you have the name of some of these boardinghouses?" I asked. "One of them might be what I'm looking for."

"I'm afraid I don't, Mrs. Sullivan. I am only charged with making sure our stars are well taken care of."

With a loud toot the ferry's paddle wheels started churning and we moved away from our dock. Liam watched this new experience with wonder. *Did he remember traveling on a ship a year ago?* I wondered. But then it had been a big ocean liner, not a small craft like this. A stiff wind whipped across the water, making me hang on to my hat with one hand, my son's jacket with the other.

"I'll take him for you," Mr. Paxton said. "Come on, boy, let's go and take a look over the side, shall we?"

"Be careful with him," I called after them. "He can be a handful."

But I watched as he held Liam firmly in his arms and pointed out various wonders to him. Our captain had to sound his horn frequently for smaller vessels to get out of his way. Strange Oriental faces looked up from sailing boats of various sizes. Larger steam vessels lay anchored. We picked a path between them until a tall tower came into view and the building proclaimed itself the San Francisco Ferry Building.

More porters swarmed aboard and again I followed my luggage down a gangplank.

"Where to now, lady?" my porter asked. He was a rough-looking fellow, unshaven, and with tattoos over his bare arms like a sailor.

"I'm not sure," I said. "I have to find a hotel room. Do you know of one nearby?"

"You're looking for a hotel room?" He started to laugh. "Ma'am, you won't find a hotel room in this whole city right now."

"What do you mean?" I demanded, staring at the grinning porter. "Surely there are plenty of hotel rooms in a city this size?"

"Sure there are, ma'am. But all of 'em are full right now. Unless you've come with a sack full of money, you're going to be out of luck."

"Are hotels so expensive in this city?"

"Not normally," he said. "Although the Palace and the St. Francis will set you back a fair bit. But frankly I don't think you'll find a room for love nor money at the moment and if you do, they'll be asking a hundred dollars a night or more."

"A hundred dollars a night? For a simple room?"

He shrugged. "It's this Caruso fellow. The whole place has gone mad. Folks have come from all over the West to hear him sing and pretty much every hotel room is taken for the next few days. And if one is still available, they are asking the moon for it—and getting it."

Mr. Paxton was still standing close by and heard all this. He came up and tapped me on the shoulder. "I've a suggestion, Mrs. Sullivan. You only need the room until you meet up with your husband, don't you? And that should not take you too long. I've a block of rooms reserved for our singers. I see no reason why you shouldn't occupy one of those until the company arrives. That won't be until tomorrow at the earliest and will give you a day or two's breathing room."

"Mr. Paxton, I couldn't," I stammered. "Not at the Palace Hotel. I couldn't afford it, for one thing."

He grinned. "The rooms are reserved and paid for, as we weren't sure when the company train would arrive. So I suggest you make the most of it. All it will mean is that the maid has to change the sheets, which she would have done anyway."

"I'd take him up on it, lady," the porter said. "You'll likely not find another room until Caruso has done his singing and gone home. And the Palace—well, you can't do better than that, can you?"

I looked at Mr. Paxton and of course it had by now dawned on me that the Palace Hotel was where I had spotted Daniel in the newsreel. It would be the perfect place to start searching for him. "Thank you," I said. "Just for tonight, I accept with gratitude."

❧ Eleven ❧

O ur bags were loaded onto the back of an open dogcart. We were assisted up to the seat and we set off down a long straight street. This part of the city was flat, in contrast to those hills I had seen from the ferry, and it was only a minute or two later that the carriage turned into a circular forecourt of a magnificent building, some six or seven stories high. Bellboys in livery swarmed to assist us and whisk away our bags as we were escorted inside. I think I gasped as we entered a central foyer with balconies rising all around it, topped by a glass ceiling. Tables and chairs were interspersed with potted palms. It was the scene I had witnessed in the movie, but the camera had not shown me the size or scope of it. Truly magnificent. But I had little time to gaze as Mr. Paxton had gone ahead. I hurried to catch him as he entered a large vaulted room with a marble tiled floor. Our footsteps echoed as we were led across to a reception desk.

I hung back while Mr. Paxton checked in and then explained that I would be using one of the rooms he had reserved for the opera company until their rightful occupant arrived. The desk clerk gave me

an appraising glance and I could tell from the look that he was reading more into this than the truth. He obviously suspected that I was
Mr. Paxton's fancy woman, even though I held a squirming baby in
my arms. But he was paid not to judge or ask questions. He handed
two keys to waiting bellhops.

We rode an elevator to the fifth floor and I was led along the cor-
ridor opening onto the central court, and then ushered into a magnificent room. Its window looked down Market Street to the ferry
building and to the Bay beyond. It was so sumptuously appointed that
I almost feared to touch anything.

The bellboy put down my carpetbag, then said, "Did madam not
bring a maid with her?"

"No, I didn't."

"Then madam will not need to be shown her maid's room." His
expression showed disappointment in me. "Will the infant be requir-
ing a crib, madam?"

"I don't think that will be necessary. You see I'm not staying long.
Probably only one night until I meet up with my husband."

"It's no trouble, ma'am. I'll have one sent up immediately," he said.
"And your trunk will be here any minute."

Then he showed me my bathroom, complete with a huge tub with
gold-plated handles. He demonstrated how to press the bell whenever I needed assistance, then he left, clearly disappointed in the size
of the tip I had given him. I put Liam down and just stood there in
the middle of that luxury, not knowing whether to laugh or cry. If I
had been visiting in other circumstances, I should have been thrilled
to be surrounded by such opulence. But all I could think was, *I have
to get out of here and find Daniel.*

No sooner had this thought crossed my mind than there was a
tap on my door and I opened it to find Mr. Paxton standing there.

"I came to check that everything was all right," he said.

"All right? Look at it!" I exclaimed. "It's breathtaking, isn't it?"

"I hope our singers will agree," he said. "Our divas are thoroughly
spoiled and require the most absurd luxury. One brings her canary

in a cage whenever she travels. Another has to have rosewater for her bath. If she doesn't have it, she complains her throat closes up and she can't sing."

"Goodness." I had to laugh. "Then I must be easy to please."

"Look," he said, suddenly serious again. "I know you'll want to find your husband right away. I wondered if you'd like me to look after Liam while you go and make inquiries."

"If you're sure you've nothing else to do right now."

"Nothing at all. As I say, after I've checked out all the rooms and rehearsal facilities then I'm free to explore the city until the company arrives. That task shouldn't take me too long. So you see I have time and would be happy to watch the little guy while he takes a nap."

"That would be wonderful." I let out a sigh of relief. "He's awfully heavy to carry around now. I wonder if the hotel has a baby buggy they can lend me?"

"I'm sure this hotel has everything you could possibly wish," he said, laughing. "I'll send down for some food and we can share a snack before you set out on your quest."

"You really are very kind." I blinked back tears.

"Nonsense. I'd want someone to do the same for my wife and child," he said. "And you did keep me splendid company on a long train ride."

I found postcards of the hotel among the stationery and wrote to Bridie and Sid and Gus, letting them know that we had arrived safely and I was about to go off to locate Daniel. A plate of cheeses and fruit, cold meats, and bread soon arrived as well as some soup for Liam. I handed the postcards to the boy who delivered the food. He assured me that they would go out with the next collection. The crib was wheeled in and I put my son down for a nap. He protested at first, but then fell asleep. I whispered another thank-you to Mr. Paxton and set off.

I hadn't walked a few yards down the hall when I was conscious of being followed. I glanced back. A tall, skinny fellow wearing a derby hat was walking behind me. As I turned the corner toward the elevator he hurried to catch up.

"If I might have a few words, madam?"

"What about?"

He was holding a pencil and pad at the ready.

"You of course. Your journey across the country."

"I'm sure there is nothing remarkable in either. Are you some kind of reporter?"

"I am, madam. Jeremiah Hicks of *The San Francisco Examiner.*"

"And do you make a practice of interviewing all the new arrivals to the city, Mr. Hicks?"

"Just the famous ones, madam," he said. "I must say you are a lot slimmer and younger than your pictures. I had always thought that opera singers were—you know—broader?" He blushed at the word.

"I'm sorry, but I think you've made a mistake," I said. "I am not an opera singer."

His face fell. "You are not Mimi Adler?"

"Unfortunately no."

"But I was told downstairs that Miss Adler would be occupying the room you just came out of."

"She will, in a couple of days' time. I have graciously been allowed to use her room until she arrives. The very kind man from the Metropolitan Opera arranged it for me after we arrived to find no rooms available in the city. Only please, let's keep this to ourselves. I wouldn't want him to have overstepped his authority and to get into trouble."

He grinned, then looking like a naughty schoolboy said, "Don't worry. I won't spill the beans."

I realized that I might have a valuable contact in Mr. Hicks. "So you interview famous people when they arrive in the city?"

He nodded. "My boss, Mr. Hearst, is very keen on getting the scoop, you see. I have to hang around the Palace and the St. Francis and be the first to get an exclusive interview for the newspaper. I get a bonus if the scoop is a good one." His face fell. "I was hoping to bag Mimi Adler before she was expected to arrive. Wouldn't that have been something?"

"I'm sorry I disappointed you."

"And you're not a famous person in your own right?"

"I'm afraid I'm not." I paused. "I am an ordinary wife and mother from New York. But I wonder if you might have come across my husband? He came out here a couple of weeks ago. Daniel Sullivan is his name."

Jeremiah Hicks frowned. "Sullivan? Is he famous?"

I was about to say that his name might be known in certain circles, but then I reasoned that he might not have wanted his presence broadcast. Before I could phrase the way I wanted to answer he frowned. "Wait. Sullivan? I did read that name recently. Where was it?" He paused, but then shook his head. "He's an important kind of guy?"

"Not really. He's a police captain in New York City. And he might not even be using his own name . . ."

"Why would that be? On the run?"

I smiled. "Nothing like that. An undercover assignment, I suspect. But I'm asking if you met him because he was photographed at the bar of this hotel, talking and laughing with a group of men."

Hicks shook his head. "I'm afraid not. I don't normally hang around watering holes like this. Too pricey for me." He looked at me with interest. "So you've come out to surprise him, have you?"

"Something like that. Actually more than that. I have important news that I have to give him so I have to find him immediately."

"Have you asked at the hotel desk here, and at the other hotels? He'd have had to stay somewhere unless he was invited to a private home."

"He did mention a Mrs. Rodriguez in his letter," I said.

"Bella?" He smiled. "If he knows Bella, then you're all set, aren't you? She'll know where to find him. She knows everyone in the city, does our Bella. She likes to think of herself as the city's hostess par excellence."

"And where can I find her?"

"She has a big house—well, mansion really—up on California Street. That's Nob Hill, where all the swells live—you know the Crockers, Mark Hopkins's widow, and those other railroad barons. Anybody who is anybody lives on Nob Hill. And they're about to open another fancy hotel up there too—the Fairmont, they are calling it. If you'd come a week or so later you could have stayed there."

"How do I find this Nob Hill from here?" I asked.

"Easy. You take the cable car from Powell Street," he said. "Just walk along Market until you come to it."

"Thank you," I said. "And if I wanted to visit the San Francisco police, where is their headquarters?"

"Justice building on Portsmouth Square. To get there it's easier to go down Market until you find Kearny Street and then follow Kearny until you come to Clay. Then you can't miss it. Fine new building on a fine new square. The city is very proud of it."

"Thank you," I said.

The elevator arrived and we stepped inside. We rode down in silence. On the ground floor I was about to walk away when he called after me, "Mrs. Sullivan, be careful where you walk in a city like this. There are parts you wouldn't want to go alone, without a man to escort you."

"I've been warned about the waterfront," I said.

"With good reason. And then there's Chinatown. It's only a block north of Portsmouth Square and I certainly wouldn't advise a woman to wander through the backstreets there alone. The Chinese pretty much keep themselves to themselves, but you never know. There are rumors of white slaving . . ." He fished into his pocket. "Look, here's my card. You can leave a message for me at the Examiner building just across the street if you need help."

"You are very kind," I said. "And if you could ask your colleagues if any of them has come across Captain Sullivan, I'd be most grateful."

"If he says he's with Bella, you don't need to look any further, do you?" He looked puzzled. "She'll have him fetched for you in a jiffy. Everyone around here dances to Bella's tune."

"So exactly who is this Bella Rodriguez?" I asked. "Another widow of a railroad baron?"

"Not of a railroad baron, but certainly a rich widow. What we understand is that her husband owned a big cattle ranch in New Mexico. I'm not sure where she came from originally, but her husband must have been Spanish with a name like Rodriguez. Of course that whole part of the United States originally belonged to Mexico, didn't it? Anyway from what we heard he died and she sold up and came here. Must have been worth a fortune. She set herself up with a fine mansion and quickly became one of the city's leading lights. She's certainly generous and knows how to throw a good party. Your husband will be enjoying a fine lifestyle if he's staying with her."

"He didn't say he was staying with her, just that he'd met her," I said cautiously. "But you're right. She would be the person to call upon."

Mr. Hicks tipped his hat to me and went off. I was about to follow when it occurred to me to ask at the reception desk first. If Daniel had been seen in the bar, it was possible he had stayed here when he first arrived. I saw a distinguished-looking man in a frock coat standing at one of the mahogany desks and went up to him.

"May I be of assistance, ma'am?" he asked.

"You may. I wanted to know whether my husband might have stayed at this hotel a couple of weeks ago."

His expression changed. "I'm sorry, but we cannot divulge the names of our guests," he said. "It goes against our policy of discretion and privacy."

"But this is my husband I'm inquiring about," I snapped.

"All the more reason, ma'am." He gave me an annoying smirk. "You have to understand that there are occasionally husbands who would not like their wives to know that they have stayed here."

"Really," I said, my annoyance now boiling over. "My husband summoned me to join him in San Francisco and you can't tell me whether he was a guest at your hotel?"

"If you are about to join him, then I suggest he tell you himself," the man said. "I'm sorry, ma'am, but it's hotel policy. We have some very important guests staying here. Guests who would not want their presence to be generally known."

"This is most frustrating," I said. "Very well. I don't suppose it's important. I'm sure Mrs. Rodriguez will know where he is. He may even be staying with her."

"Then I wish you luck," he said. I was being dismissed.

I was just about to cross the foyer to the glass doors when I heard a loud laugh coming from my right. It was almost as if that moving picture I had seen in New York was being played over again. The same shot of the foyer and then the camera sweeping across to the bar where I had glimpsed my husband. I spun around, a hopeful smile on my face. But my husband was not among the smartly dressed men who stood there, with whiskey glasses in their hands. Complete strangers. I was tempted to go and ask them if they remembered sharing a drink with Daniel but it seemed too improbable. In a hotel like this people came and went and, as the porter had said, half the world was in town for Mr. Caruso. Also, as I'd just learned from the desk clerk, men stick together on such occasions and would not confide to me if they had met Daniel. I gave the bar one last glance and realized that I did recognize someone after all. Surely that was Mr. Endicott, standing at the far end?

I hesitated, not sure whether I should seize this chance and go up to introduce myself to him. But I had more pressing things on my mind at this moment. I had to find Daniel. Mr. Endicott could wait. At least I knew where I might find him, when things were not so chaotic and when I had located my husband. I gave a satisfied nod as I passed through the glass doors. I came out onto the street and stopped in amazement. We had arrived to bright sunshine at midday. Now a dank fog hung over the street, turning the tower of the ferry building and the tall skyscrapers along Market Street into indistinct shapes. It had become colder and I wished I had brought my shawl with me. But I wasn't going to risk going back and having Liam wake up. Besides, I couldn't expect Mr. Paxton to watch him for too long.

As I crossed Market Street, dodging out of the way of a trolley car, I was still in a state of indecision about what to do next. Logic told me there was no reason not to go straight to Bella Rodriguez. Mr. Hicks, who as a reporter should know all about his city, had spoken of her as a respected citizen. He had warned me about other matters. Would he not have warned me if there had been anything suspect about Bella Rodriguez? And Daniel had mentioned how well she was looking after him. Was I being too suspicious not to take that statement at face value? I could go to the bottom of Powell Street, a hop, skip, and jump away from where I was standing, and take a cable car to her residence and might find myself reunited with my husband immediately.

On the other hand there was still that nagging doubt that I might be walking into a trap. I tried to think what Daniel would have done when he arrived in the city. He was the sort of man who did every-thing by the book. That would mean he'd introduce himself to the local chief of police. There could be no harm in my going to Ports-mouth Square and seeing what they knew about Daniel and where he was staying. So I walked along Market Street, noticing the smartly dressed women and handsome, rakish men. Trolley cars clanged as they ran along Market Street, but there was also a procession of fine carriages and even automobiles. This was clearly a city of money and progress. The shops I passed were full of exotic merchandise—silks imported from the Orient, champagnes from France. And there were also many bars, oyster houses, and even French restaurants. Lots of money and plenty of ways to spend it, I thought.

To begin with, Kearny Street also had an elegant feel to it. A large jewelry store. A department store similar to the ones we'd find in New York. But as the road climbed gently uphill the atmosphere of the street changed and I realized I was on the fringes of Chinatown.

Smells wafted toward me, smells that I recognized from my own adventure in New York's Chinatown. But that was just a tiny area, comprised of three city streets. And in New York, Chinatown had a distinct absence of women. When I looked up the side streets I passed on my left I saw a true Chinese community: newspaper vendors on the street, hawking Chinese newspapers; women with baskets over their arms haggling at a vegetable stall; and above all children—little girls with long black pigtails, wearing baggy, colorful trousers and little boys with strangely shaved heads. It looked like a place that was full of life, not danger. I would have liked to explore but I had more pressing things on my mind.

Portsmouth Square was a wide expanse, newly laid out with gardens and young trees. Spring bulbs were blooming in the flower beds and children were playing, just like they did in New York. Only some of these children were Chinese, being kept by a watchful mother or nursemaid well apart from their European counterparts. The Hall of Justice was an impressive brick building on the far side of the square. I went up marble steps and into a central foyer.

"I'm afraid the chief is in a meeting at this moment, ma'am," the constable at the reception desk said. "Might one of our lieutenants be able to assist you?"

"When might your chief be available?" I asked

He shook his head. "He's in with Mayor Schmitz and Abe Ruef, the city attorney. When those three get their heads together it would be more than my job's worth to interrupt them. What might this be about? Are you reporting a crime?"

"Nothing like that," I said. "My husband is a captain with the New York police and he was sent out here. So I assumed he would have paid a courtesy call on your chief when he first arrived. And I thought that someone here might know where he was staying."

"What was your husband's name, ma'am?"

"Sullivan. Daniel Sullivan."

"Oh, here comes Lieutenant Addison," the desk clerk said at the sound of footsteps coming down tiled stairs. "This lady was inquiring after a Captain Sullivan, sir. Do we have any knowledge of someone by that name? Daniel Sullivan?"

The older man paused and gave me the strangest look that I couldn't interpret. "You're too late, I'm afraid," he said. "The funeral was two days ago."

✵ Twelve ✵

The world stood still. There was no sound. Nothing moved. I wasn't even breathing anymore.

Then I blurted out, "There must be some mistake. I'm talking about a Daniel Sullivan recently arrived from New York."

"That's the one," the man replied. "He was from New York. They found something in his wallet indicating that he came from New York." I must have swayed because he put out a hand to steady me. "Are you all right, ma'am? Here. Sit down. Get her some water, Hanson."

I wasn't conscious of sitting or even of taking the water glass from the constable. "You've had a shock, ma'am," the officer said. "Was the gentleman related to you?"

"My husband." The words came out as a whisper.

"I'm truly sorry to be the bearer of such bad news, Mrs. Sullivan," he said.

"When did he die?" I asked.

"It would have been five days ago now, on the eleventh."

"Why wasn't I notified?" I demanded, realizing as I said it that any message would probably have arrived after I left New York. All those days sitting in a train, looking forward to seeing Daniel when all the time he was already dead. I pressed my lips together. I was not going to cry.

"I don't believe a home address was among his possessions," the man said. "He had some form of identification linking him to the New York police and I think a telegram was sent to them."

I sat there, staring down at a tiled floor, not knowing what to say next. Then I forced myself to ask, "How did he die? Was he murdered?"

"Oh, no, ma'am. A tragic accident. He was standing at the edge of a cliff, out at Lands End, when the ground crumbled and he fell with it down to the rocks below. Clearly he didn't appreciate the fragile nature of our local sandstone. It simply isn't stable, especially after the rains we've had recently."

"An accident," I repeated. "You're sure of that?"

"No, we can't be sure. It was late at night and nobody actually saw the fall. But someone was close enough to have heard a cry and called a constable to investigate. They saw where the land had given way and when a flashlight was shone down, they could make out the shape of a body on the rocks below. Of course there was no way of reaching him in the darkness but next morning a boat was launched to retrieve the body."

I sat like a statue. "And he was definitely alone? There was no possibility that he was pushed over the edge?"

I looked up to see his expression waver. "As a matter of fact a witness did come forward to say that he saw two guys together near the edge of the cliff around that time. But he didn't witness your husband falling. So whether there was someone with him, whether the other man was responsible for his demise, I couldn't say. As you probably know your husband was a guest of Mrs. Rodriguez and naturally we interviewed her afterward. Most cut up about it, she was, and couldn't think of anyone in the city who'd want to harm Mr. Sullivan."

"It was Captain Sullivan," I said proudly. "He was the youngest captain in the New York police."

"A tragic loss," he said. "But you'd probably know more than we do. What brought him across the country to our city? Was he on the trail of a dangerous criminal? Can you think of why he'd go to a remote cliff top site at night?"

"I wish I could tell you," I said, "but in truth he told me nothing. He only sent me a cryptic letter, indicating that he might be in danger and that I should come out to join him."

"Why would he want you to join him if he knew he was in danger?" The lieutenant looked troubled. "Wouldn't a man usually want his wife to remain safely at home?"

"This is what I've pondered about all the way across the country," I said. "All I know is that he was sent out here on some kind of secret assignment. But what it was, I couldn't tell you."

"That is strange in itself, wouldn't you say?" Lieutenant Addison said. "You don't send a man cross-country unless it's to snag a pretty big fish. And if the guys on the East Coast knew we had a big fish swimming in our pond, why not let us do the apprehending? At least come to ask for our help, which Sullivan obviously didn't."

"I agree," I said. "None of it makes any sense. But it doesn't even matter now, does it? My husband is dead and buried. I'll have to take my son home again and try to figure out what to do with my life. But first I'd like to see his grave."

"Of course you would. And I expect it can be arranged. But it's a good way out of the city. We'd need to have the use of an automobile."

"Why was he buried so far away?" I demanded, my suspicions rising again.

"They passed a law a couple of years ago forbidding any more burials within the city limits," he said. "So they've created these big new cemeteries way down to the south. We'll have to ask the officer who arranged the funeral and the burial. I don't think he was put in the paupers' field, seeing that we knew who he was and could expect payment eventually."

"You'd no right to bury him!" I heard myself shouting. My voice echoed in the tiled hallway and policemen passing looked around to see where the noise was coming from. "I don't want my husband buried here, so far away. He has to be buried near his home, where his father is buried."

The lieutenant looked embarrassed. "I'm sorry. I had no part of the decision. They don't like to keep bodies around more than a couple of days. And as I said I don't believe he had a home address on him."

I stood up again, not sure what I was going to do but sure that I no longer wanted to see the officer's concerned face looking at me with sympathy. "If I wanted to get his body retrieved and have his coffin shipped home, how would I go about that?" I asked.

A worried frown crossed his face. "It's a lengthy process, having a body exhumed," he said.

"I don't want the body exhumed. I just want his coffin taken out of the grave and shipped home," I said, my voice rising again. "That can't be hard if he's only been in the ground a couple of days."

"It would be up to the coroner, I suppose." He put a hand on my shoulder. "Look, Mrs. Sullivan. You've had a horrible shock. Where are you staying?"

"At the Palace Hotel tonight," I said.

He smiled then. "Well, you can't do better than that, can you? I'd say go back there, have a good meal, a good rest, and take time to let things sink in. In the morning I'll try to arrange for an auto to pick you up and drive you out to the grave. All right?"

"I suppose so," I answered mechanically. He escorted me to the door and down the steps, leading me like a blind person, which, essentially, I was. I walked into the middle of Portsmouth Square and stood among the new flower beds. Daffodils were blooming and something that smelled sweet. An accident, the lieutenant had said. A tragic accident. But my husband was a highly trained policeman. He would not have stood in the dark, alone, on a crumbling cliff top, in a place where he didn't feel safe. We had been right all along, I thought. Daniel knew he was in danger and had written to me. But had the letter not been to summon me here, but to say good-bye?

I started to walk back down Kearny Street toward the Palace Hotel, and tried to make myself think clearly. So it seemed now I had two options. Liam and I could take the train back to New York, where we would be safe, or I could stay here and try to find out who killed my husband. It only took me a few seconds to opt for the latter. Daniel was not going to have died in vain. He had come here to solve an important case, to catch a dangerous person, to stop a dangerous plot, and had come close enough that he had to be silenced. And if I started to delve into what brought him here, I'd also be putting my life in danger. Liam only had one parent now. Could I risk his future?

I stepped back hurriedly at the sound of a bell being rung furiously, and a cable car went past me, going up Clay Street toward the hilly part of the city. I made a decision. I would not return to the Palace, not yet. Liam was safe in the care of Mr. Paxton and I had not been away long. If I was going to find out more about what happened to Daniel I had a place to start. And that was Bella Rodriguez, who had a mansion on top of Nob Hill.

California Street, Mr. Hicks had said. And I remembered crossing California Street as I came along Kearny. With luck there would be another cable car line going up the hill as it had looked long and steep and in my current shaky state I didn't think my legs would carry me that far. I passed Sacramento Street and came to California with a cable car line conveniently going up the hill to be swallowed into swirling fog. A car arrived, bell clanging, and I hauled myself onboard. It was quite full and I had to join those hanging on to the step outside. On any other occasion it would have been an exhilarating experience, but in truth I hardly noticed as the hill got steeper and steeper and the cable beneath us whirred and groaned.

I stepped down when we reached the crest and stood looking around with awe. Below me was a sea of whiteness with green hills and even the tallest buildings rising out of the fog. And around me were the finest mansions, just as impressive as those on Fifth Avenue in New York. The cable car had moved away, disappearing into fog again as it went downhill and I was left alone in silence. The street was empty. No sign of anyone to ask and I certainly didn't feel that I could go up one of those flights of steps to a pillared front entrance and inquire about Mrs. Rodriguez. After the burst of energy needed to get me onto a cable car and up the hill, I felt completely drained, like a deflated balloon. If a cable car had shown up heading down the hill again I would have taken it, fled to my room in the hotel, and curled into a tight ball on my bed.

But no cable car came. Instead I heard the clip-clop of hooves approaching through the mist and a carriage came into sight. It stopped outside one of those mansions and a driver climbed down, going around to stand beside the horse's head. I crossed the street and went over to him.

"Pardon me, but I'm looking for the house of Mrs. Rodriguez," I said. "Can you tell me which one it is?"

"Further down the street, miss," he said. "She might be rich but she's not in the same league as the folks who live here at the top of the hill. These here are the railroad barons and the silver barons— Stanford and Hopkins over there and on this side you've got Flood and Huntington and Crocker. Bella Rodriguez is a lesser light. Go past the Crocker mansion and hers is the redbrick with the white trim you'll come to in a hundred yards or so."

"Thank you," I said and set off in the right direction. As I began to descend the fog crept up to meet me. I could hear the mournful hoots of boats down on the Bay. My footsteps echoed unnaturally loudly. It was like being in a world of unreality. Actually my life had become unreal when I first received that letter. Nothing had made sense since. Presumably nothing ever would again.

❧ Thirteen ❧

I took several deep breaths as I stood on the doorstep of Bella Rodriguez's house. Was this visit sheer foolishness? Nobody knew I was coming here. Shouldn't I have told Mr. Paxton of my plan so that he knew where to look if I didn't return? Or was I worrying about nothing? Nobody had anything negative to say about her. She appeared to be a respected society matron. But my husband had written about being well looked after by Bella and my husband was dead. I knew I would have to tread very carefully indeed. And that would not be easy with the current turmoil raging inside my head.

I raised my hand and tugged on the bell. I heard it jangle inside and waited a long while until the front door opened. I suppose it was stupid of me to think that Mrs. Rodriguez would open her own front door, but I certainly wasn't expecting to see a large Oriental man standing there. I had met many Chinamen in New York City but they had been small and thin. This man was a great hulk of a person with a long, drooping mustache and wearing what appeared to be black silk pajamas.

"Yes?" he said, staring at me coldly. "You want?"

The thought flashed through my mind that what I wanted was my husband alive again, but I forced myself to say, "Is this the residence of Mrs. Rodriguez? I wish to speak to her. My name is Sullivan."

I saw the flicker of response to this in his eyes although no other muscle moved on his face.

"Come in," he said.

He opened the door wider to allow me to enter an impressive hallway. The floor was black-and-white marble tiles. There were classical statues and tall potted palms rising to a stained glass dome not unlike the one in the Palace Hotel. A staircase curved upward to our right. It was as impressive as any mansion I'd seen on the East Coast.

"Wait there," he said. "I see if madam is available."

The words came out staccato fashion. He went up the stairs, his slippers flapping on the marble steps. I waited, my heart thumping so loudly that I was sure it could be heard echoing in that lofty entrance hall. Minutes went by, but then I heard feet coming down the stairs again.

I looked up but again it was not Mrs. Rodriguez who came toward me. It was another large man. This one was young and red-haired. Whereas the Chinaman looked as if he were made of granite, this one was chubby. What's more he was dressed in Western garb and looked to me as if he had come straight from rounding up cattle on a range. And the thing that struck me most was that he was wearing a gun belt with a gun in it.

"Can I help you, ma'am?" he asked. "You want to see Bella about something?"

I went to meet him. "I'm Mrs. Sullivan. I traveled out from New York to visit my husband and I've just learned that he met with a terrible accident."

"You're Daniel's wife?" There was instantly compassion on that big weather-beaten face. "I am so sorry for your loss, ma'am. Bella was devastated when she heard the news. She had become so fond of your husband."

I nodded. "He wrote that Mrs. Rodriguez was so kind to him that

I thought I should at least visit her to thank her for her hospitality before I go back to New York."

"Of course she'll want to meet you," he said. "Please, come in. We had no idea that his wife was coming out West. You must have traveled the moment you heard the bad news."

"I just heard it a few minutes ago," I said. "I am still in shock."

"I can imagine. So were we all when we heard." He went ahead of me, through double doors into a lovely octagonal room with windows looking out over the city. At least they would have looked over the city if the fog hadn't hidden it.

"Too bad the fog came in this afternoon," he said. "We normally have a lovely view. Bella had this room built on purpose to sit here and look out. She loves this city. I only wish we could have shown it to you in happier circumstances."

He motioned to a chair upholstered in yellow brocade. I sat. "I'll go and find her. I think she must still be taking her nap," he said. "It's been parties every night recently, what with the excitement of Caruso coming. Would you like some tea?"

"Yes," I said mechanically. "That would be nice, thank you."

I heard his feet clomping up the stairs. I waited. The room seemed surprisingly cold and I shivered. I hadn't heard her approaching and I jumped when a voice right behind me said, "You poor, poor dear. I can't tell you how sorry I am. Here, let Bella give you a hug."

I scrambled to my feet. She came toward me, arms open to envelop me. My first impression again was of size. It was only afterward that I realized she was not a big woman, but she created a large presence, thanks to the big sleeves and collar of her dress and a luxurious coil of black hair, piled up in the Spanish style and held in place by a gardenia. It was hard to tell how old she was. Her face was a perfect mask of makeup—white face powder, plucked eyebrows, rouged cheeks and lips. At home only women of dubious professions would wear that amount of face paint, but I presumed it must be acceptable here, if she was a beloved hostess.

Her arms came around me and for one horrible second I thought

99

I might break down and cry on her shoulder. God knows I needed a friend and sympathy right now. When she released me she must have seen the tears brimming in my eyes. "You go ahead and cry, my dear. We certainly cried enough when we heard, didn't we, Tiny?"

I looked up and saw that the chubby redhead had come back into the room. He nodded. "Bawled our eyes out. Even Francis."

"Francis?" I asked.

"My Chinese butler. I know, it's an odd name for a Chinaman but his real name is too hard to pronounce so I rechristened him. I said, 'If you're going to work for me, you can't have some heathen name. And my favorite saint is Francis so that's what you'll be.'"

She stopped talking then frowned at Tiny. "Did you not tell Ellen that we wanted tea?"

"Yes, I ordered it. It should be here in a jiffy. I'll go see." He disappeared again.

I looked after him with interest. "His name is Tiny?"

"A private joke," she said. "That's what the other wranglers called him on the ranch because of his size. He took over as my ranch manager after Señor Rodriguez died and became so indispensable to me that I lured him with me when I sold up and came to the city. Now I rely on him completely."

As if on cue Tiny reappeared, carrying a tea tray. He poured a pale liquid into dainty cups with infinite care, considering the size of his hands. Then he handed a cup to me.

"I hope you don't mind, it's a Chinese tea. We've become used to it because that's what Ellen likes to serve."

It was too hot to drink but I took a sip. The sensation of unreality returned. To be sitting with a cowboy and a Spanish señora sipping China tea in a world of white fog. Any other time I would have relished the experience and looked forward to telling Sid and Gus about it. Now all I wanted was to be at home.

I started when Bella touched my hand. "You poor little thing. You look all in. Where are you staying?"

"I have a room at the Palace for tonight."

"Nonsense," she said. "You must come and stay here."

"Oh, but I couldn't possibly . . ." I began.

She held up a white hand tipped with long, red-painted fingernails. "Of course you must stay here. I positively insist. It's the least we can do. Stay as long as you want. I expect you'll be arranging to take your husband's body home, won't you?"

"I do want to, but . . ."

"They've already buried him," Tiny mentioned.

"Then they'll just have to dig him up again," Bella said. "Don't worry. I'll have a word with them. I usually get my own way in this city." She waved an imperious hand at Tiny. "Go and have the carriage brought around, then you can take Mrs. Sullivan down to the Palace to retrieve her things."

"I'm sure that's not necessary," I said. "I'll be fine there tonight and I don't know how much longer I can stay here. Besides, I have my young son with me. A kind person is looking after him at the moment."

Bella laughed. "The more the merrier. How old is your child?"

"Still a baby. Eighteen months old. I really don't think—" but she interrupted, holding up an imperious hand. "Tiny, think who we might know with a crib to spare and tell Ellen to go down to Chinatown and find us a suitable nursemaid."

"Oh, no," I interrupted. "I really don't need a nursemaid. I won't be staying—"

"Everyone in San Francisco has a Chinese nursemaid," she said, waving my protests aside as Tiny left the room. "They're awfully good at it. He'll be treated like a young lord. So that's settled then. You go back with Tiny as soon as the carriage comes around, and he'll arrange to have your things packed up and sent up here. At least we can make your stay as pleasant as possible in such awful circumstances. Much better than staying at a hotel with strangers." She put a hand on my shoulder. "Drink up your tea. You look whiter than a sheet and tea is marvelous for shock."

I obeyed, sipping mechanically and feeling the hot, smoky liquid trickle down my throat. I tried to think of a good reason not to accept her generous offer but my mind was still refusing to work when she added, "Ah, here's Tiny with the carriage now. Off you go."

Tiny came into the room and took my arm.

"Take good care of her, Tiny," she called after us. "Bring her back to us quickly."

The carriage took off with Tiny sitting across from me. It seemed I was going to be a guest of Mrs. Rodriguez whether I wanted to or not.

❧ Fourteen ❧

I heard Liam's wails long before I reached my room at the Palace Hotel. I opened the door to see my son, red-faced and sweating, standing up in his crib while Mr. Paxton stood beside him waving his favorite bear, to no avail.

"Mama!" Liam shrieked and flung himself at me. I scooped him up into my arms.

"He's been inconsolable ever since he woke up," Mr. Paxton said. He looked thoroughly exhausted. "I've tried everything—food, drink, singing . . ."

"I'm so sorry," I said. "Waking up in a strange room with no sign of his mother must have been the last straw for him. He's been awfully good for four days."

Liam's wails had now subsided to sobs that shook his whole body as he buried himself against my shoulder. I stroked his hair, drenched with sweat, and patted his back. "It's all right," I said. "Mama is here now. Everything is all right."

Except that it wasn't. It would never be. He'd grow up not even remembering his father. He'd grow up poor unless I could find some kind of job.

"So did you manage to locate your husband?" Mr. Paxton asked.

"I did, but not in a way I hoped." I took a deep breath before I forced the words out. "He's dead, Mr. Paxton. My Daniel is dead."

He looked at me in horror and disbelief. "Dead? Then you weren't wrong in your suspicions that he was in danger."

I glanced at the door, conscious that Tiny must be lingering outside. "They say it was a horrible accident," I said. "He fell from a cliff top in the dark."

"From a cliff? Do they know what he was doing on a cliff in the dark?"

I shook my head. "I spoke to the police. Nobody seems to know anything, except that someone reported hearing a cry and found that the cliff had given way. Oh, and one person reported seeing two men standing together a little earlier."

Mr. Paxton came over to me and put a hand on my arm. "I am so sorry, Mrs. Sullivan. What an awful shock for you. Is there anything I can do?"

I shook my head, his kindness bringing me close to tears again. "Nothing. There's nothing anyone can do. I would like to have his body shipped home so I can bury him by his father's grave, but they've already had the funeral and he's already buried here. Mrs. Rodriguez says she has the clout to make them dig him up again. We'll have to see."

"Mrs. Rodriguez? So you did go to see her?"

I nodded. "I did, and she is being so kind. She's insisting that I come to stay with her until everything is sorted out. She's sent her carriage and one of her employees to help me pack everything up. He's waiting outside right now."

Tiny must have been listening because he entered the room. "Show me what's to go, Mrs. Sullivan," he said. Mr. Paxton and Liam both eyed him nervously. "That trunk can be taken down, thank you, Tiny," I said. "Then I'll just need to collect the things I took out for my baby.

They can fit in the carpetbag. Lucky I hadn't unpacked earlier, isn't it?"

Tiny hoisted the trunk onto his shoulder as if it weighed nothing at all. "I'll be right back for the rest," he said.

As soon as he was gone Mr. Paxton moved closer to me. "Are you sure you're okay with this?" he asked. "Do you really want to go to her house, after all your suspicions?"

"I don't have much option," I said.

"You do. We can send that man away saying that you've changed your mind and you'd rather stay here. I'll tell him that I am happy to put you on the train back to New York."

I looked across at the door, where I expected Tiny to return any moment.

"But I do want to find out all I can about what happened to Daniel, and Mrs. Rodriguez is being really kind. And she can get Daniel's body exhumed for me."

"If you really think that's for the best. That man . . . well, I don't like the thought of you going off with him. He doesn't look entirely trustworthy, if you want my opinion."

"We are in the Wild West, Mr. Paxton. I suppose it's only natural that men wear guns and cowboy hats and Mrs. Rodriguez herself seems very civilized. She lives in a mansion with marble statues . . ." I broke off, unable to convince myself any longer.

Mr. Paxton looked into my eyes with concern. "Well, you know where I am if you need me. I should be here at least until after the first performance at the opera house. Send a note to me and I'll come running."

"You're really very kind," I said. "I can't tell you how much I appreciate everything you've done for us. I hope to see you again before you go."

"I hope so too," he said. "I wish you all the luck in the world. You're a fine lady. And a brave one. You'll get through this if anyone can."

He took my hand and held it in his as Tiny came back into the room.

"I still need to pack my odds and ends," I said. "Liam, you better go back in the crib while I get things done."

"Give him to me," Mr. Paxton said. This time Liam went to him with no outburst.

I stuffed everything into the carpetbag. "You know where I'm staying, don't you?" I said. "Mrs. Bella Rodriguez up on California Street." I said the words clearly, wanting Tiny to hear that I had an ally here if necessary.

Mr. Paxton nodded as he handed Liam back to me. Tiny took the carpetbag and we walked in solemn procession back to the elevator and then out to the carriage.

When we arrived back at Bella's house she was waiting for me and made a big fuss of Liam.

"Look, Francis," she said. "A baby in the house. Isn't that lovely. Come and let me show you the nursery, my dear Mrs. Sullivan."

I followed her up the stairs. Then up another flight. "I thought we'd put him up here so he won't be disturbed by noise," she said. "I hold a lot of parties and they can get loud at times." She went ahead of me into a pretty, bright room with a bed covered in a white chenille quilt and a white dresser against the wall. There was a braided rug on the floor and a flowery washbasin in the corner. "We have a crib coming over and Ellen's gone to find a nursemaid. Now come and see your room."

She led me down the stairs again. "I thought you might want to sleep in the room where your husband last slept," she said. "It's definitely the nicest bedroom."

It was a fine room at the side of the house. There was a little balcony outside the window and a creeper twined around the railing. The view faced the bigger and more extravagant mansions at the top of Nob Hill. Against one wall was a big brass bed with a satin quilt on it. And there was a fine mahogany wardrobe, a chest, and a vanity table. And a radiator under the window.

"As you can see, I like my creature comforts," she said. "It's not particularly cold here but it can get damp at night and the heat comes on at six o'clock. You'll be quite comfortable and the bathroom is across the hall. I'll have towels sent up. Always plenty of lovely hot water. Have a good long soak. I always find that helps when I'm wound up."

Tiny came in with the trunk. "The crib has arrived. I'll bring it up," he said. "Oh, and Ellen's back with the nursemaid."

"That was quick. Good for Ellen. She always knows where to find the right people," Mrs. Rodriguez said. "Send them up here."

We waited and soon an elderly Chinese woman came in, dressed in the traditional manner with black baggy trousers. Although her face was wrinkled like an old prune, her hair was still jet black and pulled back severely into a bun. Behind her was a younger Chinese girl, also wearing black trousers but with a crisp white tunic over them. Both of them both bowed to Mrs. Rodriguez.

"I find good nursemaid, missus," Ellen, the elderly Chinese woman, said. "She work for white family before. She take good care of little boy. Her name Li Na."

"Who did you work for, Li Na?" Mrs. Rodriguez asked.

Li Na stepped forward and bowed shyly. "I work for English family in Hong Kong," she said. "Then my brother come here to America and say there is good money to be made in Gold Mountain so I come with him."

"This is Mrs. Sullivan and her son's name is?"

"Liam," I said.

The young Chinese girl giggled, holding her hand in front of her mouth. "That funny," she said. "Lee-na and Lee-am. We made to go together."

Then she reached out and took him from my arms and to my surprise he didn't protest, looking at her face with wonder. "We go up to your room and play with toys, yes?" she asked. And she whisked him away.

"Looks like you've hit the jackpot again, Ellen," Bella said. "Well done. And it will only be Mrs. Sullivan and Tiny for dinner tonight. I promised I'd attend a little gathering at the mayor's house and I can't really get out of it. Besides, I think Mrs. Sullivan might rather have a quiet meal alone on a tray in her room. Isn't that right?"

I nodded.

She put an arm around me. "I need to get dressed for this evening's festivities. And you should have a good night's sleep. Tomorrow we'll try and sort out all those annoying details and then get you safely back home to New York."

She left me then. I sank down onto the bed, too weak to do anything else. I lay staring at the ornate ceiling, trying not to think. Outside the window I heard birds chirping and the clang of the cable car bell as it rattled past. I don't know how long I lay there but I came to when I heard voices, then a front door slam, then a carriage going off. I roused myself to unpack Liam's things and took them up to the nursery. He seemed quite content as Li Na fed him some kind of soup.

"He good boy," she said, nodding with approval. "He like to eat. Chinese soup make him strong."

Ellen brought up a tray for me. I was rather worried that it might be Chinese food and I didn't think that I could face it, but it was an omelet, light and fluffy, some thin brown bread, a glass of milk, and some cookies. Exactly what I felt I could face. I could see what Daniel had meant when he said he was well looked after at Bella's house. Even so, I found it hard to swallow and had no appetite. Ellen clucked disapproval when she came to retrieve the tray.

"Missus need to eat," she said. "Need to stay strong for boy."

This was true, of course. As she bent to pick up the tray she added in a low voice, "Sullivan's death not accident."

I looked up at her, shocked. "How do you know?"

She nodded slightly. "Ellen has good eyes. She see things. She see man always stand waiting in shadows. When Sullivan go out, man follow."

"What kind of man?"

She shrugged. "Not always same man."

She looked up as we heard feet on the stairs. "Better go now, back to kitchen," she said and fled with the tray. I sat like a statue, digesting what she had just said. So Daniel hadn't meant he was in danger from someone in Bella's house, but from an unknown outsider, keeping tabs on him. An unknown threat, I repeated. Someone who didn't want him here. Someone who was powerful enough to have more than one man watching him. But I had no idea how I could find out more, unless I offered myself as bait. If I started asking too many questions, if I let it be known that I didn't believe my husband's death was an accident, then I might find out more. But then I might also find myself pushed over a convenient cliff. And even if I found out who killed Daniel, what chance did I have of proving it, so far from home and in a place known for its Wild West ways?

I undressed, curled up in that big cold bed, tucked the comforter around me, and lay there shivering—praying that this was a dream and that I would wake up and everything would be all right again.

❧ Fifteen ❧

I must have drifted off to sleep eventually because I didn't hear Bella return in her carriage. When I awoke sun was streaming in through my window. As if on cue there was a tap on my door and Ellen came in with another tray.

"Missy Bella say you take breakfast in bed," she said. She put the tray down on the bedside table and left. I sat up and looked at the pretty china decorated with flowers, the linen cloth, the boiled egg in a silver cup, and thin bread and butter. It was all so civilized. I forced myself to eat and drink, then got up and had a good wash. I was going to put on the same costume I had traveled in, but decided I should look my best if I wanted to achieve anything—especially to have my husband's body returned to me. So I put on the good dress I had brought with me. Outside the world was bathed in sunshine. Below me the city spread down to blue water. Sails dotted the Bay and steamships too. On the other side was the mirror city of Oakland with green hills rising beyond, and out toward the ocean the fog lingered in a band of whiteness. It was a truly spectacular scene, exactly as Daniel had written about it. Thinking of Daniel made me turn away and black despair came back to swallow me. Today I would see my husband's grave, something I never hoped to do in all my life.

I should write to Sid and Gus, I thought. I had promised Bridie I would write to her every day, but I couldn't bring myself to tell them the news and I also couldn't pretend that everything was going swimmingly. Later, I told myself. I'd try and write something later.

When I went up to Liam he was already dressed, fed, and playing on the rug with Li Na, who was building mah-jongg tiles into a tower for Liam to knock down with squeals of delight. She looked up at me, nodding with satisfaction.

"Not to worry, Missee Sullivan. Liam have good time," she said. "I take good care."

As I walked down the stairs again those words buzzed around inside my head. Was she hinting there might be danger to my son? Would those same unknown forces try to kidnap or hurt him? And again the thought hovered: Was I running a risk by staying here? What could I possibly hope to achieve?

I went downstairs to find Tiny reading the daily newspapers. He looked up as I came in. "Caruso, Caruso, and more Caruso," he said. "That's all the city can talk about. I think if the Japanese fleet was sighted off the coast, ready to invade, it would only get the back page."

"Has Mr. Caruso arrived yet?" I asked politely.

"Apparently he's arriving today. Crowds predicted to welcome him when he steps ashore at the ferry building. And his first performance is tomorrow, the seventeenth. The whole New York Metropolitan Opera is coming to join him. Ridiculous, isn't it? But then I'm not one for opera. Too much singing."

I had to smile at this.

"You must miss being out on a ranch, Tiny," I said.

"Sure do. But I'll have my own ranch one day. Bella pays me well and I'm saving up."

"Why did Mrs. Rodriguez sell her ranch and come here?" I asked.

"Bella never was one for the wide open spaces," he said. "Never happy miles from anywhere. That was her husband's idea of fun, not hers. When he died she couldn't move away fast enough. And you should see her here. Loves every minute."

"Has she gone out?" I asked.

This made him laugh. "Lordy no. She will sleep until midday. Stays up half the night."

"Then maybe you can help me," I said. "When I visited the San Francisco police yesterday they said it might be possible to have me taken to my husband's grave. Should I go down to see them?"

"No need," he said. "I'll telephone them and let them know you're safely with Bella. They'll have an auto up here in no time at all."

And so it proved to be. Within half an hour a black automobile had arrived with a constable driving it. I tied my hat securely under my chin and we set off. We turned onto a broad boulevard called Van Ness and from there onto Mission Street. This was no longer the city center with tall and elegant buildings, but rows of small wooden houses, clinging to hillsides. These gradually thinned out and we were driving between green hills dotted with spring wildflowers. Birds of prey circled overhead. For a long while we drove in silence. In truth I was too wound up for small talk and the constable did not seem too enthusiastic about his current assignment. When we finally turned in through wrought iron gates and saw the sign *Holy Cross Cemetery* I almost cried out loud and fought to remain calm. It was a lovely place, on a hillside dotted with stately trees. Many of the graves had fine monuments over them—angels and crosses and mausoleums. The constable helped me from the auto, then he led me to a section of new graves. And there it was, the earth newly packed down and beside it a temporary wooden cross with the word *Sullivan* printed on it unevenly.

It was only now that I fully accepted that he was dead. I turned to the officer who was standing respectfully a few yards away under a eucalyptus tree.

"You can take me back now," I said. I started to walk back toward the waiting auto.

"If you say so, ma'am." He took my arm and aided me over the uneven grass back to the waiting automobile.

"Do you know anything about his death?" I asked as we drove away.

"Not much to know, ma'am," he said. "From what we heard your husband was standing at the edge of the cliff. The ground gave way and he fell. That's all I can tell you."

"I'd like to see your police chief," I said.

"See the chief?" he asked. "I'm sure he can't tell you anything more than I have."

"I'd like to know if Daniel told him why he was in San Francisco."

"Why would your husband have told our chief why he was in town?" he asked.

"Because my husband was also a policeman and was working on a secret assignment. Courtesy would demand that he visited the local chief."

"I see," he said. "I didn't know that. I heard nothing along those lines. But I can take you to the chief and see if he has time to speak to you, if you like."

"Thank you. That's what I would like," I said.

We rode back to the city in silence. Suddenly I said, "No, wait. First I'd like you to show me where my husband died."

"Are you sure, ma'am?"

"Yes. I'd like to see it for myself. I need to see it."

"It was all the way out at Point Lobos, wasn't it? Out at Lands End." He looked at me as if he was reluctant to drive that far.

"I don't really know. They just said a cliff top. But I have to see for myself."

"Of course. I understand. Okay, I'll take you out there." We turned to the left and drove away from the city center again. We passed big new houses. A couple of fine churches. Then the buildings became few and far between and the fog came to meet us as we were swallowed into an unreal world. At last we came to the ocean. There was salt in the damp air that clung to my curls and eyelashes. Through the mist I glimpsed a building that seemed to be perched on top of the cliffs, ready to topple over any moment.

"Holy Mother of God, who would build a house there?" I asked. "Especially when I'm told how unstable the cliffs are."

"It's not a house, ma'am. It's a restaurant and a hotel. The Cliff House is what it's called. And down below are the famous baths. People come from miles around to swim in the saltwater."

"Do we know what time my husband was killed?" I asked suddenly.

"I believe it was around ten o'clock," he said.

"If there is a big restaurant here, not to mention swimming baths, then shouldn't someone have witnessed what happened to Daniel?"

"Ah, but it wasn't close to this area. Further out at Lands End. We've a way to go yet." And he drove off the paved surface and onto a sandy track. We passed between tall Scotch pine trees, bumping over tree roots until the track ended.

"We have to walk from here," he said.

He helped me out again and took my arm as we set off. An over-poweringly strong and pungent scent from the trees around us hung in the air. I looked up at their delicate, feathery branches.

"What are these trees?" I asked.

"Eucalyptus, ma'am. From Australia. They grow well in our climate. You'll find them everywhere."

Eucalyptus. Australia. Everything added to the sense of unreality as we picked our way over soft soil and crunchy dead leaves. At last the constable stopped me. "Careful, ma'am. We go forward slowly from here."

Before me the trees ended and there were a few feet of springy turf. Mist swirled in my face and from far below came the rhythmic clanging of a bell, echoed far away by another. "Those are the buoys that keep the ships off the rocks," the constable said. He took my elbow as I attempted to move forward.

"No further, ma'am. The cliff edge is unstable at the best of times."

I stood. Seagulls cried plaintively somewhere above the fog and from below came an extraordinary barking noise.

"What is that?" I asked because I'd never heard anything like it.

"Sea lions. A whole colony of them on the rocks down below."

"Is this where he fell?" I asked.

"Somewhere right around here. Look. See where the ground gave way?"

I took a tentative step forward. I could see that the edge had crumbled, but there was no evidence that a large chunk of land had given way. I inched forward and looked over the edge.

"Careful, Mrs. Sullivan." He grabbed the back of my skirt. "It's a long drop."

It certainly was. Through swirling fog I could make out the rocks. Waves splashed at them. A seagull wheeled below me, giving a plaintive cry. But I didn't see what I was looking for. The rocks were black from their regular exposure to water. And there were a few chunks of new sandstone and grass lying on them, but not the sort of big pieces you'd expect to find if the whole cliff top had given way.

A picture flashed into my mind of my husband lying sprawled there. I turned away hastily. Ellen had been right, I decided. Daniel's death was no accident.

❧ Sixteen ❧

As we picked our way past bushes and tree roots to the automobile I tried to make sense of what I had seen. What was Daniel doing out here at ten o'clock at night? If he had to meet someone in secret, surely there were plenty of secluded spots in the city? Why come so far, to the ends of the earth, at night? I could come up with two possible answers to this: the meeting was so dangerous, so vital that they couldn't take the risk of being seen, or he had been lured here to kill him. I think I favored the latter at this moment.

I tried to push my grief aside and to think clearly. Daniel had been sent out here by the head of the U.S. Secret Service. That meant it wasn't an ordinary crime. If it was a Secret Service matter, it might have something to do with spies, anarchists, national security. Had some kind of dramatic deed been planned? The assassination of a prominent figure? But no president or world leader was coming to town, as far as I knew. And the world would not reel from the killing of one of San Francisco's railroad or silver barons. Then it hit me: Caruso was in town. Was there a plan to kill him? To blow up the opera house? I toyed with this idea. Was Caruso a big enough fish to believe that killing him would create an international incident? And if such a plot was uncovered, why not just share the information with the local police chief and have him add extra security measures? Why was Daniel, an outsider, specifically needed here? It didn't quite make sense but I decided there was no harm in confiding these fears to the police chief when I met him.

As we drove up Market Street we found traffic ahead of us stopped and crowds milling around. My constable muttered what sounded like a swear word under his breath. "Sorry, ma'am," he said out loud. "I forgot. We shouldn't have come this way."

"Is it some kind of riot?" I asked.

"It may well turn into that later. It's that Italian fellow Caruso. He was due to arrive on today's train. I bet they're all waiting outside the Palace hoping to catch a glimpse of him. Let's see if we can cut up at the next cross street."

We did and made our way up the hill to Bush and then across to Portsmouth Square. We left the auto outside the Hall of Justice and the constable led me inside. I waited on a bench in the foyer while he went upstairs. I sat there for what seemed like a long while until I heard the tap of feet on the marble floor and the lieutenant I had spoken with the day before came toward me. I thought that maybe he had been sent to get rid of me, but instead he said, "Please come with me, Mrs. Sullivan. The chief is extremely busy with all that's going on in San Francisco right now, but he'll squeeze you in for a few minutes."

I almost had to smile at this choice of words. Squeeze me in, indeed. They had a strange vocabulary out West!

Chief Dinan was an imposing-looking man with a well-trimmed mustache and a uniform with a lot of braid on it. He rose from his desk and held out his hand to me. "Mrs. Sullivan. How very sorry I am for your loss. Please take a seat and let me know how I can help you?"

"Two things, Chief Dinan. Firstly, I understand that my husband paid a courtesy call on you when he arrived in the city."

"He did."

"Did he tell you why he had been sent here and what his mission might have been?"

"I understood it was a case of fraud. Fake oil leases in Texas. There was some indication that the perpetrator was in this area. I told him to feel free to go ahead but he needed to come to me if he wanted to make an arrest in my city."

"I see." A simple case of fraud. This had completely confounded my theories. "Did he give you any names? Were you able to help him?"

He smiled. "Mrs. Sullivan. We are up to our eyes in our own crimes here. San Francisco isn't the easiest place to keep the peace. Murders every night in the Tenderloin and the Barbary Coast. Shanghaiing. Human trafficking . . . as well as the more everyday stabbings and quarrels and robberies. And now we've the added responsibility of protecting a world-famous opera star, not to mention the whole damned opera company. I don't have enough men to start with and right now they are all working twelve-hour shifts with no days off."

I nodded, showing sympathy. "I understand. And I appreciate your taking time to see me. As you can imagine, I'm somehow trying to make sense of my husband's death. I'm wondering whom he might have gone to meet at such a remote place. Whether he was lured there to kill him. I suppose no details have come to light?"

He shook his head. "I'm afraid not. Unfortunately if it were a murder, there would be no way of proving it, unless there was a credible witness. A push over a cliff does not leave a convenient handprint on the back." He gave me a little smile.

"So you don't know any details of this supposed oil-lease fraud?"

"I'm afraid not. I told Sullivan at the time that my men were stretched too thin as it was and he was on his own." He started arranging papers on his desk, indicating that he had better things to do than talk to me.

I went to stand up, then decided to stay put a little longer. "It just crossed my mind that his presence here might have had something to do with the arrival of Caruso," I said. "A possible assassination attempt?"

He looked surprised now. "What put that idea into your head? Did your husband mention anything to you that he didn't tell us?"

"Not at all. He said nothing of his reason for coming here. It just struck me as an interesting coincidence that he was sent to a city at the same time as a famous opera singer, and was killed just before that singer's arrival. What's more I spotted my husband at the Palace Hotel, which is where Caruso and the other opera singers are staying."

"You spotted him?" He looked up sharply. "When was this?"

"At the movie theater back in New York. They were showing news from around the world and featured Caruso's upcoming visit to San Francisco. And when they went inside the Palace Hotel, I saw my husband standing at the bar."

"Interesting." I could see he was considering this. Then he shook his head. "But I can't see . . ." He broke off. "Who would want to assassinate an opera singer? A head of state I could understand, but Caruso? What would be the point?"

"I don't know," I said. "We have problems in New York with an Italian gang called the Cosa Nostra. Maybe they have some kind of score to settle with Señor Caruso."

"Why didn't he tell me this when we spoke? Why make up a story about land fraud? He would obviously have had my support in stopping an attack on Caruso."

Reluctantly I had to agree. He gave me an understanding smile. "I can only imagine how painful this is for you, Mrs. Sullivan, and how you'd like to do something to make things better, but I really don't see what there is to be done. If there were a clear hint of wrongful death, you could be sure I'd have my men onto it right away. As it is, there's really nothing we can do. So please, go home to your family and try to get on with your life."

I decided to strike while the iron was hot. "And the other thing I want, Chief Dinan, is to get permission to have my husband's coffin dug up and shipped back to New York. I want him buried beside his father. I know that's what his mother will want too."

I realized as I said it that I would have to tell her soon and it would break her heart. Her only son. Her pride and joy. But would it be kinder to wait until I returned home and then give her the bad news in person, rather than the shock of a telegram?

"I don't think that's an impossible request," he said. "But there are formalities that have to be gone through. Let us get this opera performance over and I'll have time to set it in motion."

I stood up then and thanked him. He shook my hand again. "Anything else we can do, please let me know."

I came out to the street at least feeling hopeful that I'd be able to take Daniel's body home. It wasn't much but at this moment I was clinging to any thread of the positive. I rode the cable car up California Street to Bella's house. She was dressed and sitting in her octagon room, checking a list. She looked up as I came in.

"My dear Mrs. Sullivan. How are you holding up? Did they take you to see Daniel's grave? I'd be happy to have a suitable tombstone erected for you, at my expense. All you have to do is tell me what you want."

"I want him brought home to New York," I said. "And the police chief seemed optimistic that he could arrange it."

"Well, that's good news." She patted a seat beside her. "Have you eaten? Would you like another tray in your room or shall I have Ellen prepare something for you in the dining room?"

"Thank you. I would like a little something. Just a sandwich. But first I must go up and see Liam."

"He's not there," she said easily. "Li Na took him out."

"Took him out? Where?" The words came out sharp and raw.

Bella Rodriguez shrugged. "I'm not sure. She said it would be good to give him fresh air and to allow him to run around."

"She had no right to do that," I snapped. "I thought my son was safe here. And now she's taken him God knows where."

Bella moved across and put a hand on my shoulder. "My dear

Mrs. Sullivan, please do not distress yourself. I'm sure your son is quite safe with Li Na. Ellen would not have selected an untrustworthy nursemaid."

"You don't understand," I said. "It's possible that my husband's death was not an accident. And if that is true, then perhaps someone might want to harm me or my son."

"Why would they want to do that?" She looked puzzled.

"I don't know. Why would someone want to push Daniel over a cliff? Who even knew that he was in California?"

"You're overwrought," she said. "Nobody seems to think that your husband's death was anything other than an accident, I'm sure. And Li Na will take good care of your child. So please, calm down. Would you like to borrow my smelling salts?"

"I don't use them," I said, shaking her off. "And I'm not about to faint and I'm not hysterical. It's true, I am overwrought, but who wouldn't be? If you'd traveled across the country looking forward to seeing your husband, only to find him dead and buried, how would you feel?"

A slight smile crossed her lips. "In my case I'd be feeling relieved. My husband was a dominating bully," she said. "Like most men he seemed to think that I was a helpless little lady, quite unable to think for herself and only on this earth to provide comfort for him."

"I gather from Tiny that you did not enjoy living on a ranch."

"I couldn't get away fast enough," she said. "I longed for fine dresses, good company, and all I got was a lot of cows and flies."

In spite of my tension I had to laugh. "So why did you marry him?"

"He was a slick talker and I needed to get away from home," she said. "I regretted it instantly. You are lucky to have had a happy marriage and a delightful child. I was never blessed with children."

As she said those words I was reminded of a similar conversation back in New York. Mrs. Endicott had said she had not been blessed with children and her husband was also of the dominating kind. And I'd promised I'd look out for him in California. I had spotted him at the hotel, but frankly at this moment I no longer felt up to paying him a call or delivering his wife's best wishes. All I wanted was to take Liam, Daniel's coffin, and myself back home to New York.

Bella stood up suddenly. "Here they are now. You see, all that worry for nothing."

The front door was opened and I heard Liam's laughter as they came in. I rushed out to join them. His face was sticky, his cheeks were pink, and he grinned at me.

"We running on grass," Li Na said. "And feed birds. And eat Chinese candy. Have good time."

"He certainly seems to be enjoying himself," I said and watched her carry my son up the stairs. I followed her up to see Liam settled. He showed little interest in having me around so I returned to my own room. Soon Ellen brought up another tray for me with little ham sandwiches, a pickle, and a glass of lemonade.

"Ellen?" I asked as she was about to leave. "Do you know more than you're telling me? Do you have a reason to believe my husband's death was not an accident?"

She looked around warily, as if afraid of being overheard. "When he go out at night someone follow him."

"Do you know who followed him?"

"A man. I go now." She scuttled off, leaving me wondering. Was she talking about a nameless man watching on the street, or was it someone from this household, someone who had a reason for wanting Daniel out of the way? But that was absurd, wasn't it? Bella could not have been kinder to me and could not possibly have any reason for wanting Daniel harmed. But Tiny? He had been on Bella's ranch in New Mexico, but for how long? Was it possible that he'd gone to New Mexico to hide out after some kind of crime? Was he possibly Daniel's land swindler?

❧ Seventeen ❧

fter a short rest I came downstairs again to find the household busy with preparations. I heard voices and noises of clanging and banging, the scraping of chairs. I traced it to a splendid drawing room on the other side of the front hall. Two maids I hadn't seen before were dusting, polishing, and rearranging furniture. Before I could speak to them Bella reappeared, carrying a big display of spring flowers in an ornate glass vase.

"On the piano, I think, Alice," Bella said, handing the flowers to her. She smiled when she noticed me. "I hope our noise did not disturb you, dear Mrs. Sullivan," she said. "I'm afraid we're having a little soiree this evening. The mayor and the city attorney are coming as well as some prominent people who are in town for Caruso, so I couldn't put them off, could I?"

"Of course not," I said.

"I do hope you will join us," Bella said.

"Oh, I don't think . . ." I began, but she waved this aside. "It will do you good. Make you forget your troubles for a little while. I have to say with all modesty that I give splendid parties, don't I, Tiny?"

she asked as Tiny came into the room, carrying more chairs. He only grunted and put the chairs down.

"Not there, Tiny. Over by the window," Bella said. She turned to me. "Why do men have no idea about how to arrange a room for good conversation? But I think he does it deliberately. I know he hates these gatherings, especially when I include intellectuals and thinkers. Poor Tiny. He was designed for the wide open spaces, I fear." She watched his back as he left the room again.

"Then why not let him return?" I asked.

"Let him return? You make it sound as if I keep him here. No, Mrs. Sullivan, he is here because he chooses to stay, I can assure you. Nobody else would pay him so well for so little." She took my arm. "Let's leave these girls to finish their work, shall we, and I'll have some tea sent to the octagon room. The fog hasn't come in yet and the view is quite lovely as the sun goes down over the ocean."

I was steered to the room on the other side of the house and plied with tea and small Chinese almond cookies. The view was as spectacular as she had predicted. The water in the Bay sparkled. The sun hung like a red ball above a bank of white fog. I tried to enjoy what I was seeing but I was too numb to do more than stare out of the window. Afterward I went up to see Liam, who was waking from his nap. He did seem such a happy little boy, and he was already attached to Li Na. When he was having his supper I went down to change for the evening. I really didn't want to be part of a gay soiree but Bella had insisted. "There will be some of your fellow countrymen there," she said. "Father O'Brien from Star of the Sea Church is a delightful young man. Highly educated and interested in music and theater, and he has told me that he has a distinguished professor from Dublin staying with him. The man was actually a friend of the composer Bizet, can you imagine? And of course Caruso has chosen *Carmen* for his first performance."

Neither Bizet nor *Carmen* meant much to me. I had been to a few theaters in New York but opera was outside my sphere of experience.

But I could tell that Bella thought this was most impressive, so I had agreed to come down for at least part of the evening.

"I don't suppose they'll stay long," she said. "Father O'Brien will have to be up early to say mass and the professor is very old, so I hear. But I think it will do you good to be in company, especially of Irishmen."

So I was not allowed to refuse. I put on the one evening gown I had brought with me. When I looked in the mirror to put up my hair I could imagine Daniel coming up behind me, slipping his hands around my waist, and kissing the back of my bare neck. I turned away, unable to bear it any longer.

I heard the front doorbell ring, the sound of voices and laughter. More and more people arrived. I knew I'd have to go down but I couldn't bring myself to do so. In the end there was a tap on my door and Francis was standing there. "Missy Bella want to see why you not come to join party. She send me to bring you down now," he said, and escorted me down the stairs.

The drawing room was now full of people. The overhead chandeliers were twinkling with electric lights. Waiters were moving through the crowd with trays of champagne. The noise level was overwhelming and I would have turned around and escaped back to my room had not Bella spotted me.

"Here she is now," Bella said, coming toward me with hands outstretched. "My dear Mrs. Sullivan, come and meet everyone. I have to tell you that we have here the cream of San Francisco society gathered. Our beloved Mayor Schmitz and his wife." A vibrant and handsome man with a red beard stood up to shake my hand.

"Welcome to our city, Mrs. Sullivan," he said. "And this is my right-hand man, City Attorney Abraham Ruef."

This man was dark-haired with a sallow complexion and his smile didn't quite reach his eyes. He bowed solemnly. "How do you do? I'm told you've had tragic news. I'm sorry you'll have such bad memories of our city."

"We're going to do our best to see she also has some fond memories," Bella said, whisking me away again. "Come and meet some fellow wanderers from the British Isles. Here is Mr. Douglas, from Scotland. If anyone can understand his accent, it will be you." She laughed and moved on, leaving us together.

"You're Irish?" he asked me. He had a bushy red beard that covered half his face.

"I am."

"Fellow Celts," he said, nodding approval. "This is nae my kinda gathering, I can tell you. Give me a simple ceilidh at home with whiskey and songs and bagpipes anyday. Do you nae miss your home, lassie?"

"I do, sometimes," I said. "But my home is now New York."

"New York? That was a place I couldn't wait to get out of. I don't go much for cities. Give me the wide open spaces."

"What sort of business are you in, Mr. Douglas?" I asked.

"Land, lassie. Agricultural land. I've acre upon acre planted in the Central Valley. That's where the wealth of California is going to come from. Not minerals, but crops. With the right management we can feed the nation." He gave a satisfied grin. "This is the place of opportunity all right. Take me. I came with nothing and now I have a house on Nob Hill. And one in Sacramento." He moved closer to me. "Take a look around the room," he muttered. "Everyone you see here came to California and seized opportunity. The folks you see here are worth millions. That young man with his back to you is Mr. William Crocker, with his wife. He's the son of our famous railroad baron, of course, and currently occupies that wee house on the top of the hill." He grinned, sure that I'd had the Crocker mansion pointed out to me. "And that man he's talking to is James Flood, son of the silver bonanza king. And the older man talking with Bella is Spreckels—you know, Spreckels sugar?"

I didn't really know any of them but I nodded politely.

"You enjoy mixing with these people, do you?" I asked.

He shrugged. "Like I said, these musical evenings are not my cup of tea, but every time I'm invited to something like this I'm reminded of how far I've come from that little stone cottage in Scotland."

I nodded with understanding. "I've had the same feelings in New York." I glanced at the doorway as a short and dapper man sporting a neat little beard came into the room with an elegant woman in gray silk on his arm. He was wearing a uniform with a good deal of braid on it and in spite of his height he carried an air of confidence and authority. "Who is the man in uniform?" I whispered to Mr. Douglas.

"General Funston," Mr. Douglas said in a low voice. "Head of the Presidio here. Also not the sort of man you'd expect to see at a gathering like this. He's very much a no-nonsense sort—outdoorsman. More my type. But I gather his wife likes opera and there is to be a performance this evening. Probably that will be when I'll make my excuses and leave. Can't stand the row they make."

I had to smile at this. I watched Bella come over to greet the general and his wife and I sensed the tension in the room as he shook hands with the mayor. So the army and the city were not all together happy neighbors. I had to admire the way Bella played the gracious hostess, drifting among the crowd, making sure everyone was introduced and having a good time. And yet I also noticed that her fists were tightly clenched, even though she appeared smiling and relaxed. So she too felt some strain this evening.

My Scottish gentleman had wandered off and I was standing there with that lost and embarrassed feeling one has at a party where one knows nobody, when Bella came up beside me again, this time with an older woman. "I've found someone else you have to meet, dear Mrs. Sullivan. This lady is the widow of Mr. Wheeler, a British gentleman who made his fortune in the shipping business. Trade to China, wasn't it, Elsie?"

"It was." The older woman nodded to me. "And now he goes and dies on me and leaves me in this godforsaken place." She spoke with an accent that betrayed origins in the north of England. Although she was dripping with jewels she was wearing black and suddenly it hit me. I was now a widow too. I should be wearing black as well. Thank heavens the dress I had brought with me was dark green and not my more flamboyant blue one.

"And if I might whisk Mrs. Sullivan away for a minute, I've just spotted her fellow countrymen over there in the corner," Bella said. She took my arm firmly. "Come with me."

She steered me across the crowded room. A young priest rose to his feet as I approached.

"This is our dear Father O'Brien," Bella said. "Such a talented young man. He has the loveliest tenor voice. In fact it was suggested that the opera house save its money and have Father sing instead of Caruso."

Those around us broke into laughter. The young priest blushed with embarrassment.

"Really, Mrs. Rodriguez, you shouldn't say such things," he said. "My voice is good enough for a rendering of 'Danny Boy' at an Irish gathering, that's all."

"Too modest." Bella shook her head. "And he's also a whiz at amateur theatricals. You should have seen him in *The Pirates of Penzance* last year. He brought the house down."

The young priest was still looking distinctly embarrassed. "Enough of this, Mrs. Rodriguez. Mrs. Sullivan, let me introduce you to someone who is really distinguished," he said. "This is Professor Flannery from Dublin who is staying with us at the rectory at the moment. He is an authority on modern opera and has been sent by the Irish newspapers to report on Caruso's performance."

"How do you do, Professor Flannery," I said, as the old man attempted to stand up. "Flannery is my mother-in-law's maiden name."

The young priest took his elbow and helped him to stand. "A good name, Mrs. Sullivan," the professor said. He had a shock of untidy white hair and a bushy white beard. He peered at me through bottle-thick glasses. What's more he was wearing a tweed jacket when the rest of the room was in evening attire. "I'm pleased to see a fellow countrywoman," he said in a voice scarcely louder than a whisper. "And you'll have to excuse me. I caught a devil of a chill on the train across the country and I've quite lost my voice." He pulled a big handkerchief from his pocket and held it up to his face as he coughed.

"I'll get you some water, Professor," the priest said.

"Not necessary. I'll survive," the old man said. "But I wouldn't say no to a whiskey." He turned to me. "So which part of Ireland are you from, my dear?"

"From County Mayo."

"Ah, the wild west," he said. "So you've come from one wild west to the other. Quite a journey."

"I don't live in Ireland any longer," I said. "I live in New York. I came out here to meet my husband but I don't know if they told you. He was killed in an accident, before I arrived."

"So I heard. What a shock for you," he said, and then turned away again to cough. He tapped the priest on the arm. "Father, I'm thinking this might not have been a good idea, to come out in the night air. I'm thinking perhaps we should make our excuses and go if you don't mind too much."

Bella was passing and reacted to this. "Oh, no, Professor. You can't go yet. We have some wonderful musical performances planned. Some of our local opera stars have agreed to sing for us. I wouldn't want you to miss that for the world."

"And I wouldn't want to disturb their singing with my coughing," he said. "No, it wouldn't be right."

The priest helped him to his feet. "I must apologize," the professor said. "I have to make sure I'm over this before the great performance. I couldn't disturb Caruso with a cough."

"I do understand," Bella said. "So good of you to come. You won't have a little supper before you leave?"

"I think not. Good-bye, Mrs. Sullivan. I'm sure we'll meet again soon."

The priest assisted him from the room. He must have been a big man once but he was horribly bent over and shuffled out, leaning on his stick.

"He looks too frail to have undertaken such an arduous journey, doesn't he?" someone commented.

"Ah, but he's the authority on Bizet," Bella replied. "He knew the composer when they were young music students together in Paris. It will be such a treat for him to hear Caruso sing *Carmen*."

"A treat for us all," one of the ladies said.

"If you happen to like opera," Mayor Schmitz said and got a disapproving look from his wife. "Frankly I think it would be better without the singing."

This produced a laugh from the crowd.

"You must watch what you say, Eugene," Mr. Ruef said. "Visitors will get the impression that San Francisco has no culture."

"You're not drinking, Mrs. Sullivan," the man standing next to me said. It was the Scot, Mr. Douglas. "Try the local champagne. It's not at all bad. I think California has the makings of a good wine-growing area." He reached at a passing tray and grabbed a glass for me. "It's called Big Tree, but don't let that put you off." He grinned. "I'm thinking of planting grapes myself. There are certainly enough people in this city who enjoy their wine."

I hardly heard him. I was suddenly feeling very unsettled, as if something had happened or someone had said something important but I hadn't quite caught it. I looked around the room, trying to think what I might have missed.

"So where is the great man himself?" one of the men demanded. "Where is Caruso?"

Bella spread her hands in apology. "I tried to lure him here tonight. I told him there would be lobster and champagne and caviar, but alas he refuses to leave his hotel room. He is resting before the performance, so I'm told."

"Maybe after the initial performance tomorrow night he'll be more willing to mingle with us," Mr. Crocker said. "You can invite that up-start Giannini to join us and he can talk with a fellow Italian."

"Come now, Crocker," Mayor Schmitz said. "Would you condemn a man just because of his ancestry? He is trying to make himself a fortune just like every man here tonight. Whether he will ever suc-ceed in creating a bank only time will tell."

"But I promised you opera and opera you shall have," Bella said, stepping in to intervene between the two men. "After supper we'll have the stars of our San Francisco opera performing for us. And be-tween ourselves I think they are quite as good as these people they are bringing in from New York City. I can't think why Caruso in-sisted on singing only with the Metropolitan Opera."

"He is very temperamental, so I hear," one of the ladies said. "He performed *Carmen* with them last year so he knows what to expect."

"Great men always are temperamental, especially artistes like Mr. Caruso," Bella replied. "But give him time. We'll charm him with our friendly California ways."

Now that I had been introduced I was forgotten and willingly shrank to the shadows at the edge of the room, looking for my chance to slip away. More guests arrived until the room was uncomfortably crowded and hot. I was interested to see that the police chief was among the newcomers and that Bella greeted him warmly. The police certainly did not mingle with the highest levels of society in New York. Beside him was a muscular young fellow, rather swarthy and arrogant in appearance. Unlike his chief, who was in tails, the younger man was in police uniform.

"I believe you know my young lieutenant Teles, Mrs. Rodriguez," Chief Dinan said. "I thought it wise to have a police presence here, just in case the great man himself puts in an appearance. We can't be too careful, can we?"

So he was taking my suggestion that an attempt might be made on Caruso's life seriously. "Unfortunately Señor Caruso has turned down my invitation for this evening. Maybe tomorrow at the

Crockers', after the first performance?" she said. "But do make yourself at home, both of you."

Chief Dinan looked around and nodded politely when he saw me looking at him. "I'm glad to see you're getting out and about, Mrs. Sullivan," he said. "Always better to accept things as they are and move on." Then he moved through the assembly to chat immediately with Mr. Ruef and the mayor. Very thick together, I thought.

The champagne was going to my head as I had eaten very little and I was glad when a gong sounded and we were invited through to supper. A magnificent spread was laid out in the dining room, everything from lobster and oysters to cold chicken and poached salmon. There were great bowls of fruit and all kinds of salad. I helped myself to a little cold salmon and chicken as well as various salads. It seemed that no type of food was impossible to get here. In New York there was no lettuce this early in the year. Nor grapes or peaches! Even so I found it hard to do more than nibble. My stomach felt as if it was tied into knots. I found that I still couldn't shake off that restless, uneasy feeling. Something had happened or was going to happen, I thought. Something very important. I looked around wondering if other guests had picked up my tension, but they were all drinking and laughing without a care in the world. I decided this might be a good opportunity to slip away before we were seated for the musical portion of the evening.

As I came out into the hall I saw that the front door was just closing and that several people had just arrived. Bella came flying out to meet them.

"Our opera stars are here. How wonderful," she called toward the dining room. "Welcome, welcome. Everyone is so looking forward to this." She held out her hands to them. "Madame Bernini—such an honor. And you, Mr. Richter."

"And our pianist, Mr. Dupont," the woman said. In speech she had a soft, low voice.

A thin man with a bald head and skull-like face stepped from the shadows at the front door and bowed to Bella.

Bella looked flushed. "Francis will show you where to put your coats and then we'll have the drawing room arranged for you to perform. We are so excited. It's so good of you to come. Will you not take a little refreshment first while the room is being arranged?"

As the three of them went off with Francis, Bella realized with surprise that a man still stood by the front door. He was dressed in a traveling coat and had black hair and dark eyes.

"You!" Bella said. "What are you doing here, Señor Garcia?"

"I had business to attend to in San Francisco and thought I should look up my dear old friend Señora Rodriguez," he said in slow and heavily accented English.

"So kind of you, but as you can see, I am hostess for a big party tonight. We are about to hear some opera."

"No matter. I can wait," he said. "I can join your party if you like?"

"No," she said brusquely. "I don't think that would be the right thing at all. Why don't you come back in the morning, then we can talk in peace?"

"About the old days on the ranch, no?" He smiled then. "Such happy memories."

More guests were leaving the dining room. Some of them wandered into the hallway.

"Did the singers arrive, Bella?" one woman asked. "Should we go and take our places?"

"Yes. Please do." Bella was clearly distracted. "The performance will start shortly."

Her fists, I noticed, were still clenched.

Señor Garcia still stood there unmoving. "You want me to go?" he said.

"That would be best," Bella said. "Come back in the morning. Then we can talk."

"Oh, yes," he said, smiling broadly now. "Then we can talk. I have much to tell you—about the improvements on the ranch. We do much excavation for new building. Beautiful . . . but expensive."

Bella opened the front door and he gave her an unctuous bow before he walked out into the night. He must have been wearing some kind of pomade or hair oil because a rather unpleasant sickly smell lingered in the hallway.

I realized that it must look as if I was eavesdropping. In truth I hadn't wanted to cross the hall when Bella was engaged with other people. But now she turned around and saw me. She put a hand up and distractedly patted her hair.

"Such a surprise," she said. "The man who bought our ranch. I never expected him to turn up in San Francisco. What a small world it is." And she managed to give me a bright smile. "Come. The music will be starting."

"If you don't mind, I think I'll go up to my room now," I said. "I'm afraid I have a headache. All the gaiety has been a bit much for me."

"Of course. I understand. Would you like Ellen to bring you hot milk?"

"Nothing, thank you. Please go back to your guests."

"Yes," she said. "I must go back to my guests. Of course."

And she patted her hair again before she went back into the drawing room. I was intrigued as I went up the stairs. Clearly meeting Señor Garcia again had upset her, although he seemed pleased to see her. *An old romance?* I wondered. Had Señor Garcia pursued her when she lived in New Mexico? She had certainly seemed flustered. Perhaps I'd learn more when he returned tomorrow morning.

I let myself into my room. In the drawing room a piano started to play and then a soprano voice echoed out of the drawing room and filled the front hall with sound. It was a lovely voice but so powerful. Overwhelming when it wasn't on a stage in a big theater. I wondered how long the performance would continue and hoped I'd be able to sleep. Gratefully I closed the door of my room behind me and leaned against it, feeling the comforting solidity of the wood against my bare back.

I sat on the bed for a while, then undressed and climbed into bed, pulling the covers up over me. Now that I was alone again the black despair threatened to overwhelm me once more. I would not give in to grief. I would do everything within my power to find out who wanted my husband dead. And I remembered the strange and unsettled feeling that had come over me halfway through the evening.

Think, I told myself. *What did you see or hear this evening that was important, because something happened in that room.* I went through the encounters one by one. Mr. Douglas. The mayor and the unpleasant attorney. General Funston and the police chief, who clearly did not like each other. The nice young priest and the old professor with a bad cold. But none of them had said anything that was in any way relevant to me or to Daniel. I shut my eyes and tried to sleep. "Home," I whispered. I wanted to go home. I didn't belong here. Tomorrow I'd badger the police chief to have my husband's coffin delivered to me and we'd be off.

My eyes shot open as I heard the smallest of clicks. I turned to the door but it was still closed with a strip of light shining under it unbroken by the shadow of a person who might have been standing outside. Then, as I looked around the room, I saw the French door to the balcony slowly inching open. The thought raced through my mind that I had locked that door earlier in the day. Before I had a chance to sit up I saw the shape of a man coming into my room. In the half darkness he was just a big shadow, moving cautiously. Then, to my amazement, he turned toward me and the light from the streetlamp below revealed a white beard, a tweed jacket. I sat up.

"Professor Flannery?" I demanded, shocked. I had not taken him for the sort of man who creeps into ladies' boudoirs. But at least I was no longer terrified. "What on earth?"

He crossed the room with remarkable speed and agility and sat on the bed beside me. I noticed he was no longer wearing glasses.

"What do you think you're doing?" I demanded. "Leave this room instantly. You should be ashamed. . . ."

I heard him chuckle.

"I'll scream for help. You'll be sorry. I'm not a delicate little lady, as you'll soon find out."

His hand came over my mouth. I tried to fight him off. "Molly," he whispered in my ear. "Stop struggling. It's me."

As I looked up, confused, he ripped off the beard and put his finger to his lips. It was Daniel.

❧ Eighteen ❧

My heart leaped in my chest, pounding. I stared at him as if I were seeing a ghost. Only this ghost was living and breathing. I could feel his warm breath on my cheek. Then he took my face in his hands and kissed me. His lips were warm and demanding against mine. That more than anything reassured me that this was my husband, and that he was most certainly alive.

"But you're dead," I managed to gasp at last. Tears sprang into my eyes. "They told me you were dead."

He nodded. "They think I am." He wiped a tear away from my cheek with his fingertip. "Don't cry. It's all right. It's all going to be all right."

"I know," I said, still crying. "I still can't believe it."

Daniel looked around the room. "Where is Liam? Did you leave him at home?"

"No, he's upstairs with a nursemaid. He's fine." I stared at him hungrily, taking in every detail of that beloved face. "I've seen your grave. Who did they bury in your place then?"

"The poor fool who was standing with me on that cliff top," he said. "He arranged to meet me out at Lands End. That's an area of cliffs where the Bay meets the ocean."

"I know," I said. "I went out there today."

A burst of applause came from downstairs. Daniel looked up, then back at me again. "Suddenly," he continued, "these men appeared out of the darkness and pushed us over the edge. He plummeted straight down to his death. I was lucky. I sensed a movement behind me before they struck and was slightly forewarned when they pushed me. A bush was sticking out a few yards down the cliff where I fell. I grabbed onto it and managed to stop my fall. My feet found a narrow ledge and I clung there, hoping that the bush would conceal me from anyone looking from above."

His eyes held mine and I nodded for him to go on.

"I could sense they were looking over to check that we were dead. Then I heard footsteps and voices going away. One of them was actually laughing. They were pleased with themselves."

"What monsters," I said. "What did you do?"

His eyes were sparkling in the light from the streetlamp. "As you can imagine I was battered and winded. I didn't dare move for a while but eventually I made my way down to the bottom of the cliff. It wasn't easy, I can tell you, and I thought I was done for several times when the rock crumbled and I slithered. My poor friend was quite dead, sprawled on the rocks. He had fallen headfirst and his face was a horrible mess. Then an idea came to me. We had both been wearing similar dark suits. Carefully I changed his identification for mine. Then I tossed my hat into the waves. Let them think that we had both perished."

"What did you do then?"

"I picked my way around the shoreline until I could clamber up to the path. I realized, of course, that I couldn't risk being seen again in the city. I heard the sound of a church bell tolling eleven o'clock. Then I saw the dome of a big church. I made for it and lucky for me a priest was crossing from the church to the rectory. I called to him and asked him for sanctuary. My guardian angel must have been watching over me twice that night because it turned out to be Father O'Brien. A more decent guy you couldn't find anywhere. I told him my whole story." He sighed. "Of course he wanted to know why someone had tried to kill me."

"That's what I want to know too," I said. I was holding his hand. It was warm and real and I still couldn't quite believe it. "Who were those men?"

"As to that, I couldn't tell you," he said. "Hired thugs, probably, but I have a good idea who might have sent them."

"Who?"

"Someone high up in city government. Maybe the mayor or the city attorney. They were both in the room tonight. I have to say I rather enjoyed that." He grinned, and I saw Daniel's old cocky smile.

"But why did the mayor or the city attorney want you dead?" I asked. "The police chief said you were on the trail of some kind of land fraud. Was that just a cover?"

"Yes and no," he said. He looked up as music started again below. "Good. They sound as if they'll be occupied for some time yet. I'm not sure if we could be heard through this door."

"That Tiny person seems to prowl around a lot," I said.

"He does, doesn't he? I wonder why?" He got up, went over to the door, and opened it cautiously. He then closed it again and came back to sit close beside me on the bed. "So far, so good."

"How did you get up to my balcony?" I asked. "Surely you didn't climb up the wall?"

He smiled. "I shot back up the stairs after we had supposedly left," he said, "and let myself out onto your balcony. I would have hid in your wardrobe but there wasn't much room and I was scared of giving myself away by sneezing."

I laughed. It felt wonderful to laugh again. "You were telling me why somebody would want to kill you."

He nodded, putting his lips close to my ear to talk in a low voice. "My first assignment from John Wilkie was indeed to chase up a man who had made a fortune selling land deeds. It was before your time in New York but it was a big scandal. His name was Douglas Hatcher and he was selling parcels of oil-rich land in Texas. The deeds guaranteed mineral rights. He showed prospective buyers the geological survey with oil beneath the whole area, and he promised that the oil companies would do the digging. And of course he reminded everyone that this would be the age of the automobile and everyone would need oil. They'd be rich beyond their wildest dreams. There were plenty of poor suckers back East who paid a thousand dollars each for acreage in Texas, only to find it was a desert wasteland with no hope of oil."

"And he wasn't caught?"

Daniel shook his head. "By the time the land was found to be without value he had vanished. Not a trace of him, until now."

"Here?" I asked.

He nodded. "One of the investors was a little suspicious. He paid his share with marked fifty-dollar bills. A couple of those bills showed up at a San Francisco bank recently."

"So this Hatcher man is in town? Did you find him?"

"Not yet," Daniel said. "He may well have changed his name and appearance and come to San Francisco to make a new life for himself."

"Do you have your suspicions?"

"It's a big city," he said, "but the guy is obviously rich and it seemed possible that he'd hobnob with Bella and her like. That's why I agreed to stay with her. It might have been a mistake."

"You don't think she was in on any plot, do you?"

"No, but as you can see, she's very thick with the city bigwigs. They could have asked her to keep tabs on me and notify them of my movements. I'm sure I was followed every time I went out."

"I don't understand," I said. "Why would the city bigwigs feel threatened by you? They weren't part of this land swindle, were they?"

He shook his head. "Something quite different all together. When John Wilkie sent me to California he told me also to seek out a man called Dennison. It seemed that this Dennison had been sent by the federal government to San Francisco to gather evidence for corruption charges to be filed against the mayor and city attorney. But he had not been heard from in weeks. The men in Washington were worried that something had happened to him."

"Corruption charges?" I asked. "Don't most city governments have their share of corruption?"

"Yes, but not at the level it is going on here. They are raking in millions in bribes, paybacks, protection money . . . all the brothels and bars as well as the legitimate businesses. It's been going on brazenly and there have been so many complaints that Washington decided to put a stop to it. Dennison was ready to file charges against the mayor and city attorney in federal court."

"And then he vanished?"

"As you say, he vanished."

"He was killed, do you think?"

"Not until later, when he met me on a cliff top."

"Oh, he was the man you met that night?"

"He was. He had gone into hiding after threats against his life, and was waiting until the case came to court before he could reappear to nab the city fathers. He told me the preliminary court date was arranged for April 18 and he asked me to be there, just in case something happened to him and needed to be reported back to Washington."

"How horrible," I said. "Something did happen to him."

Daniel gave a long sigh. "I feel guilty. I rather think that I was the bait. They followed me hoping I would lead them to him. And I did and they took care of both of us."

"So what will you do now?" I asked. "If they are prepared to kill so ruthlessly I don't want you trying to take over the case."

"Someone has to," he said, "but obviously I can't in current circumstances. It's far better that they think I am dead. I've been trying to retrieve the evidence that Dennison was going to present and take it back to Washington but the problem is that I can't go rushing around the city in my current disguise."

I had to smile at this. "Daniel, how did you come up with such a ridiculous alter ego?"

"Thanks to Father O'Brien. He is not only a good, reliable fellow, but as Bella told you, he is remarkably keen on amateur theatricals. He actually puts on plays for the parish children. He was able to raid their costumes and props, as well as the clothing in the poor box, and came up with this. We decided on an old Irishman as there would be little chance of bumping into anyone who might move in musical circles in Ireland. And people don't get too close to an old man with a nasty cough, do they? The beard and hair covered most of my face. And the thick glasses disguised my eyes well."

"And you took the risk of coming to a gathering where you knew you would meet your enemies."

He nodded. "It had to be done. And of course I came to see you. I couldn't believe it when Father O'Brien let me know that Sullivan's widow had arrived in the city."

"You did send for me, didn't you? I didn't read that letter wrongly?"

"No, you didn't read it wrongly. I did want you to come," he said. "At least part of me hoped you would come, and another part wanted you to stay home safely in New York."

"I really wasn't sure I was doing the right thing," I said, pausing, as there was more applause downstairs. Then I heard voices in the front hall and the sound of the front door slamming.

"I suppose I was feeling desperate when I wrote that," he said. "I realized that my every move was being watched and I might well be in grave danger. I wanted you to know, just in case something happened to me. I didn't want to disappear without a trace and have you never knowing."

I smiled at him. "All that nonsense about embroidery and opera and being a good little wife," I said. "I wasn't sure whether you were being funny or deadly serious."

"I thought there was a good chance that any letter I wrote would be read by the wrong people," he said. "And since I was pretty sure that any mail would be intercepted and read, I couldn't risk writing to Wilkie either. The problem was that Bella wouldn't leave me alone. If I went out, she sent Tiny with me. I couldn't tell whether she was just being a solicitous hostess or whether she'd been asked by the mayor to keep an eye on me at all times."

"She seems so nice," I said, "but who knows. The mayor and attorney are powerful men. She may enjoy being in their social circle."

"We don't know whether she owns businesses here. Most of those respectable folk have their fingers in all sorts of shady pies. She may enjoy considerable kickbacks too."

"So what do we do?" I asked. "Admit defeat and leave the city as quickly as possible?"

"I'd still like to get my hands on the evidence that Dennison gathered," he said.

"Did he leave it in his hotel room?"

"Absolutely not. He wasn't stupid, poor fellow. He had a safe-deposit box at a bank."

"And you'd need the key for that."

He nodded. "I have the key, except that I haven't dared to use it yet. My old Irish professor is a wonderful disguise, but I would certainly be noticed if I went to the Crocker Bank and claimed to be young Mr. Dennison."

I took his hand, stroking it lovingly. All I wanted to do was to touch him and reassure myself that he was real. "Let's just collect Liam and go home," I said. "There is nothing more to be done here."

Daniel shook his head. "I can't just give up and go home with nothing," he said. "I'd feel like a failure. I'd feel I let Wilkie down."

"Daniel, they tried to kill you. If they got any hint you were still alive, your life wouldn't be worth a brass farthing. You know where the evidence is being kept. You have the key. Nobody else can get at it. Go back to Mr. Wilkie and tell him what you know. That's all you can do."

Daniel looked doubtful. "I could at least try to find Hatcher," he said. "That was my primary reason for being sent here. Or at least their excuse for sending me here."

"You say he might have changed his appearance and name," I said. "Do you have any suspicions?"

"Only one, so far," he said. "That Scottish man. Douglas."

"Why him?"

"He claims he came to America with nothing, and yet now he's bought up large tracts of the Californian Central Valley. One has to ask, where did the money come from?"

"Anything else?"

"His name is Mr. Douglas. The man I am seeking is called Douglas Hatcher. Convenient, don't you think?"

"But not in any way conclusive. Douglas is a common name for a Scot."

"Ah, but if you wanted to disguise yourself what better way than a luxuriant beard and a strong Scottish accent. He's rather young for such a beard, don't you think?" He looked at me suddenly. "You could help me there, maybe. Do you know much about Scotland? Perhaps you could ask him some questions about his homeland and catch him out?"

"I don't know that much detail," I said, "but I could give it a try. What did Douglas Hatcher look like? Are they physically about the same age and size?"

"Close enough. I had a couple of photographs of him in my valise."

I was suddenly alert. "Bella must still have your bags here, presumably. I'll ask for them."

He nodded. "Good idea. And this is an ideal chance to find out about people. There are parties every night because of Caruso. Everyone is trying to lure him to their particular party and everyone is attending in case he turns up. So please agree to attend and I will too and between us we may find out a thing or two."

Downstairs there were more voices in the hall, then the sound of the front door shutting again, and soon after the sound of an automobile cranking up and then driving away.

"How are you going get out?" I asked.

"Wait until the middle of the night then climb down the creeper."

"Daniel. That's dangerous."

He chuckled. "Much of my life seems to involve danger at the moment, my darling. But luckily not many windows overlook this side of the house, nor does it face the street. I will be fine."

"When will I see you again? How will I get in touch with you?"

"Better not try to contact me at the moment. You never know, they may have put someone to follow you, although I can't see why. But they may think I've told you more than is prudent. They may see you as a threat."

"Then let's just go home now," I said. "They won't be surprised if I want to leave. We'll take tomorrow's train and put this all behind us."

"First I must do some more checking on Douglas," he said. "I can't abandon a task simply because there is some danger involved. And you can help me this time." He grinned. "I never thought I'd say that. I'd really like you to chat with him yourself. Pretend to know Scotland well and see how he reacts. And also . . ." He paused. "I'd dearly like to know if Bella was in on the little plan with the mayor and Ruef. Did she tip them off that I was going to meet Dennison? Does she have something to lose if corruption charges are brought against the city fathers?"

"The Chinese servant Ellen told me that men were watching the house all the time you were here," I said.

He nodded. "I thought as much. But in a way that's a relief. It means that they were not relying on Bella to watch me."

"I hope not," I said. "She has been really kind. I can't picture her sending someone to his death."

"Perhaps she didn't know the full circumstances or what they planned to do. She may have been an unwitting accomplice."

He took my face in his hands again. "God, Molly, it's so wonderful to have you here with me. I love you so much."

And then he kissed me again, with passion and urgency. I felt my own passion arouse. I wanted him badly, but I was also conscious that I was in a house where our mortal enemies might still be downstairs.

"No, Daniel," I whispered. "Not here." I looked at him and started to laugh. "And I couldn't make love to a man with such awful white hair."

He smiled too and kissed me on the forehead, tenderly this time.

"You're right. We can't get carried away. Move over." He lay down beside me and I rested my head against his chest. I could feel his heart beating. In utter contentment I closed my eyes.

❦ Nineteen ❦

I blinked as a bright light shone down on me. I sat up, heart thudding, only to see that it was the morning sun, shining directly into my face. Memories of the night before came rushing back to me. I turned to look at the bed beside me. Daniel was not there. There was no indication he had ever been in the room. I began to wonder whether I had dreamed the whole thing. Whether it was my subconscious wanting him alive again. But then I noticed a strand of white hair against the red coverlet. I picked it up, cradling it in my hand. He had been here. He was real. Then I noticed that my lip tingled when I ran my tongue over it. So that part had been real too.

I got up, feeling energized and excited. I'd help Daniel in any way I could and then we'd go home. I washed, dressed, and went up to see Liam. How strange it was to have someone else taking care of him. When he was in my care at home I'd never have allowed myself to sleep late. His cries would certainly have awoken me if I had dared to sleep a minute after he had woken up. I found him up and dressed, being fed a boiled egg for his breakfast. He gave me a delighted grin as I came in.

"Look at you, eating like a big boy," I said, going over to kiss the top of his head.

"He eat good," Li Na said, nodding approval. "Soon he be big and fat and strong."

"He has certainly taken to you," I had to admit. Then saw her looking puzzled. "He likes you a lot," I corrected.

She smiled. "I take him out again, all right?" she asked. "He like to run and feed birds."

"Yes," I said. "That would be fine."

I left Liam to finish his breakfast and went downstairs to have my own. Ellen looked pleased to see me.

"You look better. I make breakfast for you?"

"Thank you," I said, and went through to the dining room. The room had already been cleared of last night's food and it struck me that someone must have stayed up very late or gotten up really early. I took a seat and with miraculous speed a pot of tea and an egg and toast appeared.

"I go shopping in Chinatown this morning," she said. "I make you good chicken soup. Chinese soup. You like."

I nodded that I probably would like it. I was still eating when I heard voices.

"You know why he's here." It was Bella's voice, raised and strained. "There can be no other reason."

"Don't worry about it. I'll handle it. It will be all right. We've made it this far." The other voice was Tiny's.

I was surprised that Bella was up so early, but then I remembered that she had told Señor Garcia to call on her in the morning. I came out of the dining room to greet her. She started with a shocked look when she saw me.

"Mrs. Sullivan. I had no idea you were awake. How wonderful." The smile was forced.

"I thought I should go out this morning and see if the police chief is making arrangements to have my husband's coffin returned to me," I said. I realized as I said it that this was no longer true. I couldn't be responsible for moving another man's remains. But it did give me an excuse to be out and about.

"Yes, yes, of course you must. Good idea," she said. I noticed she didn't offer to have Tiny escort me.

"Oh, and my husband's effects," I said.

"His effects?"

"I thought he must have left his luggage and clothes at your house when he went out that night and didn't return. I should like to have them for sentimental reasons."

"The police came for them," she said. "I expect they wanted to see if they could find his home address and send the bag home to you."

"Oh, I see. Well, I can ask Chief Dinan for them when I see him, can't I?"

"Of course you can. Well, that's settled then." She patted her hair, smoothing it down. "I must tell Ellen what I need when she goes to Chinatown. She brings me a perfect face powder, so much better than one can find at the City of Paris or the White House. Shall I have her fetch some for you?"

"I rarely wear face powder," I said.

"Ah, but you have that lovely, clear Irish complexion. You don't need it."

I grinned. "I wouldn't say that. I have freckles in the summer. I'd dearly love to cover them."

"Then I'll have her buy some for you too. My little treat," she said. She looked around, almost as if she was confused. "Dear me. What a complicated day. And the big performance tonight. I'm so very sorry you won't be able to attend, but there isn't a ticket to be had for love or money. But at least you'll come with me to the party before the show. Now you'll know everybody there. And I hope to persuade Caruso to join us here tomorrow. Won't that be something?"

She gave me a bright smile. Then she walked through to the kitchen.

So I was obviously free to go as I pleased. I was half-tempted to linger and observe the encounter with Señor Garcia when he returned. But I wanted to make use of my freedom too. I put on my coat as the day was brisk and blustery. A chilly wind was blowing off the ocean and I had to hold on to my hat as I came down the steps onto California Street. I looked around carefully as I climbed onto the cable car. There was no sign of anyone following me. I felt an absurd sense of relief and freedom. I alighted on Kearny and walked the two blocks to Portsmouth Square and the Hall of Justice.

I didn't have to ask to see the police chief this time as he was just coming out of the building as I approached it. I intercepted him.

"Chief Dinan," I said.

"Mrs. Sullivan." He gave a perfunctory bow. "A fine party last night, didn't you think? Although I'm not one for opera myself. But the food was good, as always. Bella puts on a grand show."

"She does," I agreed. "I'm sorry to bother you but I wondered how I would have to proceed to have my husband's coffin dug up and released to me. You said there would be formalities."

"Yes, you mentioned you wished to have his coffin shipped home. There will be certain formalities to go through. We'd have to get permission from the coroner to dig up a coffin after burial. I'll see what I can do, but I'm sure you can understand that I have a lot on my plate at this moment. Extra security for Caruso and those New York opera singers for one thing. And then I might have to testify at a rather tricky court case . . ."

"I do understand," I said. "Maybe in a few days . . ."

"Of course." He nodded. "I'd really like to help you."

He started to walk away.

"One other thing," I called after him. "My husband's effects. Bella tells me that one of your men took away his luggage. It was a small leather suitcase with some clothes in it. Obviously I'd like that back for sentimental reasons."

He frowned. "I don't remember giving any order to remove his suitcase. He had identification on him when we retrieved the body." He shook his head. "No, I'm sure we didn't take the suitcase. I can't help you there."

And he went on his way, leaving me staring after him. Either he was lying or Bella was. And what could she possibly want with a couple of changes of shirts and underwear? I should ask Daniel next time I saw him whether there was anything incriminating in that case. Then I remembered he'd said he had photographs of Hatcher. So perhaps the real Hatcher knew that Daniel was on his tail and had asked the police to help him out. In which case pushing Daniel and Dennison over the cliff had conveniently killed two birds with one stone.

I realized I was alone in the city with time on my hands. What could I do to help Daniel? I decided I should first go to Mr. Paxton, just to let him know I was all right. Of course I couldn't tell him the truth, that Daniel was alive. Nobody else could know that. But he had been so kind to me and was clearly worried when I went off with Tiny. That was understandable too. Tiny was a formidable-looking fellow, and quite an enigma to me. Bella relied on him but bossed him around. He longed for the open spaces yet he chose to stay in the city. *Just what was their relationship?* I wondered. Had he been more than her ranch manager? Her lover maybe? But I had not detected that spark that flashes between two people who are intimate with each other.

I followed Kearny back to Market Street and then to the Palace Hotel. Today there was a ring of policemen, some of them on horseback, surrounding the entrance to the hotel and I had to state my business before I was let through. Then I had to wait in the reception area while a message was sent up to Mr. Paxton. While I was waiting I looked up to see the journalist Mr. Hicks also loitering.

I went over to him. "Hello, Mr. Hicks. Have you found some real opera singers to interview for your newspaper?"

His face broke into a grin. "Oh, it's you. Nice to see you again. Yes, I managed to collar a couple of them when they arrived yesterday, but I'm still hoping for a chance to chat with Mimi Adler and of course with the great man himself. He's not venturing out of his suite and he's giving us reporters the cold shoulder. But I'm told he has to go to the opera house later this morning to familiarize himself with the stage. So I'm planning to swoop then." He looked at me with concern, as if he was just recalling the details of our previous encounter. "Did you find your husband? Weren't you looking for him?"

"I'm afraid I had bad news. The worst, in fact. My husband was killed in a tragic accident. He fell from a cliff top."

"I am most sorry to hear it. What a terrible shock for you, Mrs. Sullivan. Now I come to think of it, that's why the name was familiar to me. I remember we printed something about it in the paper."

"Can you remember any details?" I asked. "Were there any eye-witnesses to the tragedy? I'd dearly love to know exactly what happened. All I've been told is that my husband might have been seen there with another man and then the cliff top gave way."

He gave me an apologetic smile. "I'm afraid I did little more than glance at the article. But we have back copies of the paper in our archives. Come into the Examiner building and look for yourself. It's just down the street."

"Thank you. I will." I turned to move away then a brilliant idea came to me. "Mr. Hicks," I said. "You might be able to help me in another way. My husband was on the trail of a man called Douglas Hatcher. You might have read about him. A few years ago he made a fortune selling fake oil land in Texas."

"Yes, I remember that." He nodded. "And absconded with the money and was never seen again."

"It seems there were marked bills used in one of those transactions and a couple of them have shown up here in San Francisco. So it's possible that Hatcher is here. The speculation is that he has changed his name and appearance. So I'm wondering—you must know most people in the city, especially rich people. Can you see if your paper has any photographs on file of Douglas Hatcher and whether his face resembles anyone here in the city?"

He hesitated before saying, "That's not really my beat, Mrs. Sullivan. And while Caruso is here."

"I know," I said. "But if you could help to nab a man who has been wanted by the federal government for years, then wouldn't that be your ultimate scoop?"

I could see the wheels turning in his brain. He nodded. "You're right. It would. Let me see what I can come up with. Where can I find you?"

"I'm staying with Mrs. Rodriguez," I said.

"So you are staying with Bella? Then you're meeting the richest people in the city already. You're sure it's not one of those?"

"I gather most of them have been here for a generation or more," I said. "But I was curious about the Scottish man, Mr. Douglas. For one thing his name . . . Those wanting to change their identity have used their Christian names before. And he seems to have come to this country with nothing and now owns vast tracts of land."

"Jimmy Douglas?" He frowned. "That's interesting. You're right. I don't think we do know much about his past. At least, I don't. And he's certainly well-heeled now. Building himself a new mansion further out in Pacific Heights. Says he's getting the prime view over the ocean."

Over the ocean, I thought. Further out. Could he have had anything to do with following Daniel to a cliff top?

"Mrs. Sullivan," a voice called across the marble foyer, and Mr. Paxton came toward me. "How good to see you again. I've been quite concerned."

"I'm being well looked after, Mr. Paxton, and plan to go home shortly," I said.

"You're Paxton. The guy from the Met," Hicks said. "Any chance of a cozy chat with Mimi Adler? I work for the *Examiner* and our readers are dying to hear what it's like to sing with Caruso."

"Miss Adler is unfortunately occupied all today. She will be going to the opera house any minute now to run through scenes with Caruso," Mr. Paxton said. "And this afternoon of course she has to rest before the performance."

"Maybe tomorrow then? 'My experience singing with Caruso'? It would make the front page."

"I'll ask her," Mr. Paxton said. "Mimi is usually not shy about publicity. Come and see me in the morning."

"Terrific. Thanks, Paxton. I'll be here." Mr. Hicks shook his hand. "And I'll be in touch about our little matter, Mrs. Sullivan."

Mr. Paxton looked at me inquiringly as Hicks wandered off to take up his position by the elevators. "He's looking into a person Daniel was supposed to find here," I said.

"Is it wise for you to get involved in your husband's business?" Mr. Paxton asked. "Wouldn't it be better to go home?"

"Don't worry. I will be going home shortly. I just thought . . . I wanted to know the truth."

"You won't be going anywhere for a day or so," Mr. Paxton said. "The trains are fully booked with those who came to hear Caruso. Tonight is the night, as I'm sure you are aware."

"I am. Bella wanted to take me with her to the grand performance, but there are no tickets to be had."

"I wish I could help out," Mr. Paxton said. "But every seat in the house is taken."

"That's all right. I had a taste of opera last night and I don't think I could handle a story of great tragedy in my current situation."

He gave a commiserating smile. "Is there anything else I can do for you?"

"Yes," I said as a sudden thought occurred to me. "Could you find me a pen and writing paper and mail a letter for me?"

"Of course." He went to one of the reception desks and came back with stationery headed with the Palace Hotel crest. I sat on a bench and wrote a letter to Sid and Gus. I told them that they might hear news of Daniel's death, but that he was alive and well and we'd both be home soon. But they were to tell nobody that they knew he was alive. It was absolutely vital that nobody knew for now. I sent love to Bridie. Told them that Liam was flourishing and would soon be talking fluent Chinese.

I sealed the letter and wanted to give Mr. Paxton the money for a stamp, but he refused. I promised to look him up when I was back in

New York. I would have liked to tell him that Daniel and I would have him to dinner, but of course I couldn't. He took my hand. "You are a brave woman, Mrs. Sullivan. I am so sorry for your loss."

We were about to part company when a voice shouted, "Stand aside, please. Out of the way. Señor Caruso is coming through."

The elevator doors opened and a bodyguard came out, followed by a big man with dark hair and striking features. Although he was corpulent he could certainly be described as handsome and I could tell immediately that he was used to adulation. He waved regally as he crossed the foyer. He blew kisses to certain females. He had flashing dark eyes that crinkled at the sides when he smiled.

"I see you tonight," he called to the mob of admirers. "Tonight you hear what Caruso can do. Tonight I sing my heart out for you."

A worried-looking man rushed ahead to make sure the door was open for him.

"My automobile is here?" Caruso demanded. "I cannot stand outside in cold air. And I hope there is none of that disagreeable fog. So bad for the voice."

Then he swept through the doors and was gone. There was a collective sigh from the spectators, as if they had just witnessed a miracle, then they broke into excited chatter.

"Are your singers just as temperamental, Mr. Paxton?" I asked.

He rolled his eyes. "Even more so. Picky. Superstitious. One has to witness the stage being swept before she'll step onto it. Another won't allow the color purple on the stage at the same time as her."

"I'm glad I'm a normal person," I said. "So much easier."

"Ah, but you are not normal. Most women would not have dared to do what you have done. And not have borne devastating news so stoically. You are a heroine, Mrs. Sullivan. I admire you greatly."

I gave him a weak smile. It was not easy accepting praise for something I didn't deserve. I only wished I could tell him the good news. When we're all safely back in New York, I thought. Then I'll surprise him.

❧ Twenty ❧

When I arrived back at the mansion on California Street I was admitted by Francis. There was no sign of Bella. I wondered whether Señor Garcia had come to call and what had transpired. I went into the octagon room to find Tiny sitting there. He looked up when I came in.

"You're back, Mrs. Sullivan. Did you accomplish what you set out to do?"

"I'm not sure," I said. "The police chief says he will try to help me have Daniel's coffin exhumed, but he's too busy at the moment to think about it."

"Of course he is," Tiny agreed. "The whole city is in turmoil for various reasons. But things should quieten down when Caruso goes."

I nodded agreement and was about to tell him that I'd seen Caruso in person when I realized it was more prudent not to let anyone know I was at the Palace or that I had written a letter and asked Mr. Hicks for help.

"So has Mrs. Rodriguez gone out?" I asked.

He grinned. "No, back to bed. She wants to rest so that she's at her best for this evening."

"Did the Mexican gentleman come back to visit?"

"Oh, yes. He came back. All smoothed over." Tiny picked up the newspaper again.

"Will you be going to the opera tonight?" I asked.

"Unfortunately yes. Bella insisted. Between ourselves I don't think she really likes opera either. But it's the done thing right now and everyone has to be seen at the opera house tonight."

I almost found myself regretting that I could not go. It would be the sort of thing that people would tell their children—how they heard Caruso sing. But then I remembered that he came to New York quite frequently. I'd make a point of taking Daniel sometime. And I felt a thrill of pleasure in being able to have that thought.

"You'll be staying until they dig up your husband's coffin, will you?" Tiny looked up from the newspaper again.

"I'm not sure. It depends how long it will take."

"Could take ages unless you come up with the right sort of bribe."

"Bribe? To dig up a coffin?"

"That's how things seem to work out here. Money talks. Laws can be bent in the right circumstances. Give the police fifty dollars to get things moving and things will miraculously be speeded up. There's not a business in San Francisco that doesn't exist by paying bribes."

"That's terrible," I said. "What if Washington finds out how things are done out here? Won't they step in?"

"They might try to." He grinned. "Luckily we're a continent and two mountain ranges away from Washington. General Funston has tried to poke his nose into local affairs, without much success so far. After all the Presidio is federal land and outside of the Presidio it's Mayor Schmitz who calls the tune."

"And Mayor Schmitz is okay with bribes and corruption?"

Tiny laughed. "How do you think he got himself elected? This place is not for sissies, as your husband found out."

•

"My husband?" I said sharply. "I was told his death was an accident. Do you know something?"

"I know he asked a lot of questions," Tiny said. "I'm not quite sure what he was doing here but certain people in high places didn't like it."

"I see." I nodded blankly as if all this was a shock to me. "Then I'd better take my son and go home as soon as possible. We might not be safe here."

"I think that's a wise decision, Mrs. Sullivan," Tiny said.

I went out of the room and stood in the silence of the hallway for a moment, collecting my thoughts. So the corruption was common knowledge here. And from the easy way Tiny talked about it, he was not involved in it. I glanced back into the octagon room. Tiny was engrossed in the newspaper again. I was tempted to ask him if he remembered what happened to Daniel's suitcase, but I decided to keep quiet for a while. It seemed more likely that the police had found something incriminating inside that suitcase and had destroyed it.

I sniffed as a waft of that unpleasant scent came to me. Señor Garcia's perfume obviously lingered longer than the man himself. I went up to visit my son. He was not there and again I felt a wave of panic. I went outside and wandered around until I found him on a nearby green. He had bread in his chubby little fist and Li Na was showing him how to throw it to the pigeons. He greeted me with delight at this newfound skill.

"*Niu!*" he said, pointing at a pigeon. "*Niu.*"

"Yes, it's new," I agreed.

Li Na giggled. "He say 'bird' in my language. In Cantonese."

"Goodness," I replied. "He's learning Chinese before he learns English."

She looked pleased, then turned to Liam, who had his empty hands held up to her and was making impatient sounds. "No more bread," she said. "We go home, have food now. Okay?"

He held out his arms to be picked up by her and I followed them back to the Rodriguez house. I found myself thinking how nice it would be to take her back to New York with me.

Back at the house I ate my own lunch, alone in the dining room. True to her promise Ellen had made me a Chinese soup. It was spicy with bits of mushroom and other vegetables in it, but it tasted wonderful and I could almost feel it doing me good.

After lunch I went up to kiss Liam before he fell asleep and then took a rest myself. I had slept so well the night before that I wasn't tired and lay on my bed listening to the sounds of the city—the clanging of the cable car bell and the rattle of the cable as it passed us, the clip-clop of hooves as a smart carriage went past or the coughing spluttering of an automobile as it negotiated the steep hill. And closer by the cooing of a pigeon.

"*Niu*," I muttered and smiled to myself. It was so wonderful to be able to smile again. This evening I'd go to the party and ask a few discreet questions and presumably Daniel would be there, disguised again as the old professor. I had a long soak in the luxurious bathtub and was dressed for the party by five o'clock. Bella appeared soon afterward looking splendid in black lace with a silver and pearl choker at her neck and a white gardenia in her hair. In her hand she carried a large ostrich feather fan. She looked so quintessentially Spanish and yet I had been told that she was originally an East Coast American girl who married a man of Spanish descent. The exotic persona suited her well, I thought. I wondered if she would have stood out as well if she had been the widow of a Mr. John Smith.

"How do I look?" she asked.

"Magnificent," I replied.

"You are too kind." She smiled. "I'm hoping to catch the eye of Señor Caruso. I hear he is quite one for the ladies."

"The ladies in the plural," I pointed out. "You wouldn't want to be one of many, would you?"

"I haven't seen him close up yet but I understand he is very handsome. San Francisco is lacking in sophisticated European gentlemen."

"You should move back to the East," I said. "New York is full of sophisticated and handsome men."

"I could never do that," she said quickly, then frowned and added, "but you will be able to find yourself a new husband, will you not?"

I remembered I was supposed to be the grieving widow. I had quite forgotten. "How can I even think of that now?" I asked indignantly. "Daniel is the only man for me."

"Of course you feel that way now, but you are young and pretty. You will want a new man in your life, I am sure."

"Maybe. But let's not even talk about it. We'll go to the party and I'll try to have a good time. Then you'll watch Caruso and it will be wonderful."

She took my hand and patted it. "I wish you were coming, my dear. I did try to find you a ticket, but even the scalpers say that no one wants to sell to them. The event of the new century, they are calling it here."

Tiny came down the stairs, looking uncomfortable in a white tie and tails. "I don't know why you want me there," he said.

"I might need a bodyguard if there is a riot," Bella said. "Besides, it will do you good to acquire some culture." And she laughed. "Go and summon the carriage."

"You don't have an automobile yet," I commented. "It seems they are becoming more popular."

"My dear, with hills like ours can you imagine trying to climb them in an automobile? There have already been occasions when engines have cut out at the wrong moment and the automobile has slid backward to destruction. Give me a reliable horse any day."

The carriage arrived, Tiny helped us inside, and off we went, a few yards up the hill to the Crocker mansion. If Bella's party had been glittering, it was certainly overdazzled by this: a magnificent ballroom—ablaze with electric light—with a small orchestra playing in one corner. A fountain of champagne played in the middle. An endless stream of waiters in smart black jackets brought around trays of tiny vol-au-vents, crab claws, oysters, minute lamb chops. At least

I wouldn't have to eat dinner when I went home, I decided. The room was already quite full and I looked around for Daniel. I felt a wave of disappointment when I didn't see him. But I did notice Mr. Douglas, standing close to the bar with a glass of whiskey in his hand. Now was my chance. I squeezed through the crowd to him.

"Good evening, Mr. Douglas."

He looked up from his contemplation. "Mrs. Sullivan. Good to see you again. Are you ready for the night of the century?"

"Alas I won't be attending. I don't have a ticket," I said.

"I imagine there are many men in this room who would willingly give you theirs, only their wives won't let them." He smiled.

"You are not married yourself?" I asked.

"I was." The smile faded. "She died in childbirth ten years ago. That was when I decided to leave old and bitter memories and come out West. I've done well for myself."

"You certainly have, from what I've been told. How did you manage it?"

He smiled again. "The Scots are naturally frugal. I worked on a ranch here. I found out how things are done. I saved my money, bought a small plot, and started growing fruit. That's when I found there was an insatiable market for peaches and soft fruit. I made money and bought up more land. Some of it was considered useless marsh, but I drained it, built dykes, and now it's the best soil you can imagine."

"So how did you know about soil?" I asked. "Did you live on a farm in Scotland? Exactly where in Scotland did you come from?"

"Nae, lassie. I didn't come from the land. My father ran a pub in Glasgow," he said.

"Really? Where exactly in Glasgow? One of our best friends in New York is from that city."

"Near the Gorbals. Not the part of the city your friend would have ventured to. That's why I got out of it as soon as I could. Made my way to Canada, then heard about California and came here."

"So you were never in New York, or any of the East Coast cities?"

"Never was. Toronto, then Winnipeg. Can't say I've ever enjoyed big cities."

"They say you're having a house built closer to the ocean than this."

"Aye." His face lit up. "You should see the view from up there. Nothing around me and the Bay and ocean at my feet. If you're staying on, I'd be happy to motor you out to see it."

"I'm not sure how long I'll be here," I said. "I just have a couple of loose ends to tie up and then I'll be going home. There's nothing to keep me here any longer."

"I understand, lassie," he said. "The world seems empty and pointless, doesn't it? It felt that way when my wife died. And the bairn. Hard work. That's what you need. Make yourself too tired to brood."

"Thank you. I will," I said, as a noisy group of young people swept past us to the bar.

I took a glass of champagne I was offered and moved away. Mr. Douglas had come across to me as completely genuine and I was sure that the story of his wife's death was real. It would be easy enough to check ships' manifests, as well as records across Canada. But I would have to tell Daniel he was barking up the wrong tree. Another idea came to me. I came back to Mr. Douglas, who was now standing with General Funston. I hadn't realized until I stood beside him what a small man the general was. No taller than I. And yet he was the one who'd waged such a successful war in the Philippines. Mr. Douglas introduced me and the general bowed. "We met last night at Mrs. Rodriguez's, although we had no chance to converse. So how do you like San Francisco, Mrs. Sullivan? Do they have such parties where you come from?"

"I live in New York, and I'm sure they have such parties, but I am not among the Four Hundred who are the elite in society and thus not invited to them. But you yourself, General, how do you enjoy California? I take it you are not from here?"

"Born in Ohio, raised in Kansas," he said. "And I have to confess that my quarters at the Presidio are decidedly cold and damp after the sweltering heat of Manila. I'm a man of action, Mrs. Sullivan. I feel myself champing at the bit here."

"Waiting for the next war, General?" Mr. Douglas asked.

"You could say that." The general grinned.

I looked around the room, deliberately staring at the chandeliers, the silk wallpaper, the sheer opulence of it all. "It's hard to believe that Crocker was a self-made man," I said. "This is all truly magnificent."

"It is quite impressive," General Funston agreed, "although to one used to Spartan army conditions I find it almost overwhelming. I'm told there's nothing in San Francisco that money can't buy."

"And I hear that most wealthy people in San Francisco are self-made," I said.

The general nodded. "So I've been told. Railroads and silver, isn't it?"

"Are there still chances to make millions?" I asked. "Any new gold or silver rushes? Any new millionaires arriving in the city?"

"I don't know about silver rushes," Funston said. "But still plenty of chances to make money here, I'd wager. Shipping to the Orient and now more trade with the Philippines, and pineapples coming from Hawaii. We're the gateway to the world here."

"So is anyone else building a house like yours outside the city center, Mr. Douglas?" I asked.

"Not yet. I expect they will when they see my situation and my view. There's no more land to build on Nob Hill. The city will have to spread out toward the ocean."

"But much of that land is sand, isn't it? Do you think they can build on sand dunes?" the general asked.

"They could create a park on sand dunes, so why not build houses," Douglas said.

I tried another tactic, looking around the room. "Presumably you must know everybody here," I said. "The Four Hundred in New York all know each other."

163

"San Francisco is not like that," Mr. Douglas said. "People come and go all the time. It's a convenient stopover from the Orient."

I gave a little sigh. Of course this was something we had not considered. Daniel's land fraud perpetrator could merely have stopped over in San Francisco on his way to points East. He might only have been in the city a few days and was now long gone. In which case the reason Daniel was pushed over a cliff was entirely to do with the corruption charges being brought against the city fathers, and I was standing in a room full of them. Against one wall I saw Mayor Schmitz throwing back his head in laughter as if he hadn't a care in the world. Even City Attorney Ruef was smiling at the joke. I didn't know which one of them had ordered Daniel to be followed but if the federal government wanted to bring corruption charges, then this was a dangerous place. I looked around once more, hoping that Daniel might still arrive, but I couldn't see him.

"I was hoping to meet your friendly priest and the funny old Irishman again," I said when Bella came up to me.

"I should think last night was a bit much for the poor old boy," she said. "That nasty cough—I hope he doesn't come down with pneumonia. And . . ." she paused, looking around the room, "I hope he doesn't cough during Caruso's performance."

"It looks as if people are already leaving for the opera house," I said. "Would you like me to walk back to your house? It really isn't far."

"Walk? Of course not. I'll have the carriage take you first then come back for us. Tiny?"

She looked around in annoyance and spotted him standing at the bar, looking morose and out of place. "Tiny! The carriage for Mrs. Sullivan."

He went, probably glad to escape from the room.

Bella smiled. "Poor Tiny. How he'll hate the opera."

The carriage arrived and I slipped away without seeking out Mr. Crocker to thank him for the party. I doubt if he noticed I was there in the first place. We went a few short yards down the hill and the coachman helped me out. Francis was waiting at the front door.

"Do you require dinner, Missy Sullivan?" he asked.

"I don't. Thank you, Francis," I said. "I ate enough canapés at the party."

"Then I go take my dinner with Ellen in kitchen," he said.

"Please do. I need nothing else," I said. "I may read for a while in the octagon room and then go to bed."

"You want me to bring you drink first?"

"Oh, no, thank you. Go and enjoy your dinner, Francis."

"Thank you, Missy Sullivan," he said. "If you want drink, you find on sideboard in drawing room."

I nodded, took off my wrap, and went through to the octagon room. I looked for the newspaper but couldn't find it. Probably it had already been cleared away. There was just a possibility that it had been taken to one of the other rooms. I wandered first into the dining room, then into a library, then the drawing room. In the latter the sideboard, well stocked with decanters and bottles, caught my eye. I had hardly sipped my champagne at the reception and decided that a small glass of brandy might be settling to my stomach after the rich fare. I found the decanter, poured myself a little, and started to carry it back to the octagon room. I suppose I could have sat in the drawing room, but the smaller room felt less overpowering.

As I crossed the hall on my way back my nose picked up a whiff of scent—the faintest whiff of the unpleasantly sickly smell of Señor Garcia's pomade still lingered. I stood alone in the hall, realizing I was alone in the big, empty house apart from the servants somewhere in their quarters at the back. And an idea came to me. I could take this chance to search for Daniel's bag. It could have been disposed of, but if not, where might it be hidden? Was there an attic? I knew there was a cellar because I had seen . . .

I realized at that moment that I was standing close to the cellar door. I opened it and was relieved that there was an electric light switch, even down here. Such an efficient and modern house! I placed my brandy glass on the top step then tiptoed down the stairs. The cellar was full of the normal jumble one stores away—packing cases, broken lamps, cleaning materials . . . and in one corner a small brown leather suitcase. I opened it with trembling hands. The loud click echoed around the cellar. It was Daniel's all right. I lifted out various items of his clothing and shaving equipment, puzzled. Why had Bella claimed the police had taken it away? Unless she didn't know it was still here. Maybe Ellen or Tiny had taken it down to the cellar without Bella's knowledge. I reached the bottom of the case and found nothing suspicious. Nothing that would have raised a red flag to anybody. Then, when I went to replace Daniel's neatly folded shirt, a piece of paper fell out onto the dusty floor. I picked it up. It was a photograph of a fine figure of a man in Western garb and a cowboy hat standing at the gateway to a ranch. He had an impressive mustache and from the way he stood and smiled at the camera he was feeling very pleased with himself. He was holding the bridle of a horse in one hand and his other arm was around a woman. She was a mousy little thing, skinny and bony, wearing an apron over a plain cotton dress, clearly uncomfortable having her photograph taken as she was looking away from him at the ground. It was hard to tell whether she was his wife, sister, or mother.

And on the back of the picture someone had written, *Douglas and Lizzy Hatcher, Texas 1889.*

Hurriedly I stuffed it into my skirt pocket and searched the case for more such pictures, but found nothing. I replaced the suitcase, realizing that I should not give any hint that I was anything other than the grieving widow. I was about to creep back up from the cellar when I caught another whiff of that obnoxious perfume. What could Señor Garcia have been doing down here?

I started to poke around, my nose trying to pick up where the smell was most potent. There were trunks and valises stacked against the far wall. My nose wrinkled as the smell was at its strongest here.

Most unpleasant, in fact. Cautiously I opened one of the trunks and let out a small gasp of surprise. It was full of money. Hundreds and hundreds of bills of various denominations. Hurriedly I closed it again. Then I opened the trunk beside it and found myself staring down at Señor Garcia's lifeless body.

❧ Twenty-one ❧

I put my hand to my mouth to stifle my gasp. Señor Garcia had been stuffed into the trunk like a rag doll. His eyes were wide and bulging. His mouth was open in surprise. The scent of his pomade was sickly sweet and overpowering. I closed the trunk again with a shudder. I had to get out of here immediately. I tiptoed up the stairs, listened for a long moment, then turned off the electric light switch and opened the door, an inch at a time. Nothing moved. There was no sound except for the heavy ticktock of the grandfather clock across the hall beside the drawing room. I retrieved my brandy glass, came out of the cellar, and shut the door carefully behind me, trying to make no sound as I lowered the latch into place. I had only gone a few steps across the hall when I heard the slap of Chinese slippers and there was Francis coming up behind me.

"Missy Sullivan? You need something? We hear you walking around," he said, his face expressionless as always.

I smiled. "No, thank you, Francis. I just went to help myself to a little brandy to settle my stomach. The food at that party was rather rich. I think I'll take it up to my room and read up there."

"Very good," he said and watched me walk up the stairs.

Did he know I'd been down to the cellar? In which case was I liable to end up like Señor Garcia? I must let Daniel know immediately. He would know what to do and could decide whether to go to the police. But Daniel was at the opera with the rest of San Francisco. I could not send a message to him until morning. In the meantime I would play the innocent and watch my back. Since I had no idea why Bella or anyone in her household might want Señor Garcia dead I had no way of judging whether I might be in mortal danger. Just in case I locked my door.

I undressed and curled up in my bed. After the initial shock had worn off I started to see the complicated nature of our predicament. How could Daniel go to the police, when he was supposed to be dead and buried? And if he did reveal that he had survived, who exactly might not be pleased to learn that news? For all we knew he might become a convenient suspect in Garcia's murder. In the morning I'd tell Bella that we had decided to return home immediately. I'd pack up our things and take Liam across to Oakland, where I'd send Daniel a message to join us as soon as he could. Then we'd be safely on the next train heading East and Daniel could choose whether to tip off the police about Señor Garcia's murder or not.

I drifted off to sleep and half awoke at the sound of a carriage coming to a halt outside, then Bella's animated voice floating up to my French windows. I had left them unlocked, just in case Daniel chose that way to visit again. Bella was laughing merrily as I heard the front door slam, the footsteps coming up the stairs, past my door. They did not pause but went on down the hallway.

I lay there, holding my breath until I heard a door close behind her. Bella had seemed so carefree and gay. Was she privy to the fact that a body lay in her basement? She had clearly been upset when Señor Garcia arrived, but had she ordered his murder? Even taken part in his murder? She seemed like such a warm and generous person. I could envision both Francis and Tiny killing someone if necessary, but surely not Bella. Had Tiny killed Garcia to somehow protect

Bella? Or had I got it wrong and was Tiny under the control of Bella somehow? And what about the trunk full of money in the cellar? I'd often found that money and murder go together. Had Bella decided to keep her life savings here, rather than in a bank? And had Señor Garcia learned of the money and tried to steal it? In any case it appeared that Francis had not had a chance to tell her that I had been down to the basement tonight. I was safe until morning and then I'd make my escape.

I was awoken by being thrown violently across the bed. Someone was shaking me awake with considerable force. I opened my eyes in terror. My first thought was that Tiny or Francis had come up to my room to finish me off.

"Holy Mother of God!" I heard myself exclaim as I looked around me in panic. It was still quite dark outside. From what I could see I was alone in the room, but I was still being pitched around like a rag doll. From deep below came a rumbling sound as if a freight train was passing close by. But there was no train line in this part of the city. Then I heard other sounds: creaking and clattering, wood splintering, glass breaking, heavy thuds. I clung on to the bed frame as the bed skittered and danced across the room as if it was possessed. I had no idea what was happening or how to stop it. In truth I wondered if I was in a nightmare and might awaken at any moment. Then a picture crashed down from the wall. Plaster fell from the ceiling in large chunks. The light from a streetlamp outside allowed me to see only a hint of flying shapes. I glanced around the room in time to see the wardrobe against the wall teetering. I managed to scramble out of bed as it crashed where I had been lying.

Liam! I thought. *Have to get Liam out of this.*

I tried to reach my dress, which I had left lying over the back of a chair, but it was now covered in plaster and the chair had tipped over. I retrieved the dress, brushed it off, and tried to put it on, but it was impossible to stand. It was like being on the back of a bucking horse. And now the sound of screams and wails rose up from the city below. I didn't bother to do up the buttons, just slipped my feet into shoes and managed to pick my way over broken glass and plaster to my door. I turned the key in the lock but the door wouldn't open. I yanked at it. I kicked at it. Then in frustration and panic I staggered across the room, picked up the wrought iron lamp that now lay on the floor, and used it as a battering ram. A panel in the door splintered. I hammered some more and finally shattered the lock.

And all the while the shaking continued. A light had been left on in the stairwell. Now it flickered and jiggled around, sending crazy shadows dancing over the stairs. As I came out onto the landing someone was running down the stairs ahead of me. It was Li Na, with Liam in her arms. Thank heavens that sensible girl was carrying him outside to safety.

"Li Na. Wait. I'll take him now," I called.

But she didn't stop. She wrenched open the front door and ran down the front steps.

"Li Na. Wait for me!" I shouted after her and ran down the stairs as fast as I could, clinging to the shaking banister. The grandfather clock fell into the hall with a great clang and crash. Statues were toppling onto the marble floor, which was springing up in chunks as if with a life of its own.

"Earth Dragon. Got to stop Earth Dragon!" Li Na shrieked as she ran out of the house.

Liam spotted me. "Mama!" he cried, struggling in her arms. But she didn't stop. She was already out of the front door, down the steps, and running at a great rate up California Street.

"Wait!" I shrieked, but she was striding out ahead of me, her cotton trousers not hampering her movements in the way that my dress over my nightgown did. What was she doing? Where was she taking my son? The world had stopped shaking but from the city below came the wail of sirens, cries for help. Electrical wires lay across the street, hissing and writhing like snakes as they sparked in the darkness. Some of the streetlamps had gone out. It was horribly eerie. The mansions I passed seemed unscathed, with people in night attire standing outside them, but bricks had been flung across the sidewalk from the almost-finished Fairmont Hotel. The first streaks of light appeared in the eastern sky.

Li Na had reached the crest of the hill where California Street drops down sharply toward the Bay but still she didn't stop. She jumped over piles of bricks with the ease of a gazelle and kept running down California Street. I followed, stumbling and tripping over the debris that littered the sidewalk, unable to see more than a foot or two in front of me. A pall of dust rose up around us, getting into my nose and throat. I read the street names as I passed them. Past Powell Street. Past Stockton. A sharp pain shot through my side and I gasped for breath. It was hard to run in my dainty shoes while she wore flat cotton slippers. The buildings on this side of the hill had clearly suffered more. Cornices had been shaken down and chunks of decorative stonework lay across the street and sidewalk. On some houses whole fronts had fallen, oil lamps had tipped over, starting small fires that revealed rooms with furniture hurled around, as if by a giant hand. Paving stones had popped up from the street and the rail for the cable car had buckled like a switchback. Until now I had not had to encounter people but ahead of me the street was full of them, standing dazed, in nightclothes, with bleeding heads and damaged limbs. One building had collapsed completely and a man had been buried up to his neck in fallen bricks. "Help me," he implored as I ran past.

Crowds were now coming up the hill toward us. And among those crowds now were Chinese people—men in baggy trousers, with skullcaps on their heads and long pigtails down their backs. They carried bundles of possessions or cages with small birds in them. Behind them women hobbled pitifully, trying to keep up on bound feet. We reached Grant Avenue and the beginning of Chinatown. I caught a glimpse of Li Na's white tunic, far ahead of me. She turned left at Grant Avenue and vanished. I followed. I was thoroughly winded and finding it hard to breathe now in the dust and smoke that hung in the air.

We were now in the midst of utter destruction. The pall of dust gave everything an indistinct and unreal quality in the half-light. Flimsy buildings had slid off foundations and were lying at drunken angles. Shops had spewed out contents, with vegetables and fruit rolling under our feet. What had been streets were now littered with fallen bricks and debris. From around me came the sounds of constant moaning, and in the distance the ringing of fire truck bells, as small fires had broken out, creating pockets of hazy glow in the darkness. One of them was on my right—some kind of temple building had collapsed, its green and gold pagoda-style roof now lying pancaked a few feet from the ground with smoke curling up around the edges. Further away black smoke was rising all around.

Grant Avenue was crowded with Chinese people. Some were trying to flee, dragging small carts of children and possessions. But others were kneeling on the ground, digging away furiously. Some were holding up pieces of paper to which they had set fire, then dropping them into holes in the ground. It would have been fascinating had I not been so terrified. I stepped gingerly past the burning papers and ran on. How would I ever find my son in this chaos?

"Li Na!" I shouted over the wails and sirens. It was impossible.

Then I spotted a policeman. I ran up to him. "Help me. My nursemaid has run off with my son. She wouldn't stop."

He was a young man and he had that look of utter bewilderment in his eyes. "Ma'am, I'd get out if I were you. This place is going to go up in flames."

"What are they doing, lighting all those papers?" I asked.

"Appeasing the Earth Dragon, I gather. That's what they do when there's an earthquake."

Earthquake. Of course. The word took shape in my mind. It was the first time it really sunk in that I had just experienced a massive earthquake. And that's what Li Na had shouted. Earth Dragon. That meant she would be digging and burning paper somewhere close by. And I remembered Portsmouth Square. A big, newly planted garden with plenty of room to dig in the soil. I turned down a side street, pushing past fleeing Chinese and heaps of bricks and stone. Another fire was crackling away in what had been a restaurant to my left. *Sam Woo's Chop House,* said the drunken sign on the collapsed awning. The park was ahead of me now and I could see hundreds of Chinese scrabbling in the dirt. Then without warning the rumbling came again. Cobblestones started popping up like popcorn; buildings around me creaked and groaned. People screamed and ran in panic, pushing past me to get to the open space of Portsmouth Square. I ran with them, swept along in the tide. Out of the corner of my eyes I saw the wall to my left start to fall. I tried to put on a spurt but I was hampered by the crowd ahead of me. As if in slow motion it came. Bricks floating toward me. All around me. Then something hit me on the back of the head and I knew no more.

❧ Twenty-two ❧

I came to consciousness slowly to see a face peering down at me.

"This one's not dead," said a male voice.

I blinked. The light hurt my eyes, even though it was muted. From around me came sounds: low moans, groans, an occasional scream.

"Where am I?" I asked.

"Mechanics' Pavilion, my dear," the male voice said. The words meant nothing to me. I had never heard of a Mechanics' Pavilion. I stared up at him. I could just make out a drooping mustache and a round face. "The hospital was too badly damaged so we've been bringing patients here. You're lucky they found you. You were under a collapsed wall and everyone around you was dead. It was in the middle of Chinatown so as you can imagine there weren't that many volunteers wanting to help with rescues there. The Chinese were all fleeing as fast as they could. And the whole area is going up in flames."

I tried to sit up.

"What were you doing in Chinatown anyway so early in the

morning?" He was looking at me suspiciously. "Why didn't you get out after the first quake?"

"I was . . ." I paused. What was I doing? Chinatown? I toyed with the word. Wasn't that where Chinese people lived? How could I live there then?

"Where do you live, my dear?" the male voice sounded kinder now.

"I live . . ." I tried to think but my head hurt. "I forget."

"What's your name?"

My name was . . . I wrestled with that one and then it came to me. Molly. That was my name. I tried harder, screwing up my eyes. Molly . . . Murphy. "Molly Murphy from Ballykilleen," I said.

"Ballykilleen, where's that?"

"Ireland."

"From Ireland, are you?" He looked at me with sympathy. "You're a long way from home."

"Yes," I said, realizing this to be true. "I'm a long way from home and I'd like to go back there."

"You just rest on that cot for a while and then we'll see about getting you out of here." He patted my shoulder gently. "So where were you staying? Which hotel?"

"Hotel?" I shook my head. I couldn't picture a hotel. Frankly I couldn't picture anything except a schoolroom. A nun was standing at the front of the class and she had a pointer in her hand. "Molly Murphy!" she said in her sharp voice. "Don't tell me you've forgotten your catechism?"

"I must go home," I said, struggling to sit up. "I forgot my catechism. Sister will be angry."

The man was looking at me with concern now. "You just rest. You've had a nasty bump on your head."

Another man came up, this one in a white coat. "Has this one recovered enough to send her out?" he asked. "We've just had another wagonload brought in and we need the bed."

"She's from Ireland," the mustache man said. "Talking about her sister."

"Who was she staying with here?" He looked down at me. "Whom were you staying with, ma'am? With friends or in a hotel?"

For some reason I found the word "ma'am" funny and wanted to giggle. "I can't remember," I said.

"Were you with your family?"

There was a flash of memory. A baby. "My baby brother was with me," I said.

"Anyone else?"

I thought but no images would come.

The man in the white coat nodded. "The blow to the head has caused some amnesia. We'd better leave her here and give her time. We can't turn her out like this. Bring her a drink of water."

"I can't do that, Doctor," the mustache man said. "There's no more water. The main must have ruptured. You turn on the faucet and nothing comes out."

"Dear God." The doctor sighed. "If water mains are ruptured, how the devil are they going to stop the fires?"

They walked away. I heard them say, "This one's gone, poor devil." And a body was lifted from the cot beside me. I lay still. My head was throbbing and I felt violently sick. Even the dim indoor light hurt my eyes. When I opened them I could make out that I was in some kind of auditorium. It reminded me of a concert hall I had been in with a glass-domed ceiling high above and tiers of balconies running around the walls. So what was I doing in a concert hall and what had happened there? From what I could see the place was now full of makeshift cots and beds and every one was occupied by someone who lay still, or groaning.

I closed my eyes and tried to think. Molly Murphy from Ballykilleen. That's who I was. But how did I know about concert halls? Surely there was nothing bigger than the church hall in Ballykilleen? A school trip to Westport? Was there anything as big as this building in Westport? It hurt to think. Clearly something catastrophic had happened. A war. A plague. Something terrible. But try as I might, I couldn't remember what it was.

I must have drifted off to sleep again because I was being shaken awake. "You need to try and stand up," a male voice said. "We have to get out of here. The fires are coming closer. Here, let me help you."

I was hoisted unceremoniously to my feet.

"She seems okay," the voice said. "No broken bones that I can see."

"Can you walk by yourself to the cart, my dear? We've still a lot of patients to move and we're racing against time now."

"Where are we going?" I asked. The room swam around as I stood and I felt violently nauseous. All I wanted to do was lie back on that bed again.

"Golden Gate Park. They're going to be setting up tents there. It should be far enough away to be safe."

Golden Gate Park. That name meant nothing to me either. But tents? Why did we need tents?

I allowed myself to be led past the rows of cots. Because wherever we were, something catastrophic had happened and I was in some kind of infirmary. I looked down at myself. My arms and legs seemed to be there just fine but I was finding it hard to walk straight. Whoever was with me held my arm firmly as I staggered.

"You'll be quite safe out there," the man said kindly.

I blinked as I was led into the open air. The light hurt my eyes and I closed them. Ahead of me was some kind of open cart. It was already full of poor souls with bloody bandages around their heads, arms in slings. I put my hand up to my own head and touched the unfamiliar fabric of a bandage there too. So I had been hurt. Wounded. But how? Where?

"Got room for one more?" a voice called. "Just a little one this time."

Hands reached down to hoist me up and I was squeezed onto a few inches of wooden bench. The driver shouted a command to the horse and the cart lurched forward. I was being taken away to a park I had never heard of to live in a tent. It all felt too absurd to be real.

"Are you okay, miss?" The woman sitting next to me touched my arm gently. "You look as white as a sheet. You hang on to me if you feel you're going to pass out. We'll be much better when they get us to the park. If only the streets are clear enough for us to make it that far. What a terrible business. I've no idea where my husband is. I was bleeding so bad that they took me to the hospital and he said he'd find me again. He was going to try and save some of our possessions. I brought my mother's good china all the way out here from Ohio and somehow it hadn't fallen off the shelf. Was your own house badly damaged?"

I looked at her. She had a round face, now half-covered in white bandages with only one eye showing. A flash of memory returned. "Things were falling," I said. "The grandfather clock."

"They certainly were. But your family got out okay?"

I tried to think about this. "I'm not sure," I said. My parents—were they all right? I could picture our cottage with its scrubbed pine table in the center of the one living room, but did we have a grandfather clock? I could picture it toppling over with a horrible crash onto a marble floor. We had never had a marble floor. That was for palaces and fine churches. Obviously not in my own home. The man I had spoken to when I was lying on the cot had asked if I was staying at a hotel. All of these elements seemed too luxurious to be real.

The only thing that was real was that I was in a place of terrible destruction. We set off along a street littered with bricks and glass. Pillars had fallen from the front of a bank and now lay in chunks across the sidewalk. I thought I saw a dead hand protruding from a pile of rubble. Ahead of us was an enormous building with a dome that rose up into the sky. At least it had been a dome; now only the top part was intact, gilded and shining while beneath it was a skeleton of the tower that supported it. The ribs of the building with no bricks or stone attached to them.

"Would you look at our poor City Hall," the woman said. "And only just completed too. The most expensive in the land, they said, and all that money wasted. What a terrible shame. I don't know how the city will ever hope to rebuild after this."

She broke off as a fire engine came toward us, its bell ringing furiously. There was no room among the debris for two vehicles to pass but bystanders rushed out to move away enough pieces of brick and stone so that the fire engine could squeeze by.

"Not that it will do any good," one of the firemen called out to us. "We can't find a danged water main that isn't ruptured. If we don't do something soon the whole city will be up in flames by nightfall."

We turned onto a broad boulevard. Here there were fine houses, relatively unscathed.

"We may be in luck," the carter said. "It doesn't seem to be quite as bad out to the west. And the dampness of the fog by the ocean will make things harder to burn."

Our cart joined a steady procession of people, laden with what they could carry in bedsheets or blankets slung over their shoulders. The able-bodied helping the injured, the young, and the elderly. And all of them heading in the same direction as us.

I shut my eyes as the horse picked up his pace on the broader boulevard and the cart lurched back and forth. The kind woman with the bandaged face put an arm around me. "Won't be too much longer now," she said. "If Geary is clear, we should be fine and soon at the park."

As we moved toward the ocean we left the dust and smoke behind. The air became clear. Ahead of us was a clear sky with the sun shining into our faces. And in this part of the city there was less sign of damage—a fallen chimney lying in a pile of bricks beside a house. A wooden framed house leaning precariously as it had slipped from its foundation. People were coming out of their houses, bringing pieces of broken furniture or crockery to dump on the sidewalk. Others were loading up possessions onto carts. But most of them were setting up home on the sidewalk. Pots were balanced over small cooking fires while people sat around on packing cases and children played, climbing over the rubble. I still hadn't quite worked out the meaning of all this utter destruction. The only thing I was quite sure of was that I wanted to go home, as quickly as possible.

"I have to get back to Ireland," I said. "They will be looking for me."

Even as I said it I realized that it sounded strange to me. Something wasn't quite right but I couldn't put my finger on it. My mother would be worried about me, I thought. And then like a flash of lightning through my brain came the conclusive knowledge that my mother was dead. I remembered her funeral. It had rained hard and the newly dug earth had turned to slippery mud and my father had nearly slid into the grave with her, which the women with us had taken as a bad omen.

So it couldn't be my mother who was worried about me. Then who? I could feel a sense of urgency cutting through the layers of fog in my head. Somebody important. Something I had to do.

"Why are they taking us away?" I asked.

"Because of the fires. They are spreading out of control downtown and in the Mission," the woman said. "They say that Union Square is already gone, and Market Street." She shook her head as if this was a tragedy too hard to bear. "They reckon we'll be far enough away in the park. I hope they're right. I told William to take the ferry to Oakland, if ferries are still running. He'll be safer on the other side of the Bay."

"William?" I asked.

"My husband. William Clancy. I'm Mary Clancy."

William. I toyed with the name. I could hear a voice saying, "I baptize thee William Joseph Sullivan."

Suddenly a small boy darted out into the street. His mother gave a cry of alarm and rushed to grab him as a fast-moving vehicle went past. She swept him up into her arms and carried him to safety. "Don't you do that again, young man. You stay close to me, you hear? Your mama doesn't want to lose you." Her voice floated up to us as we clip-clopped past.

I baptize thee William Joseph Sullivan. Your mama doesn't want to lose you. It was as if a bolt of lightning had struck me. Clarity seared through my brain. I struggled to my feet. "Liam!" I shouted. "Let me down. I have to find my boy!"

❧ Twenty-three ☙

I stood up, almost falling over as the cart swayed. Hands grabbed at me.

"Careful, ma'am. Sit down," someone said, trying to pull me back into my seat.

"I've got to find my boy," I pleaded. "My Liam. Please let me down."

"You can't get out here," my kindly neighbor said. "You've had a nasty head wound, my dear. Let them take you to the park and rest a little."

"But you don't understand," I pleaded. "I have to find my son. The nursemaid ran off with him. I was trying to catch them when the wall fell on me. I've no idea where they are now but I have to find him."

"You're in no condition to go running around, ma'am," said the man who had tried to pull me back down to my seat. "I'm sure his nursemaid will be taking good care of him and you'll all meet up in the park."

I was conscious that the sun was now tinged with red and was sinking into a band of white mist. It must be late in the day. How many hours had it been since I'd lost Liam and been hit on the head? How long had I lain unconscious? And where could Li Na have taken him?

"I have to go back," I shouted. "Please let me down."

"Go back where?"

"Chinatown."

They were looking at me as if I had lost my mind.

"The poor thing, she's had a nasty blow to the head," the kind woman said.

I shook myself free of a hand that was holding on to me. "No, you don't understand. We were staying at a big house—" I broke off as my memory failed me again. What was that place called? A clear image of those mansions swam into my mind. "On Nob Hill," I continued. "And then the nursemaid ran with Liam to Chinatown." I could hear from my voice that I was on the edge of tears. "I tried to follow them. That must have been when the wall came down on me."

"You can't go back to Chinatown now," someone said. "It's too far. And in your condition you'd never make it. Much smarter to go to the park and then try to find your son. If the nursemaid is sensible she'll have taken him to safety with the rest of us."

I was horribly conscious that with every second I was being taken further and further away from the city. It was no use. If Li Na really had taken my son to Golden Gate Park, then he was safe for now. But if she hadn't . . . if for some reason she was keeping him in Chinatown, then I had to get to him somehow before the fires caught up with them. The cart came to a lurching stop as an automobile cut across in front of us, driving fast. It careened away, weaving and bouncing over rubble, its horn blaring out.

"Danged fool," someone shouted.

"That was the chief of police," someone else muttered. "Now that's one person you don't want to criticize, if you know what's good for you."

Suddenly I decided it was now or never. I stood up, pushed my way past the two men at the rear of the cart, swung myself over in a most undignified fashion, and took off, running. I realized it was a mistake almost immediately as the world swung around me and I thought I was going to pass out. How many miles away from China-town could I be and how could I possibly get back there?

I started to walk back in the direction we had come. My legs felt wobbly and didn't want to support me but I forced myself forward. My eyes still didn't want to focus properly as I staggered along, not sure where I was going. It seemed as if the whole world was fleeing out of the city. I felt like a salmon swimming against the stream as I battled my way around handcarts and mothers leading toddlers and men carrying great bundles. As I reached the wide boulevard down which we had come there was suddenly an enormous explosion that rocked the ground and sent dust flying. I looked around in terror.

"What's happening?" I asked the man who was passing me, with his son sitting piggyback on his shoulders.

"They're dynamiting the houses along Van Ness to stop the spread of the fire," he said. "Danged silly idea if you ask me. Seems like they're starting more fires with that dynamite than they hope to put out. Still, the army's in charge now and you can't tell them any-thing. But watch yourself, ma'am. You've made it through the quake. You don't want to get yourself blown up now."

"Come on, John. We've got to make it to the park before it gets dark," his wife urged. She was holding a small baby in her arms and a toddler clung to her skirts. He nodded to me and on I went. I watched them walk away, again wrestling with my own memory fog. New and disturbing thoughts were now surfacing in my brain. My fear for my son had wrenched me back to consciousness but now it came to me with full force that I also had a husband. His image flashed into my head. Daniel. My Daniel. And he was here somewhere among this chaos.

I hesitated. I knew he had been staying with the priest at the Star of the Sea Church. And he had reached that church after being pushed down the cliff at the place they called Point Lobos, at the far tip of the land . . . Which must mean that the church was somewhere out near the ocean. And since the amount of damage seemed considerably less in that direction I could reasonably hope that he had survived the earthquake. I stood rooted to the spot in indecision. Should I try to head in that direction and find Daniel first? Then he could help me look for Liam.

Another great boom came from across the street and what had been a fine, solid house collapsed in a pile of rubble. Horses neighed and bucked in fear as drivers tried to calm them. Flames flickered up and the air was choked with dust. I put my hand up to my mouth and tried to hurry past without breathing. It was one absurdity after another, a living nightmare that seemed to have no ending. I had been through some frightening moments in my life. I had been accused of murder. I had been in a train crash. My home had been bombed. But never had I felt so frightened and lost and alone as at this moment. How could I possibly find my husband and my son when I could hardly stand up straight or see in front of me?

A loud and imperious honk made me jump as an automobile tried to make its way past the slow procession. A lone driver sat in it, his face obscured by his goggles. As he was momentarily stopped by the wave of humanity I ran over to him.

"Please help me," I begged. "I have to get to Chinatown. I think my son is there. Could you take me?"

"Chinatown is burning."

"I have to get there. I'll pay you."

"How much?"

"I don't know. Whatever you want."

His head was tilted up toward me. Appraising me. "I'll do it for a hundred bucks."

"A hundred dollars?" I stammered.

"Take it or leave it. There's plenty of folks willing to fork out at the moment."

"Look," I said. "I have no money on me, but I'm staying with Bella Rodriguez on Nob Hill. She will lend me the money to give you, I promise."

He stared at me for a long hard minute.

"Please," I implored. "My baby boy. The Chinese nursemaid took him away and then I was hit on the head. I have to find him. If you've a child of your own, you know what I must be feeling."

"All right," he said. "Hop in. But a hundred bucks, mind."

He opened the door and I slid into the seat. It felt so good to be sitting as my head was now aching violently. The motor roared and we lurched forward. I had driven in an automobile with Daniel many times before and the ride had been smooth enough. From the way we lurched along I began to think that this young man had not had much experience in driving. I looked at the quality of his jacket and began to suspect that he had stolen or somehow acquired this vehicle and was using it to make some fast money. Perhaps he was intending to keep it. Who would ever find out in this chaos?

As we turned onto California Street the sky ahead was black. The smell of smoke was overpowering. We drove into the pall. Here and there figures darted out of houses and across the street, carrying bundles. One of them bent down to a body lying on what had been the sidewalk. I thought he was going to try to help but to my horror he was attempting to wrench a ring from a finger. Shots rang out and the man ran off, disappearing around the corner.

"Looks like they're shooting looters," my driver said. "They say the army has taken over."

The engine grumbled and jerked as we made our way up the hill. The mansions all appeared to be standing, almost unscathed apart from tiles that had fallen from roofs or decorative stone facades that had been shed like an overcoat. "That's the one," I said, pointing at Bella's house. It looked exactly has it had, apart from the chimney that lay in a pile of bricks.

He slowed as if meaning to stop.

"No. Take me to Chinatown first," I said. "I must find my son before it's too late. Then we'll come back here. You'll get your money, I promise."

We continued up the hill, past the mansions: the Huntingtons', the Crockers', the Hopkinses'. Then we came to the crest and I gasped. Below us was an inferno. In every direction the city was burning, great tongues of flame leaping into the sky. From all around came the sound of explosions as a building collapsed or a gas main burst. And those flames were creeping up the hill toward us. My eyes stung as the black smoke curled upward.

"That's Chinatown for you, right down there in the middle of that," the young man said. "I'll wager your kid ain't there. Nobody's there anymore. And if they are, they're toast."

I nodded, biting my lip to fight back tears. Surely she wouldn't have stayed. She was a sensible girl, or had been until she ran away with Liam so irrationally. But she cared about him. She'd have tried to save him.

"Very well," I said. "Take me away. I've seen enough."

"Don't forget. I still need my money," he said.

"I said I'd pay you," I said. "We'll go to Mrs. Rodriguez's house. She might still be there and at the very least . . ." I was going to say I knew where there was money. But could I bring myself to go down to that cellar? Could I use money that wasn't mine?

We pulled up beside the house. The front steps were cracked and buckled. I went up them and hammered on the door. Nobody answered. The street was eerily empty.

"Hello!" I shouted. "Is anybody there?"

"They've gone," a voice called up from the street. It was a young man in footman's livery. "They've all gone. The whole lot of them. I saw the Rodriguez carriage leaving at the same time as Mr. Crocker. They were piling as much stuff as they could get into their carriages— jewels and silver and the like. Scared of looters, you see. They left me to watch over the house, but I'm not staying here another minute. The fire will be up here before you know it. You'd best get out too."

"Did you happen to notice whether they had a baby boy with them?" I asked. "I'm looking for my son. We were staying here. I was hurt. And now I don't know where he is."

"I didn't see a baby," he said. "But then I didn't notice exactly when they took off. Just that cowboy type loading up the carriage to the gills."

"Do you have any idea where they were going?" I asked

"Heading south, I should think. The Crockers have a hunting cabin in the hills near Santa Cruz. I expect your Mrs. Rodriguez might be heading for the same kind of place. Safely far away from this, at any rate." He looked around him. "I'd get out now. Orders or no orders."

And with that he started running down California in the direction of Van Ness. I glanced back nervously. The smoke was now billowing up the hill.

"Get a move on, lady," my driver said. "I need my money now. I don't plan to stick around to be burned to a crisp. But I'm quite happy to leave you here to get out on your own if you don't pay me. And I don't think you've got it in you to outrun this fire."

I looked at him with distaste. "Did you steal that automobile?" I asked.

He shrugged. "Didn't exactly steal. Borrowed it. It was my boss's and he ain't going to be needing it anymore. He fell through the floor at our business and broke his neck. So I did the right thing by getting his auto safely out of the Mission District. And if I happened to make a few pennies along the way by giving rides to people, then that's what enterprise is all about, ain't it?"

"More than a few pennies if you've charged other people what you want from me," I said. "But if they've gone I don't see how we're going to get into the building."

I hammered on the door again. No answer. In fact nothing now moved on this hilltop except for the swirling smoke rising to meet us, blotting out the sky.

"Easy enough," the man said. He picked up a brick and smashed the stained glass panel beside the front door. When I looked at him with horror he grinned. "Who's to know? This whole lot will likely be destroyed anyway."

He tapped out enough glass then reached inside for the lock. The big front door swung open. "After you, ma'am," he said with what I took to be sarcasm, not courtesy.

I stepped into the front hall. No attempt had been made to clear up the chaos inside. Those marble statues still lay broken and headless. The grandfather clock lay on its face beside them. Potted palms with soil had spilled over the white marble floor. And in the middle were tears of crystal where the chandelier had fallen.

Now that I was inside I tried to think what I should do. I kept thinking of that trunk full of money in the basement. The simplest thing would be to borrow a hundred dollars, and then repay it to Bella when normality returned. But I didn't want this man to even glimpse a trunk full of money. And certainly not to see Señor García's body.

"My purse is in my room," I said. "I have probably around fifty dollars in it. You can take it all."

"Seems like they left some good stuff behind," he said. "When you're up there, see if you can find the odd ring or brooch."

"But that's stealing!" I exclaimed.

"Lady, this is the place of no law. And the folks who live in mansions like this—they're not even going to miss the odd pearl or diamond. Trust me. They'll be the ones who have the money to rebuild. It will be poor suckers like me who have lost everything for good. That's why we have to make the most of it. Now get going."

I made my way up the stairs. Chunks of plaster lay on the steps and I went carefully to the first-floor landing. Now that I was in the house I found myself looking up the stairs to what had been Liam's nursery. Of course they wouldn't still be here, would they? Everyone had gone. They would have left too, if they ever made it back here. But I couldn't leave without checking. I went up that last flight of stairs cautiously, as the banister was lying drunkenly sideways, and reached the top floor. The skylight had collapsed and pieces of bright stained glass littered the floor. I heard glass crunch underfoot as I made my way down the hall.

Liam's nursery was silent and empty. I felt a wave of disappointment, tinged with relief. I had to believe that he had been taken to safety. His crib now lay on its side and beneath it I spotted his stuffed bear, his favorite toy, which I had to tuck into his bed beside him every night. I wrenched it out from under the crib and put it to my cheek, inhaling the milky baby smell of my son. I was going to believe that he was safe. I was going to find him. I grabbed a few random items of his clothing and diapers from the table. He'd be sorely in need of a change when I caught up with him. Then I made my way back to the first floor and my room.

Now that I saw my room I realized how lucky I was to be alive. The wardrobe had smashed itself across my bed. Great pieces of ceiling lay everywhere. The picture had fallen and sprayed glass over the floor. I picked my way carefully, retrieved my purse from the vanity, and then wrestled my overcoat out of the collapsed wardrobe. The armoire had shot out its drawers so I snatched up my clean underwear, my hairbrush, conscious that time was precious. If he drove off without me, it was quite possible that I couldn't outrun the fire.

I couldn't find my carpetbag so I rolled everything into a bundle. Perhaps there was some kind of bag in Bella's room that I could use. I went down the hall. Her door was half-open. Inside was the same kind of chaos: toppled furniture, smashed pictures. I caught a glimpse of myself in her vanity mirror and recoiled in horror. I looked like a walking ghost with the bloody bandage around my head, cuts on my forehead and cheek, and a deathly white face. Then as I started around her bed to reach her wardrobe, which was still standing, I stopped, recoiling.

On the floor I could see Bella's black hair beneath the drawers of her armoire.

❧ Twenty-four ❧

"Jesus, Mary, and Joseph," I muttered, half exclamation and half prayer. I put down my bundle on her bed and crept closer. It was just possible she was still alive. After all, I had survived the collapse of a brick wall.

I lifted away the top drawer, then the next. Then I stood staring, laughing with relief. It wasn't Bella who lay there. It was a black wig of Bella's hair. I picked it up. It was perfectly intact with Bella's impressive roll of hair. So that was why she touched her hair so often, I found myself thinking. She was unconsciously checking that her wig was in place. Poor thing, if she'd had to flee without her wig, she'd be really missing it. I added it to my bundle, looked around but couldn't find any kind of bag or valise, and left the room, carrying my bundled possessions.

As I came down the stairs my driver was emerging from the living room.

"They left some good stuff behind," he said, grinning. Now that he wasn't wearing his goggles I could see he was really young, with a cheeky sort of face. The sort of face that could easily get into mischief.

His jacket was bulging where he had crammed it full of items he was presumably hoping to steal.

"I don't think you should take things," I said. "You can charge people what you like to drive them, but stealing is wrong."

"Lady, the fire will be here tonight. It will all go up in flames," he said. "And tell you what—since I made out so well here, I'll let you off with fifty bucks. Now let's get out of here while we can."

I found I was looking at the cellar door. It had unlatched itself and was partially open. I was so tempted to go down and check on things. Then I thought—if they were loading everything they could into their carriage, that trunk of money would have gone with them. There was no way they were leaving it to burn. Or that Tiny was leaving it to burn if Bella didn't know about it. I was beginning to think more and more that Tiny had some kind of hold over Bella and was using her, like a puppet master. And now it was probable that I'd never know the true nature of their relationship.

My driver went ahead of me, out of the front door. The world outside was now in gloomy twilight—the rays of the setting sun glowing red through the smoke from the fires like the light coming up from hell. My eyes watered and stung from the soot that hung in the air. I had stopped for a second on the threshold to wipe them before I came out of the house. At that moment a shot rang out. There was a cry and my driver pitched forward down the steps, candlesticks and a carriage clock spilling from his jacket as he fell and clattering down the steps to the street. Men in uniform walked up to him. One of them kicked the body.

"Seems like they'll never learn," one of them said. "What do we do with the loot? Put it back in the house?"

"Pity to let it melt," another said and threw the candlesticks into the back of a horse-drawn vehicle that was standing nearby. It looked like a delivery cart that a grocer or butcher would use—light and fast.

I had remained in the shadow of the doorway, not daring to move. Suddenly one of them spotted me.

"There's another of them!" one of the soldiers called out. He raised his weapon in my direction. I had a split second to think. I could retreat inside again, locking the door, or I could face them and tell them the truth. It flashed through my head that if I locked myself in, they could storm the place and have a good reason to shoot me. Being trapped seemed worse than facing them.

"Don't shoot!" I cried as I came out through the front door.

There was the crack of a rifle and a bullet whizzed past my head.

"Don't shoot. I live here. I'm just taking my own possessions," I screamed. "Come and look if you like. That man you shot has nothing to do with me. I paid him to drive me here, looking for my baby."

I guess the panic in my voice and the bandage around my head made them hesitate.

"It's a woman," I heard one of them say.

I came down the steps and walked right up to those weapons pointed at me.

"Look at what I'm taking," I said. "My baby's change of diapers. The toy he sleeps with. My own hairbrush and change of clothes." I dropped the bundle in front of them and it fell open.

They could clearly see nothing sparkling or shining.

"I came back here because I've lost my baby," I said and I heard the catch in my voice. "I thought the nursemaid might have brought him back here. She took him to Chinatown and now it's all up in flames. I don't know where to find him. I don't know what to do now." And to my embarrassment I burst into tears.

It seemed the soldiers were human after all. One of them put a hand on my shoulder.

"You'll find him," he said. "Everyone is in one of the parks. Now you need to get out of here. The fire will be over the hill before you know it. Is that your automobile?"

I looked at it. If I left it here, it would be burned. And there would be time to return it to its rightful owner when things settled down, if things ever settled down again. And if I told them it belonged to the man they had just shot, they might well commandeer it, leaving me to walk.

"I was allowed to borrow it by its owner," I said.

"Then you should get going right now. You know how to drive it?"

"Yes," I said. This was a lie but I had been with Daniel enough times to have some idea of how to drive an automobile.

I gathered up the bundle again and stuffed it into the passenger seat.

At that moment more shots rang out farther down California Street and dark figures could be seen, running in our direction. The soldiers scrambled back into their cart and off they went, guns at the ready, leaving me quite alone in the gathering murk. From over the hill came the crash, crackle, and roar of the approaching fire. I looked back at the house. Should I close that front door before I left and try to lock it again? Then I realized there was nothing I could do to save the house. It would go up in flames with its neighbors.

I went around to the driver's door and climbed into the seat. *Think*, I told myself. How did Daniel start an automobile? Then I remembered. He inserted a handle somewhere in the front and cranked the engine. Did all automobiles require such a handle and where would I find it?

I searched around and found it lying on the floor behind the seat—a bent handle that should be inserted somewhere at the front of the vehicle. Was there something that needed to be done first? I stared at the dials and knobs on the dashboard. At the back of my mind there was something to do with "choke," but I could not recall what it was. I was having enough trouble trying to make my brain think clearly. The fog still lingered in my head, making any thought physically painful. And now, after the scare of watching my driver shot and the bullet missing my own head by inches, I was overcome with tiredness. I'd have liked nothing more than to curl up on that seat and just sleep.

The fire had now reached the top of the hill. The outline of the newly built Fairmont Hotel was now highlighted against a sea of red and black. I had to make a decision right away. Either I started the automobile or I ran. I went around to the front of the hood and looked for a hole. It was there, plain and obvious, right under the radiator grille. The crank handle fitted into it with ease. I held it and yanked with all my might. Nothing happened. I yanked again. Nothing. Not even a cough or a hiccup. How many times would I have to turn it before the engine fired? I remembered Daniel swearing on occasion when the auto had not started right away or the handle had jerked back, hitting him.

I was crying now. Tears of frustration were running down my cheeks. Then I thought—wait, it's facing downhill. If I release the brake won't it roll forward? *And if I want to stop it again?* a voice asked. I pictured myself gathering speed and crashing into a pile of rubble, or worse still, a fleeing family. But it was my only hope. If I could coast down the hill, I'd be able to outrun the fire. I climbed back into the automobile. With trembling hands I released the handbrake. The vehicle started to move forward. The street ahead of me was devoid of life. If I could make it to the bottom of the hill, I'd reach Van Ness and be safe . . . if I could stop it again.

I pressed the foot pedal I thought might be the brake and was pleased to feel the auto slowing. I stared ahead of me, grim determination on my face, and inched the automobile down the hill. I was aware of a man running up the hill toward me and it struck me that perhaps this was another soldier and I'd be shot for stealing the auto. He was a young man in a dark suit, not a uniform, and it wasn't until he ran right past me that I recognized him.

I jammed on the brake with all my might. The auto didn't want to stop and slid for a good while, creating a horrible smell of burning rubber. But I put my whole weight into it, and tugged on the handbrake as well and eventually the tires hit the curb and stopped. I stood up in my seat. The man was still running up the hill.

"Daniel!" I screamed. "Daniel, it's me!"

He turned, peered down through the gloom, presumably not recognizing the person with the bandaged head. I waved. Screamed again. He was still staring. Then suddenly he ran back to me.

"Molly? Oh my God. What happened to you? What are you doing here? They evacuated everybody. I've been searching all over. Going crazy with worry about you."

He came around to the driver's door as he shouted at me. I climbed out and he wrapped me into his arms. "You poor thing. Your head . . . Are you badly hurt?"

"I was knocked out for a while. Quite a long time actually. And I lost my memory. I thought I was still a girl in Ireland."

"What happened to you?"

"A wall fell on me," I said. "I was trying to find Liam."

"Liam? Where is he? What happened to him?" His voice was sharp with fear.

"The nursemaid ran off with him when the first quake hit. She ran with him to Chinatown. Something about their belief in the Earth Dragon. I don't know. I ran after her but I couldn't catch her. And then another quake came and I saw a wall falling onto me. And when I woke up I was in some kind of makeshift hospital. So I've been trying to find him. Chinatown is all ablaze. Nobody can still be there."

"And the auto? Where did you get it?"

"A long story," I said. "But I didn't know how to start it. I was going to coast down the hill and hope to stop at the bottom."

"Thank God you didn't. You'd have burned out the brakes and ended up crashing. Here. Go around to the passenger seat and I'll get it started."

"The crank's still in the front," I said. "I wasn't strong enough."

"Did you pull out the choke first?" he asked, reaching in to touch one of the knobs.

"I knew there was something I should be doing, but I wasn't sure what." I climbed into the passenger seat, taking my bundle onto my lap.

He bent and jerked the handle. On the second try the engine coughed, then roared into life. With a satisfied smile Daniel climbed into the driver's seat.

"Now let's get out of here while we can," he said and we drove down the hill just as the first sparks started to fall like rain.

❧ Twenty-five ❧

I think we both held our breath until we crossed Van Ness. The soldiers at the checkpoints were surprised to see us, the area having been evacuated. They waved us to a halt, and then stood around the auto. I saw a couple of them fingering their guns.

"Daniel Sullivan, New York police," Daniel said. "I don't have my identification badge. It was lost with my clothing, but I have to get this injured woman to safety."

I had often admired his confidence that bordered on cocky arrogance and I certainly appreciated it at that moment. One of them murmured, "Yes, sir." They stood back and let him drive across Van Ness, continuing along California Street. I sneaked a glance at him. "You gave them your real name. And you're not in disguise. Isn't that dangerous?"

"They are army from the Presidio. Nothing to do with the city. And I figure the local authorities have too much on their plate at the moment to bother with me. We need to find Liam and then get out of here as fast as we can. Where did the automobile come from? Did Bella lend it to you? I didn't realize she had one."

"No. She and Tiny made their escape this morning," I said. "In their carriage. This auto had been stolen by a young opportunist, who was making money by giving people rides at inflated prices. He asked me for a hundred dollars."

Daniel whistled. "I suspect you didn't give it to him."

"Luckily I didn't have to."

"And where is he now?"

"He was shot by the soldiers for looting as he came out of Bella's house," I said. "Frankly I wasn't too sorry. They tried to shoot me too, only they missed. And I managed to convince them that all I was taking from the house were my personal effects and my baby's clothing. I think even they believed me when they saw a pile of diapers." For a moment having Daniel beside me again had made me forget my biggest worry. But with the mention of Liam's diapers my smile faded and he saw the anguish in my face.

Daniel reached across and covered my hand with his. "We'll find him," he said. "Don't worry. It will all be all right. At least we've got each other now. I've been looking for you all day. I came to the house as soon as I could get there after the quake and it was deserted but with apparently little damage. So I thought, naturally, that Bella had taken you off to safety with her. Then I checked the nearest parks where people were setting up tents. And then I thought, no—Bella wouldn't want to sleep in a tent. She'd have vacated the city for somewhere safer. I was picturing you and Liam safe across the Bay in Oakland or in one of the towns down the Peninsula. And I told myself it was only a matter of time before we found each other again." He glanced across at me. He had not had a haircut or a shave in some time and his head was a mass of wild dark curls. His chin was dark with stubble. He looked incredibly roguish and handsome. "But when they said the fires were coming I thought I had to make doubly sure that you had not come back to Bella's house."

"Thank heavens you did or we wouldn't have found each other," I said. "It's a miracle really. Now if we can find our boy, that will be the second miracle." A small sob escaped unbidden. "Oh God, Daniel. What are we going to do?"

"We'll find him." Daniel repeated. He sounded confident but the way he pressed his lips together showed me that he too was fighting with emotion.

"But where? He could be anywhere."

"The Chinese will stick together. They always do," he said, nodding as if he was just thinking this through. "So if this Chinese nursemaid has him, he'll be with the rest of Chinatown. Someone will know."

Night was falling fast. Along the sidewalks—or what remained of the sidewalks—campfires were burning, as families tried to cook a meal outside their damaged homes. These were the only form of light as there were no streetlamps and it became harder to pick our way forward. But behind us, looking up to Nob Hill, the sky was lit with a red glow. I had no doubt that Bella Rodriguez's mansion was burning, and I found myself thinking about Señor Garcia's body in the trunk. Surely they hadn't taken that with them. And if it was still there it would be burned with everything else and nobody would ever know that a murder had been committed, or why.

These musings were rudely interrupted as a voice yelled suddenly, "Hey, they've got an auto. Come on, boys." And a dark shape lurched toward us. There were several of them and one tried to reach for my door, while another went around to Daniel. The crankshaft lay on the floor at my feet. I grabbed it and struck out at the man running beside me. He swore and let go of my door. Daniel pushed the accelerator lever and we shot forward into darkness. The sound of feet receded behind us.

"That was lucky." Daniel turned to me. "Well done. You wield a nifty crank handle."

I grinned. It felt strange and I realized that I hadn't smiled in a long while.

"Are you taking me back to the church where you have been staying?" I asked.

He shook his head. "We're not allowed to go back until it's been inspected and we're told it's safe. Father O'Brien and the other priests went to Golden Gate Park with everyone else. They're setting up a makeshift altar and planning to hold masses there and offer comfort—if any can be offered at a time like this. I don't see how this city can ever recover. How will ordinary people ever get the money to rebuild their homes? And all the public buildings and churches. It's hopeless."

"And if the government is as corrupt as you say it is, then donated money might well go into their pockets rather than to the people who need it."

"Quite possibly." He sighed. "With this chaos I wonder if the officials will ever be prosecuted now. It could not have been better timed, could it? Almost as if they ordered the earthquake."

We were now inching our way forward, the auto's headlights cutting a narrow beam of light through the blackness. We had reached the outskirts of the city. Only the occasional cooking fire burned beside the road. Daniel managed to read a street sign and we turned left. The auto's headlights shone onto what looked like a forest. And beyond the trees lights were glowing. We came to a meadow and Daniel brought us to a stop.

"Having seen how keen those guys were to acquire this vehicle, I think I'll hide it among the trees here," he said. "And take the crank handle with me."

"Where are we going?" I asked. "What are we doing here?"

"This is Golden Gate Park, where you'll find most of the city camping out. The army delivered some tents earlier today and more are promised as soon as the trains are running again to bring in supplies." We bumped and lurched as he steered us between big trees. They had a distinctive strong smell, not unpleasant.

"Eucalyptus, I believe," Daniel said. "And plenty of bushes. This should provide us with enough cover. I don't think there's any chance that we'll get a tent, so we may as well sleep beside the vehicle."

"I'm awfully hungry," I said. "I haven't had a thing to eat all day. And my head is really throbbing again."

Daniel nodded, looking at me with concern. "You've been doing so splendidly that I almost forgot you had been injured. Of course you should have something to eat. And I wonder if there is a make-shift hospital of any sort to take a look at your head wound."

He helped me out of the automobile. I left my bundle, stuffed under the seat, except for my purse, and Daniel took the crank handle with him, just in case he needed to defend us or someone wanted to steal the automobile. I stood uneasily on the soft ground, still feeling the world swaying around me, and realized something else.

"I need to relieve myself," I whispered. "Do you think it would be all right to go here among the bushes?"

Daniel laughed. "I don't think anyone is concerned about niceties right now. I'll stand guard for you."

I crept between large bushes. I realized then, of course, that I was still wearing my nightdress under my dress, and none of my proper undergarments. But I didn't dare to remove clothing, just in case we were surprised. I did what I had to and rejoined Daniel. We walked through the trees and brush toward the lights and came out to a meadow, now lined with rows of tents. Several campfires were burning and from one side came an appetizing smell. A long line of people stood patiently, some with dishes or bowls in their hands, while soldiers served something from a big pot. We joined the line, conscious that we had no bowl, no utensils. When we finally reached the front of the line the soldier grinned.

"You're in luck," he said. "We're about to run out of tin plates. And we're down to the last of the stew too." He scraped around with the ladle and then handed us each a tin plate with a small amount of food on it. "I don't have spoons. Sorry," he said.

"It's all right. We've got extra you can have," a woman behind us said. "Hang on a minute." She darted over to a tent then came back with two spoons. "Here. Take these. You'll need them."

"But we can't take your spoons," I said.

"We were lucky enough to save some of our possessions," she said. "And all our family got out safely. I figure this is a time of share and share alike." She touched my arm. "You're welcome to join us. We've a loaf of bread as well. I'm Martha Hoffman."

"Mr. and Mrs. Sullivan," Daniel said. "Visiting from New York."

"New York? My my. Fancy that. Such a long way from home and your poor wife injured too. Come along. We're camping over here. We were lucky enough to get a tent. There's many poor folks sleeping on the grass tonight. Let's just pray it doesn't rain."

We went to sit with them, a family with four children ranging from a gangly teenage boy to a chubby toddler. Looking at him I couldn't stop thinking of Liam. I ate mechanically because I knew that I needed to keep my strength up. But it was hard to swallow.

"You don't have any children of your own yet?" our benefactor asked.

"We have a boy," Daniel said before I could answer. "We got separated from him and we're still trying to find him. The nursemaid carried him off and then my wife was hit on the head and knocked unconscious."

"Deary me. What a terrible thing to have happened." The woman looked at me with compassion. "We'll all help you look for him as soon as it gets light. He'll have to be here or on the Presidio."

"Not necessarily, Martha," her husband said. "There are camps in some of the smaller parks and squares, you know."

"Depends how far the fire is going to reach," Martha said. "People may have started out there and thought they were safe but then found they'd have to move again."

"They were bombing houses all along Van Ness," the husband said. "That should have contained the fire, God willing. I know our house has gone. There was no stopping it in the Mission. Jumping from street to street like a live thing."

"So unfair," Martha said, showing a catch in her voice for the first time. "We were almost untouched in the quake. Nothing really collapsed except for a few dishes off the shelves. And then they came to tell us the whole neighborhood was going to go up in flames and we needed to get out while we could."

She looked at her husband, who reached across and touched her hand. "At least we're all safe and sound. Can't ask for more than that."

"But how will we ever get the money to rebuild?" For the first time I heard desperation in her voice. "They say all the banks burned with everything else. Does that mean the money we've saved is gone forever?"

"Let's not think about that now," Mr. Hoffman said. "Let's give thanks to the Lord for sparing us and eat this food before it gets cold."

We ate. The children sat silent, still awed by the tragedy that had befallen them. The little girl was lamenting her lost doll. "She had beautiful real hair," she told me. "And she was made of china."

I nodded with sympathy but couldn't think of anything encouraging to say. Who knew if the family would ever be able to afford to buy her another one? I leaned close to Daniel. "Can we start spreading the word about Liam tonight? If the whole camp is looking for him, we'll have a better chance of finding him quickly."

Daniel shook his head. "This park is huge, Molly. This may be one small campsite among many. And you may be sure that the Chinese are off on their own somewhere. I know it's hard but let's wait until daylight. The nursemaid will be taking good care of him, I'm sure."

"I hope so," I said bleakly.

Suddenly there was the sound of commotion, raised voices, and, surprisingly, applause. People scrambled to their feet.

"It's the mayor," someone said, and the word was passed from site to site. People began converging on the place where the food was served and a lantern still burned.

"My fellow San Franciscans," a voice bellowed through some kind of magnifying device. "I applaud your bravery and fortitude. I want you to know that I am with you, every step of the way. We have suffered a major blow. We have been brought to our knees, but we will rise up again, I promise you. Your homes are in ashes. Our fine new city is all in rubble. But we will rebuild. And do you know what? We will rebuild it better than before."

There was a great round of applause and cheers.

"The new San Francisco will be better than the old one. It will be a marvel that the whole world will come to see. So don't despair. General Funston, of the United States Army, is having supplies brought in from all over the West. We'll have enough tents, enough food to see everyone through. We've work for every able-bodied man clearing away the rubble, getting the streets and cable cars working again. We'll get federal loans. We'll get donations. We'll get banks to invest in us and before you know it, we'll start building."

He paused. "Are you with me? Will we do this together? Will we show the world that you can't defeat the great city of San Francisco?"

From across the meadow and through the trees came a great shout of "Yes!"

Folks streamed forward to shake the mayor's hand as he moved through the crowds. Then someone touched his shoulder. "We should be going," the other man said. "You've many more camps to visit tonight, Mr. Mayor."

"You're right," the mayor said. "I have to spread the word of cheer to all the other camps. So keep smiling, okay?"

They came toward us. I could see the mayor's handsome features clearly in the light of that kerosene lamp. He looked strong and confident and I could see why people would believe in him. Beside him the other man came into view. He was still in uniform and I recognized him as Police Chief Dinan. And at his side were several more policemen, including the young lieutenant he had brought to the party. Chief Dinan and the lieutenant went ahead, clearing a way through the crowd, while other policemen followed the mayor. As they disappeared into the trees the mayor caught up with the two policemen ahead of him, clapped a hand on the chief's shoulder, and made some kind of comment. The chief and the young lieutenant turned back to him and laughed.

Then they were gone. I turned to say something to Daniel to find him standing with a look of shock on his face.

"What's the matter?" I asked.

"That laugh," he said. "I heard it once before. He was one of the men who threw me over a cliff to my death."

❧ Twenty-six ❧

T he chief of police?" I stared into the darkness where the figures were still retreating. "Are you sure, Daniel?"

"I wasn't sure which of them that particular laugh came from," Daniel said. "Either the chief of police or his young henchman there. But I'm quite sure about the laugh. It was rather distinct, wasn't it? And when you're clinging to a bush, halfway down a cliff, and you're terrified it will give way at any second or that your assailants will spot you hanging there and finish you off with a bullet, you have heightened emotions. You remember every detail. I particularly remembered the laugh because it was so callous. He had just sent two men to their deaths and he had enjoyed it."

"Surely police chiefs don't do their own dirty work. I have met the young lieutenant before and he had that arrogant, self-satisfied look about him. Yes, I could picture him pushing someone over a cliff."

Daniel gave me a grim sort of smile at those words, but I touched his arm. "Then you're still in terrible danger," I whispered. "If they find out you're still alive, they'll want to finish you off as soon as they can. And they have perfect chances right now. They can shoot you when they like and say you were looting. You must stay hidden until we find Liam, Daniel."

"I'll not hide away like a coward when my son is missing," Daniel said.

"Don't be silly. What good would it do Liam if you're spotted and finished off with a bullet one night?" I put my hands on his shoulders. "I thought I'd lost you once and life didn't seem worth living without you. I'm not going to risk losing you a second time." I took his arm. "Come on. Let's get back to our auto's hiding place while we can. And we'll be ready to go after Liam at first light."

We made our way back through the trees and found our auto, untouched. I was going to spread my overcoat on the ground for us to lie on, but the fog had rolled in off the ocean, blotting out the stars and coating everything in dampness. So instead we climbed into the auto and wrapped the coat over us. I snuggled up to him, savoring his familiar smell, trying to feel safe when I was now consumed with worry for him as well as Liam. Now that I was no longer active my head started to throb again, and the food I had just eaten—a perfectly passable stew of some sort—sat like a leaden weight on my stomach. I felt desperately thirsty and realized I hadn't drunk anything for as long as I could remember. Maybe they'd bring in water trucks tomorrow.

I tried to sleep, but of course I couldn't. Who could in such circumstances?

"Are you asleep?" I whispered to Daniel.

"No."

"I can't sleep either. I can't stop thinking about Liam. I can't bear to be lying here doing nothing, wondering if he's safe or if he's dead. I can't bear it, Daniel."

He hugged me tighter to him. "I know. I'm feeling the same way. First thing tomorrow, when it's light, we'll go looking for him. I promise. We'll find him, Molly."

"But you can't go anywhere, can you? Those policemen might spot you and then you'd be dead too. And I feel so weak, I don't know how much I can go running around the city looking for Liam on my own."

"I'll come with you wherever you want to go," Daniel whispered, his lips brushing my cheek. "I won't let you go alone, my darling. I'll take care of you now."

"But, Daniel," I protested. "You just said yourself that the police chief or his lieutenant . . ."

"They'll be too busy trying to keep order in the midst of chaos to notice me."

I lay there, snuggled against him, feeling the comforting warmth of his body, and tried to think clearly. I didn't share his confidence that the man who pushed him down a cliff would not spot him again and would not hesitate to use the current chaos to put a bullet in his back.

"Is there any way you can go back to your church and find that disguise you wore?" I asked. "You could move around safely in that."

"The authorities have condemned the building," Daniel said. "Nobody is to go inside until there has been a thorough inspection."

"I don't suppose you could slip in without being noticed?"

"When I left they had soldiers posted on the street outside. I'd likely be shot as a looter."

"What are we going to do?" I said. "Somehow we have to get you out of here."

"Molly, I have to say that running away leaves a bad taste in my mouth. I was sent here to do a job and I've achieved nothing, except for almost getting myself killed, and the poor fool who came to meet me smashed on the rocks at the bottom of a cliff."

"So who do you think ordered your death?" I asked. "Do you think that Douglas Hatcher is here in the city and was in cahoots with the chief of police, and maybe paid him to get rid of you? Or do you think that they somehow knew you were asked to look into the federal corruption charge?"

"I'm not sure how they'd have found that out. I didn't share that information with the chief of police, since his name was on the list of those to be indicted. But they may have been watching Dennison all the time, using me as bait to get him out into the open."

"Who suggested meeting by the cliffs?" I asked.

"Not me. Dennison did."

"Then it's possible that you were pushed over the cliff just because you were there and they couldn't let you go free. It was the man you met who they wanted dead."

"Yes, that is possible," Daniel said.

"So it had nothing to do with Douglas Hatcher."

"Probably not. Even in San Francisco I can't think that an individual could bribe the police to hurl two men over a cliff. Although I suppose it is not beyond the realms of possibility. But we haven't any proof that Douglas Hatcher is still in town, have we? He could have passed through on his way to God knows where."

Silence followed as I went through everything that had happened before the quake.

"So do you think now that Mr. Douglas really was the man you were looking for?"

"I've no idea."

Another long silence while I tried to put my thoughts in order. With my aching head and the all-consuming worry about my son I really hadn't had time to formulate what I had seen at Bella's house. I pictured Señor Garcia's body—sightless eyes bulging—lying there stuffed in the trunk. I hesitated. Should I tell Daniel? Or did I not want to inflict more worry on him at this time of overwhelming worry? I decided it might be good to give him something to think about that wasn't his missing son. God knows I wanted to talk about something else myself.

"There's something you don't know," I said. "Because you were at the opera with everyone else last night." My God, I thought as I said the words. Last night. Was it only last night before the world changed forever?

"You found out something?" he asked.

"I found a body. At Bella's house."

"Whose body?" I felt the arm around my shoulder tighten its grip.

"Nobody you'd know. A Mexican man called Señor Garcia. It was all very strange. He arrived during the party you attended. Bella was clearly annoyed or even distressed to see him. He wanted to talk to her but she told him that she couldn't leave her party guests and he had to come back the next morning."

"And did he?"

"He must have done. I was out but he wore some kind of obnoxious pomade or cologne and the smell of it was definitely lingering when I returned. I thought he had come and gone. But that evening, when everyone else was at the opera listening to Caruso, I started to look for your suitcase. Bella said the police had taken it. The police said they hadn't. So I wondered if it could possibly be hidden away somewhere. I went down to the basement and I found your suitcase there, but I also noticed that unpleasant smell again and when I opened a trunk, there was Señor Garcia's body stuffed inside."

"Good God," Daniel said. "So I was right in thinking that Bella wasn't exactly just the sweet and generous hostess that she seemed. I really was being treated like a prisoner there and my every move being watched. I wonder what her game is—or rather was, since her mansion will have been destroyed with the rest."

"Maybe it wasn't Bella who killed Señor Garcia," I said. "Maybe it was Tiny or even Francis. They seem devotedly loyal to her. If someone showed up on her doorstep who was clearly distressing her— maybe knew something incriminating about her, wanted money—I can see that Tiny would have thought he was doing her a favor by killing that person."

"Possibly," Daniel agreed.

"Don't you think there was something odd about that relationship?" I asked.

"Bella and Tiny? A relationship, you call it? Was it that and not just mistress and servant?"

"I don't know rightly," I said. "More than mistress and servant. She definitely bossed him around and he told me that he longed to be back in the wide open spaces on a ranch but that he wouldn't leave Bella. Why was that, do you think?"

"She treated him well? He was putting away money for his future?" Daniel suggested. "Or he was secretly bleeding her of her money? Maybe he saw her as a cash cow and was robbing her blind behind her back."

"And if Señor Garcia knew something about her and threatened to expose her to the authorities, Tiny got rid of him in a hurry because he was protecting his own future," I said.

"Yes, that's possible," Daniel replied. "I wonder what she might have done? They say that everyone who comes to San Francisco is running away from something or has something to hide."

"She did tell me that her husband was a bully and she was well rid of him," I said. "What if she persuaded Tiny to help her kill her husband? Then they sold the ranch in New Mexico and now she can't let Tiny out of her sight because he knows too much. And she's paying him well for his silence."

"Possible again," Daniel said. "But I'm not sure how any of this could be proved. Especially now after the fire. The house will be ashes and presumably Señor Garcia's body with it. And if his charred remains are found, it will be assumed that he was a servant who got trapped in the house by the fire. Or even killed in the earthquake and left there."

I nodded, realizing this was exactly what would happen. Bella would have escaped once again, and if she had taken that trunk of money with her, she would be able to resume her role of society hostess in another city. Except that . . . "I have one of her wigs," I blurted out. "It's here with my belongings."

"Bella wore a wig?" Daniel sounded amused. "And I was so impressed by her hair. What is the betting that her own hair is turning gray or falling out and she's so vain that she wants to keep her youthful looks?" He paused. "Why did you take her wig?"

"I don't know. I thought if I caught up with her she might be grateful to have it back. But she obviously has more than one because she and Tiny were seen loading things into their carriage and then leaving the house after the quake and before the fire reached them." I started to chuckle. "You could wear it, Daniel. Another perfect disguise."

"Oh, definitely." Daniel laughed too. "And my several days of stubble wouldn't give me away." His grip around my shoulder tightened. "Oh God, Molly. What are we doing here? How did I ever get you into such a mess?"

"You wrote me a strange letter and I surmised that you wanted me to come out to you."

"I don't know what I was thinking, bringing my wife and son into such danger," he said. "But I thought if you came to visit me, then I'd be—"

"Safe?"

"Not safe, but at least I'd have another pair of eyes to watch my back. And a witness should anything happen to me. And an aura of respectability with my wife and family around me. And since I'd had to promise the president and Wilkie that I'd tell no one where I was going or what I was doing, I had to hope that my very astute wife would pick up the clues in my letter. And you did, dammit."

"You're not allowed to swear, Daniel." I slapped his thigh.

He laughed at this. "I'm hiding from people who tried to kill me once. I've lost my son. My wife is injured and the whole city is burning around us, but I'm not allowed to swear? Molly, I'll say 'dammit' if I like."

From beyond the trees came the sound of an accordion and voices singing. It all sounded very cheerful and jolly, like a regular campout. But I knew that those people must be feeling the way we were and singing to keep up their spirits. I rested my head back against Daniel's shoulder. "I wish it was morning," I said. "All I want is to have Liam safely back with us."

"And to be far away from here," Daniel said. "If I could find a way to move around without being noticed, I'd go to General Funston and tell him what I know. I'm sure he'd be interested to know that the beloved mayor and city attorney had lined their pockets with graft and corruption and that the respected police chief was a cold-blooded murderer."

"He might be in cahoots with them," I said.

"I doubt it. He's a tough warrior. Don't forget he distinguished himself fighting in Cuba with the president, and then he conquered the Philippines before he was posted here. I expect he is as straight as they come and disgusted by corruption."

From beyond the trees the sound of applause came toward us. And shouts and hoots. It was going to be a long night. Probably the longest night of my life.

❧ Twenty-seven ❧

I suppose I dozed from time to time but I was aware of any small movement through the forest—the hoot of an owl, the crack of a twig, the sounds of men going to relieve themselves among the bushes—far too close for comfort. The damp cold of the fog crept under the coat we had draped over us and it was impossible to get warm. The fog covered any exposed part of us with a layer of moisture and more drops dripped down from the branches above us. Daniel seemed to be breathing regularly so I didn't want to move and wake him. By morning I had a horrible crick in my neck to add to the throbbing in my head and the dry mouth from a whole day without anything to drink. I was never more glad to see the first signs of dawn, although the fog was blotting out the rising sun and the sky beyond the branches. Birds started singing in a raucous chorus, crows cawing loudly to drown out lesser songbirds. Daniel sighed and tried to sit up.

"My arm under your head has gone to sleep," he complained. "What a miserable night. Shall we go and see if anyone is awake and has possibly made coffee?"

"Do you think anyone will have had the foresight to rescue coffee from a collapsed house?" I asked. "And besides, you can't risk being seen, Daniel. You must stay here while I go looking for Liam."

"I don't want you wandering around alone," he said. "I'm coming with you. I'm sure our noble police chief and his lieutenant will be occupied elsewhere."

"Be sensible, Daniel," I snapped. "It's not just those two. You said yourself it was a group of men who pushed you over that cliff. Any one of them could recognize you and inform the chief that you're still alive."

"There must be some way of disguising myself," he said.

"We could take off my bandage and put it around your head," I suggested.

"Don't be stupid. And expose your own wound to the dirt and air?"

"Maybe we could share it? Let's unwind it and see how long it is. And you could also see if my wound really needs to be covered."

"Molly, I don't really think . . ."

"Let's just try it, Daniel. If the wound looks bad and there's not enough bandage, then you can wind it back on again."

"I suppose . . ." he said and untucked the end of the bandage. I grunted as he came to the back of my head. I had obviously bled through and the dressing had stuck. This unwinding was pulling at it. "I'm not doing this," he said.

"Jesus, Mary, and Joseph," I exclaimed. "It's your life, Daniel. Keep going and let's see."

Slowly, painfully, he tore apart layer after layer. "There's quite a good amount of it," he said. "And a nice big gauze pad over the wound itself. That seems to be well and truly stuck, Molly. You certainly bled well. But we'll not try to remove it until there is a clean dressing to take its place. And you're right—they were quite generous with the bandage. There may just be enough for both of us. Hold on, let me get my penknife out of my pocket."

Soon he was rewinding my bandage around my head and then it was my turn to wind it around his.

"I'm sorry, I know this is rather revolting," I said. "At least the blood has dried."

"I've had worse things happen to me recently," he said dryly.

I made sure the bloodstained section went over part of his face. I examined him critically. "Yes, that might do the trick," I said. "I think you could be recognized if someone really studied you, but with a quick glance all they'd see is the bandage and the blood."

I secured the end of the bandage.

"Ready?" Daniel climbed stiffly out of the driver's seat and came around to open my door. I stood up, my limbs also stiff and aching. My face, hair, and the bandage were all clammy with damp fog. The world around us was hazy and indistinct, all sounds muffled. Daniel tore off ferns and branches and covered the automobile pretty well.

"I hope we can find it again." I smiled as I said it. It felt strange to smile, as if it was a skill I had forgotten.

"I hope so too," he said. "But we'll make sure we remember our route to the meadow. Starting with that big tree with the bark peeling off it."

He took my hand and we walked cautiously through the swirling whiteness toward where we hoped the meadow lay. The tents lay still for the most part. Beyond them families were curled together in sleep on the grass, their possessions piled around them. Only a few people here and there were awake, standing and staring out at the scene, arms wrapped about themselves to fend off the cold. At the table where stew had been served the night before, some soldiers were now setting up a new cauldron. We went over and found it contained oatmeal. This discovery made us go back for our plates and spoons and soon we had some warm breakfast inside us, also a drink of water, as a barrel had also been delivered with a dipper attached.

I asked the soldiers if they knew where we might find the Chinese camping.

"I heard that most of them went across the Bay to Oakland on the ferry," one of them said.

"They couldn't all have got out that way," another replied. "Those ferries were packed to the gills and the Chinese would have been the last they would have allowed to board, even for money."

"I heard there were Chinese camped down near the Panhandle," a fresh-faced young soldier said, turning red when we all looked in his direction. He looked absurdly young to be in uniform and I found myself thinking about Liam. What if he wanted to go off and be a soldier one day? How could any mother let her son go to fight at such a tender age?

Today I will find him, I told myself. *Any minute now I will find him and he will be safe and unharmed and all will be well.* Now all I had to do was believe it.

We learned that the Panhandle was the name given to the narrow strip of green at the city end of the park. We had no idea if the fire had reached that first part of the park and if the Chinese were still there.

"We should go in the automobile," Daniel said. "This park stretches for many miles."

"I think we have to go on foot," I said. "We've already seen what desperate people will do to get their hands on an automobile and be able to escape from the city. Next time they may have guns."

"But you're still badly hurt, Molly. A blow to the head is no matter to be taken lightly. I don't think you should walk."

"We can take it slowly and I'll rest if I have to," I said. "Besides, how do we know there are tracks suitable for an automobile through the park?" I managed a confident smile, more confident than I felt, as my eyes hurt me and my head throbbed every time I turned it. But desperation to find my son outweighed anything I may have been feeling.

I could see he was still hesitating. "Daniel, I'll be fine, honestly. And we're right in the middle of the park here, so it can't be too far to either end. And you know how far I used to walk back home in Ireland. Five miles a day to school for a start."

"You're not a schoolgirl anymore, Molly," he said, looking at me with concern. "I say we risk the auto. There are plenty of soldiers around who will come to our aid."

"And if they stop us because they think we've stolen the vehicle? Or they want to commandeer it? Or the police see us and recognize you?" I shook my head. "Too dangerous, Daniel. We'll go on foot. I'll make it just fine."

He shook his head. "You're a stubborn woman, Molly Murphy Sullivan. But I have to admit you may be right." He held out his hand. "Come on, then. Let's get going."

A watery sun was beginning to push through layers of fog, surrounding us with a glowing and unreal light. The fog proved a useful ally as we walked through our own little world, not seeing or being seen. Amid the sweet and pungent smell of eucalyptus leaves we could detect the smell of smoke. As we came to more clearings we found more camps with people just stirring, but they were white folks like ourselves. No Chinese among them.

And then finally someone told us that he had seen Chinese in a dell beyond the giant tree ferns. We hurried forward and came to the tree ferns, looming out of what had now become a smoke-tinged haze, strange and beautiful, taller than our heads. And then there was the dell beyond them, a circle of green grass surrounded by tall trees. Chinese people huddled together, most of them still sleeping. Some were already squatting beside campfires, attending to cooking pots. From birdcages, placed beside sleeping owners, or on top of piles of possessions, came early morning songs. I scanned the scene, looking for Li Na's white tunic and black trousers. There were several such but each proved to be another woman, not her.

More and more people were waking. We found Chinese who could understand English and asked, our question becoming more and more desperate each time. No, they did not know anyone called Li Na. No, they had not seen a white child. I remembered that she had only come to the city recently. She wasn't born and raised in the city so fewer people would know her. I tried to tell myself that she was a sensible girl. Perhaps she was one of the first to get out of the city on a ferry. Perhaps she had taken my son across the Bay to Oakland, where they would have been quite safe from fire. All we had to do was find a way across to that city.

"Do you think she managed to cross the Bay to Oakland with the other Chinese?" I asked Daniel. "Should we see if we can reach a ferry and go across to look for Liam there?"

Daniel frowned. "I doubt if we can reach the ferry building," he said. "That whole area of the city along the waterfront has gone up in flames. Surely they won't be allowing people in where it has burned."

We were about to walk away when I heard someone calling my name. I turned to see Ellen coming toward me. "Missy Sullivan!" There was a look of concern on her face. "What you do here? You get hurt?"

"Yes, Ellen," I said. "I got hit on the head when I was trying to stop Li Na from running away with my son. Now I'm looking for them. You haven't seen him, have you?"

She shook her head. "Your boy? No, we thought you had your boy. After earthquake you were gone and we thought you took him to safety. Li Na took him, you say?"

I nodded. "She ran with him down to Chinatown. Something about the Earth Dragon."

"Ah. Earth Dragon." She nodded as if this made sense to her. "I don't see Li Na since the earthquake," she said. Then suddenly she recognized Daniel.

"Mr. Sullivan?" she stammered. "But they say you dead."

"Not quite, Ellen." Daniel smiled at her. "But please don't tell anyone you've seen me. There are still people around here who might want to kill me."

"Wah!" she said, shaking her head. "Too many bad people. But I'm happy you are still alive. I see those men follow you all time. And then they say you fall from cliff and I don't think this is true."

"Quite right," Daniel said.

"Ellen, we'd love to come back and talk to you later," I interrupted before Daniel could tell her the whole story of what happened to him, "but right now we're desperate to find our boy. Could you ask your friends and family if they know anything about Li Na and our son? We don't know where to look."

She nodded and went across to where a group of women were sitting around a campfire. A cooking pot was emitting a pungent and not too pleasant odor. She squatted beside them and an animated conversation took place. At last she got to her feet and came back to me.

"They say Li Na dead."

"Dead? Are they sure?"

"They say they see body of girl from Hong Kong. One who wear black and white of amah."

"And was my boy with her? Did they see his body?"

More Chinese was shouted back to the campfire. Heads were shaken. Then one of the women let out a stream of Cantonese, waving her hand for emphasis.

Ellen turned back to us. "That woman say she saw a European child in a wagon with some Chinese women. He was crying. She heard they were going to take him to the place where they putting orphans."

"Orphans?" I demanded. "Where is that?"

Blank faces stared at me. "Can she point out the women who had my son with her?" I asked.

I was feeling like Alice who had fallen down a rabbit hole and at each twist and turn things were becoming more frightening and unreal. The request was made. The woman got to her feet, slowly and painfully, and I realized that she was one of the bound-foot women. Had she had to walk all the way here on those deformed little stubs? She shaded her eyes and stared around the encampment. Then she said something to Ellen.

"She's not sure. She said the woman was with a man with a long mustache and a little girl, maybe her daughter, was trying to make

the white baby stop crying. The girl had a long braid and was wearing a red and white flowery tunic and trousers."

"And they were heading here, toward the park?" I asked.

There were nods of affirmation.

"I help you find them," Ellen said. She started off, picking her way
between the bundles of possessions and sleeping people across the
dell. Every now and then she stopped to ask someone. At last a woman
pointed, nodding.

"She says a girl wearing such a tunic played with her daughter last
night. They played where there is a waterfall by the trees."

We hurried toward that spot and sure enough, an elderly man,
with a very long mustache, was tending a campfire. Ellen went up to
him. He had set up a lean-to of sorts from rugs draped over boxes.
He called into this and a woman emerged, her eyes still bleary with
sleep. She looked alarmed at seeing us. Ellen asked the question. The
woman looked at us nervously, and then blurted something out.

"She says she was going to hand the child over to the soldiers so
they could put him safely with the other orphans but then his mother
came and claimed him."

❧ Twenty-eight ❧

Disappointment flooded over me. Then it couldn't have been my son after all. My boy, my beloved Liam, was still missing or dead. Probably the latter if Li Na was dead too.

"What did this child look like?" Daniel wasn't giving up so easily.

The woman still looked scared and embarrassed. She muttered to Ellen, who turned back to Daniel. "She says the boy had dark curls, like yours. And he was chubby and healthy looking and he had a loud voice when he cried."

Daniel looked at me, anger blazing in his eyes. "That's our boy, Molly. Someone has stolen our boy." He turned back to the Chinese woman. "What did this woman look like? Where were you when she took the boy from you?"

The woman was clearly frightened now. "She says she's very sorry," Ellen translated. "She thought she was doing the right thing. Was this woman not his mother?"

"Almost definitely not," Daniel snapped.

"What did she look like?" I repeated. My heart was beating so violently now that it felt like a frightened bird imprisoned in my chest. "And where was this? Do you know where she was camping?"

More words were exchanged. Ellen turned to us. "It was on the strip they call the Panhandle," she said. "On our way to this place. The woman was big. Not young. She wore black silk and she had pearls around her neck. A rich woman."

"Will you come with us to help identify her?" Daniel asked.

The woman looked down at the ground, ashamed and mumbling a reply.

"She says she cannot walk so far. She has the lotus feet. Walking is impossible for her," Ellen translated, giving the woman a look of scorn. Her own feet were big and broad. In China she would have been the despised one, but here in the new world lotus feet were not a blessing or a mark of status.

"I understand." I nodded to the woman. "Thank you."

"Wait," she called after us in English as we were ready to go. "I send my daughter." She shouted into the lean-to and the girl in the red and white tunic emerged. She stared at us with frightened eyes and when questioned she answered in little more than a whisper, looking down at the ground. Ellen questioned her and yes, she had seen the woman take the child. And she would help us to find him.

"Perhaps they misunderstood," I said as Daniel, Ellen, and I hurried along a soft bridle path toward the Panhandle. "Perhaps she meant that she would find his mother for them."

"Who knows?" Daniel's mouth was set in a grim line. "What better time to help yourself to a baby than when the world is in chaos."

I wished he hadn't said that. I now felt violently sick, as if I would throw up at any minute and I couldn't tell whether it was because of my head wound or because of my terror. I stumbled forward, finding every step painful now but not daring to stop. We came out of the trees and saw that the park had come to an end but a narrow strip of green continued toward the city between two roads. So this was the Panhandle. It was now covered in tents. Smoke rose from cooking fires to mingle with the smoky haze that hung in the air, making our eyes sting. And when we looked beyond, toward the city, the sky was still a black pall.

The little Chinese girl, whose name, we had learned, was Mei Ling, went ahead of us, like a dog following a scent. She peered among the tents until finally she stopped abruptly and pointed, whispering something to Ellen.

"She says that is the woman," Ellen said.

We looked where she was pointing. A large woman in black had come out of a tent. She wore a tortoiseshell comb in her hair and pearls around her neck. She wasn't young, in her thirties, or even forties, and her sallow complexion hinted at Mediterranean ancestry— Italian maybe? Or Mexican or even Jewish.

"Let me handle this," Daniel said, holding up a warning hand to me. He strode forward with that confident stride of his.

"Good morning, ma'am," he said. "Captain Sullivan, police. I understand you were good enough to rescue a baby boy from some Chinese people. Did you take him straight to the place where they are holding rescued orphans or do you still have him with you?"

"You must have the wrong person," she replied, staring haughtily at Daniel. "I don't know who told you that, but they were wrong."

"So you don't have a baby boy with you? You've never rescued a toddler?"

"No," she said defiantly. "No. Never."

As if to dispute this a wail came from inside the tent.

"My own son," she said. "Not the boy you're looking for."

"Can we see him?"

"Certainly not. That tent is my private property. If you go near it, that's trespassing and my husband will shoot you."

By now people had gathered around us.

"What's happening?" someone asked.

"This woman won't let us see whether the child she has in her tent is mine," I said. "She threatened to shoot us. I think she might have my little boy in there. I just want to look."

"I've told them it's my own son," she said. "Why do they try to stir up trouble? Don't we all have enough troubles?"

There were murmurs from the crowd. From inside the tent came a plaintive cry of "Mama!"

"You see. He hears me and he wants me," she said. "I must go to him, if you'll excuse me."

She headed for the closed tent flap. I went to follow her and she spun around. "If you don't go away I'll call the police," she said. "I've heard about people like you, trying to steal babies. I'm a respected person in this community. The mayor and police chief are good friends. Do you want me to summon them?"

Of course I couldn't risk the police chief seeing Daniel. I saw the blank despair on his face.

"It may be her child, Molly," he said quietly. "We may have gotten this wrong."

"Wait!" I commanded as her hand was on the tent flap. I turned back to the watching crowd. "Liam!" I called. "Liam, darling. Are you in there?"

And from inside the tent came a plaintive wail. "Mama! Mama!"

A new murmur went around the crowd.

"You see. She has got my child." I wrenched the tent flap from her. She tried to prevent me from entering. She was a big woman, but I fought like a wild thing, pushing past her. "Go ahead. Call the police. You're not taking my child from me." She grabbed at my clothing. I hit out wildly. I heard her give a whimper as I must have punched her nose. She released her hold on me and I was through. There among pillows and trunks at the back of the tent my own dear boy stood, his face red and tearstained. His arms were held out to me.

"Mama. Up," he said.

I swept him into my arms and carried him out. "Do you need any more proof?" I demanded to the crowd. They stared at Liam, clinging to me like a limpet.

"It's her boy all right," one of the men said. "This woman is a kidnapper."

"They shoot kidnappers," someone else said.

The woman's eyes darted around nervously. "I am not a kidnapper," she said. "I found this child in the street beside a dead woman. I saved his life."

"No!" Mei Ling said in her high, shrill voice. "She take him from my ma. She say she his mother! She tell lie."

An angry murmur now passed through the crowd. The woman stared at them with defiant contempt. "He'd have a better life with me than with this . . . this gypsy."

"I'm his mother," I said calmly. "That's all that matters. Given the circumstances I'll not press charges. I'm just happy to have my boy back with me." I turned to Daniel. "Come on, Daniel. We can go now. Let's get out of this place and go home."

We walked with Ellen and Mei Ling back to the Chinese encampment. Liam clung to me fiercely, small sobs still shaking his body. His undergarments were soaked and I couldn't wait to wash and change him. I was still in shock over how close I'd come to losing him. If he'd been asleep, or hadn't responded to me, or that woman had really summoned the police, I might never have gotten him back. I tried to understand what had made this woman act so rashly. Perhaps she had assumed his mother was dead and didn't want to leave him among the despised Chinese. Perhaps she had always wanted a child and saw this moment of chaos as her one opportunity. Strange times create strange deeds, I thought. I wondered how many other similar cases had happened since the earthquake, how many children were now separated from their parents and would never be reunited?

Daniel fell into step beside Ellen. "So tell me," he said. "Is there anything I should know about Mrs. Rodriguez? Why did she have me watched all the time?"

"I don't know, sir," Ellen said. "I know nothing about her. I was just the cook. She was good to me and to Francis. She paid me well. I never knew where she came from or how she got so much money. She say she rich widow. She sell husband's ranch. That's all I know."

"Then why was she keeping tabs on me?" Daniel asked. She clearly didn't understand the meaning of "tabs" so Daniel repeated. "Why did she have me watched all the time and not let me go out alone? What was she afraid of?"

Ellen shrugged. "Maybe someone tell her or pay her to watch you."

"Possibly." Daniel nodded. I could tell he thought that person would be the police chief or the mayor.

"And what about Señor Garcia?" I asked, wondering how much she knew about this matter.

She frowned. "I don't know this name."

"The Spanish-looking man who came to visit before the earthquake."

She shrugged. "Ah, him. I bring them coffee. They were chatting. But not happy talking. Missy Bella upset. That's all I know. When I went to clear away the cups he had gone."

Yes, I thought. Gone down to the cellar in a trunk.

"So you don't know where she's gone now?" Daniel asked.

"They went in carriage," Ellen said. "When we hear that fire is coming she decide to leave. I helped her carry out valuable things. Paintings. Her jewels. Silver. Then she gave me fifty dollars and said thank you for my work and told me to save myself before the fires came."

It seemed all too believable. Ellen didn't appear to be on edge or worried about the questions. On the contrary she was happy to talk to us. So it looked as if we might never find out why Señor Garcia was killed or if Bella had any dark secrets of her own. We reached the dell where the Chinese were camped and delivered Mei Ling back to her mother, thanking her profusely. If they had not wanted to help us, if they hadn't rescued the baby in the first place, and if Mei Ling had not found Liam's kidnapper, then we would never have found our son. I reached into my purse. "I'd like to give you something," I began but the woman held up her hand angrily and said something to Ellen. Ellen turned to us. "She say this bad time for all people, white and Chinese. We must help each other when we can."

I smiled at her then and took her hand. "Thank you," I said again. "I wish you all the best. And you, Mei Ling."

The girl smiled shyly. We set off again. Ellen led us back to her campsite and offered us tea and rice with vegetables, both of which we accepted gratefully. I suspected that the green stuff was in fact nettles and ferns culled from the surrounding forest but they were most welcome at this point. Liam was hungrier than any of us and opened his mouth like a little bird as I shoveled in rice and broth. Then we thanked Ellen again and took our leave.

❦ Twenty-nine ❦

We were still walking down the wide path when we heard the tramp of boots ahead of us and a group of soldiers came into view, and following them a straggling line of men of all shapes and sizes. They stopped when they drew level with us.

"General Funston has given an order to round up all able-bodied men to remove the bodies and clear the streets in the areas where the fire has already gone through," one of the soldiers said, eyeing Daniel.

"I'm afraid my husband isn't able-bodied," I said before Daniel could answer. "He and I both received bad head wounds, as you can see from his bandages. He's not up to any kind of work. The doctors at the hospital only released us when the fire came close. He should be resting but we had to find our little son, who was taken from us." I used my most humble and pleading voice.

"All right. On your way." The soldier waved his rifle at us and the troop marched on. Some of the men looked anything but able-bodied.

Daniel turned to look at me as the last of the feet died away. "I feel rather guilty about that, Molly. I am able-bodied. Perhaps I should be helping."

"Have you lost your senses?" I demanded. "You can't risk being seen, Daniel. We've been taking a big enough risk walking through the park to find Liam. But there will be police on those streets and nowhere to hide."

"You're right," he agreed. "And that was quite some performance. Sarah Bernhardt has nothing on you."

"I do what it takes to save my family," I said. "And now we've got Liam again there is nothing to keep us here. Let's drive that automobile to the first place where we can catch a train."

"I think we'll have to wait at least a day or two," he said. "I heard the train lines were disrupted. And we can't leave the city with that automobile. It's not ours. We'll turn it over to the military when we go and they can hold it until a rightful owner claims it."

"But the rightful owner is dead," I said. "The man who borrowed it told me. He'd fallen through the floor."

"But he'll have family. Next of kin. It's not ours."

I shook my head, smiling. "The only police officer in New York City who won't accept bribes and won't borrow automobiles."

"Not that it's done me any good," he said. "I wonder if I'll still have a job when we return home?"

"We'll face that when we come to it." Liam must have fallen asleep against my shoulder and I hoisted him up, noticing how big and heavy he had become. And how wonderful it was to feel him in my arms again. Compared to what we had just gone through, nothing else mattered.

We retraced our steps to our hidden automobile and placed sleeping Liam on the seat. I left Daniel with him and went to the water barrel in the meadow, coming back with a wet cloth to wash him. His poor little bottom was bright red from not being changed for a whole day and night. Some mother she would have made, I thought. What had made her steal a child? She was no longer young. Then I decided to think charitable thoughts. Perhaps she had lost her own.

Perhaps she could never have one of her own. And I found myself thinking of Mrs. Endicott. I wondered where her husband was now, if he was still in the city, if he had managed to take the ferry to Oakland while there was still time and was now on his way back to her. Or if he had been one of the unlucky ones, buried under a mountain of rubble and she would never know what happened to him.

Daniel was pacing up and down like a caged beast. "I must find General Funston before I leave," he said. "I must tell him what I know. He's in charge of the city now. It would be up to him to bring charges against Mayor Schmitz and the police chief. And they can add murder and attempted murder to those charges too."

"How are you going to find him?" I asked. "I expect he's still overseeing the firefighting. From that black sky on the Panhandle the fires are far from out yet."

"Then we must wait until we can see him," Daniel said. "I can't go home a complete failure. I've accomplished nothing."

"You didn't exactly expect to be killed, did you?" I looked at him with sympathy. "And you now have personal proof that the police chief was part of the city fathers' corruption."

"All the same I don't want to go home empty-handed," he said. "My career hasn't been exactly stellar lately. I need to know that I have helped to see justice served here. And since we obviously can't travel for a few days, until the train line is restored, then I'll make sure I do find General Funston before we leave." He nodded, as if satisfied that he had made up his mind. I was not so satisfied with his decision. I was thinking that every day we stayed here was another chance for the police chief or one of his men to recognize Daniel. Or for Daniel to be rounded up for one of the work parties.

By the end of that day more tents had arrived and the whole meadow resembled a neat white city. I suppose we could have applied for one of the tents ourselves, but it made more sense to stay hidden, and close to our vehicle if we needed a hurried departure. More food was served that evening. People lined up without complaining. Those who had rescued supplies brought them out to share. It was all very orderly and civilized, in contrast to the awful looting and anarchy in the streets I had witnessed earlier. I suspected that General Funston, in spite of his diminutive size, must be a leader of great strength and well respected by his men. After our bellies were satisfied with a sort of chowder, we played with Liam, who had recovered from his ordeal remarkably quickly. To hear him laugh as Daniel chased him among the bushes was the best thing I could have hoped for. The fog came in again, and the cold dampness forced us into the automobile. We snuggled together under my coat for another night's sleep.

In the morning the sky was overcast and heavy with the promise of rain. That would not be good news for the thousands camping out, especially those who hadn't yet been allocated a tent. It would turn fields into seas of mud and ruin possessions folks had managed to save. On the other hand it would extinguish any fires that were still burning—so a mixed blessing. I wasn't exactly looking forward to it myself as we had no real shelter apart from tree branches. I wondered if the army might be handing out blankets or tarpaulins anywhere and left Daniel and Liam to do some scouting on my own.

"See if you can find out where I might locate General Funston," Daniel called after me. "And see if there is a field hospital. You need that head of yours attended to. The dressing should be changed."

"I've needed my head attended to since the first moment I met you," I replied. It was good to see him grin. It was even better to be able to joke again.

I crossed the first meadow, now filled with rows of tents. Beyond it a field kitchen had been set up in a small glen and several soldiers were engaged in butchering a steer ready for the evening meal. I looked with interest. One of the soldiers caught my eye. "This fellow broke out of a slaughterhouse yard after the quake. They were stampeding through the streets, trampling people willy-nilly, until they were shot. At least he's proving useful now."

I asked him about General Funston. He was a humble private, not privy to the comings and goings of a general. "He could be anywhere," he said. "He's been driving around all over, making sure the fire lines hold and the looters get what's coming to them."

But I did learn that his own headquarters at the Presidio had held up pretty well in the quake and he'd likely be back there by nightfall. As I went to turn away I spotted a familiar face. My newspaper friend, Mr. Hicks, was standing with a photographer as the latter recorded the butchering of the steer. It took him a moment to recognize me when I called his name. I suppose I must have looked a sight with a bloody bandage around my head.

"It's Mrs. Sullivan," I said. "We met at the Palace when you thought I was an opera singer."

"Mrs. Sullivan. Why yes. That seems like another world ago, doesn't it? The Palace is no more, alas. And the opera house is gone, and the Examiner building too. It's like a dead zone along Market Street. Just blackened shells and rubble. It would break your heart, I tell you."

"What happened to the opera singers, do you know?"

"Ran away as fast as they could." He had to smile. "Mr. Caruso was out of the Palace and onto the ferry to Oakland long before the fires took over. So were his friends from the Metropolitan Opera. All safely far away by now if the train lines are up and running again."

"Well at least you're getting the scoop you dreamed about now, aren't you?"

He nodded. "As soon as the telegraph wires are up I've plenty of stories to send out to the world. I might even make my name. But your own story is also an interesting one. You came looking for your husband and found he had died, did you not? And now it seems as if you were hurt yourself."

"I was lucky to survive. A wall collapsed onto me and I was knocked out. And I've a fascinating story to tell, but I don't think I'd better tell it to you now. Not until we're safely far away."

He raised an eyebrow. "You intrigue me, ma'am."

I stared at him, wondering how far I dared go. "Tell me, Mr. Hicks.

What do you know about corruption among the highest levels of city government?"

I was surprised by his reaction. He burst into a hearty laugh. "What do I know? What does everyone know? The city fathers here are up to the elbows in corruption and graft. Mayor Schmitz, Abe Ruef, Police Chief Dinan—all as twisted as a corkscrew. And open about it too. If you want to run a business in San Francisco, you need to grease their palms to get the permit. Then more money to stay open and to have the police turn a blind eye to prostitution and gambling. They were about to be indicted, you know. There was a federal investigator sent from the president himself."

"You knew about that?"

"Yes. He met a fellow newspaperman, Fremont Older, who had been leading the campaign to expose corruption in the city. Mr. Older attracted the ear of the president, who sent a man out to confirm what he had been told."

"And what happened to this man?" I asked.

"Don't know. We assumed he had returned to Washington to make his report and apparently a grand jury was to be appointed."

"I see." I didn't tell him that the man he spoke of had died at the bottom of a cliff. "What will happen now, I wonder?"

He shrugged. "It's my belief they'll walk away smelling like a rose. All the papers of evidence destroyed. City Hall in ruins. Who can ever bring charges against them now?"

I remained silent.

"So you'll be off home as soon as you can, I take it?" he asked.

"I will. I can't wait to be gone from here. It's brought nothing but grief."

As I started to walk away he called after me, "It was a grand city, Mrs. Sullivan. And we'll rebuild it bigger and better. You'll see."

I kept walking until I came to a large open space, bigger than any of the other meadows. A wooden sign read *The Polo Field* so I presumed that sport was played on it in happier times. However now tents were also in the process of being erected here. I was offered an unoccupied tent, but turned it down, coming away with two blankets and two tin mugs. I was also directed to a place where a hospital of sorts was operating. I joined a line of walking wounded, most of them more gravely injured than I. So many people with broken bones, makeshift splints, primitive bandages. At last it was my turn and the pad was soaked away from the back of my head without too much discomfort. When the wound had been cleaned the doctor nodded. "Not too bad at all," he said. "Just try to keep it clean and you'll heal nicely." He put a fresh gauze pad on it and wound a new bandage around me. When he went to throw the old one away I retrieved it from him.

"As a souvenir of the earthquake," I said. "I've nothing else to remember it by." Actually I was thinking that two bandages around Daniel's head would be better than one at keeping him disguised.

As I was about to stand up the doctor asked, "Did the blow to the head knock you out?"

"Yes, it did."

"Then you should be resting now. Concussion is a serious matter. Go back to your tent and lie down. Rest and sleep. That's the best remedy. And don't try to do too much for several days."

I smiled to myself as I walked away. If he could have seen me yesterday, running around like a mad thing in search of Liam. Still, I was tough. I had survived so far and I was actually feeling halfway normal again. I started back for our hiding place, hoping I would remember the way. It was indeed a huge park and I had only seen the half of it. I was passing along a line of tents when a man came out of one—a distinguished-looking man, still wearing a jacket, shirt, and tie, although the jacket was now wrinkled, dusty, and rather the worse for wear. He brushed himself down with distaste. I realized then that I recognized him.

"Mr. Endicott," I said, going over to him. "You won't know me, but I am a friend of your wife's in New York. She will be so relieved to find out you've survived the quake."

He stared at me coldly. "I think you have made a mistake, madam," he said. "My name is Rutherford. Edwin Rutherford."

"I'm so sorry," I stammered, "but you must have a double. I was at a picture show with Mr. Endicott's wife. They showed moving pictures of San Francisco and she pointed you out to me. Or at least she pointed out someone who looked like your twin. She was surprised to see her husband in San Francisco because she expected him to be on the East Coast."

"I'm sorry to disappoint you," he said. "But I am a resident of this city and have been for some time. If this woman expected her husband to be on the East Coast, then that was probably where he was."

"What's going on, Eddy?" A woman came toward us, leading two small children by the hand, a fair-haired boy of four or five and a little girl who still toddled rather than walked. She was also young, but somehow more cheap in her appearance than the man. She looked at me suspiciously.

"This lady took me for someone else," Mr. Rutherford said. "Understandable, I suppose, with all this chaos."

"A friend of mine in New York saw him on a newsreel at the movies. She pointed him out to me as her husband and was surprised to find him in San Francisco."

"Well, he's my husband and these are our children," the woman said aggressively.

"I see that now," I replied. "I'm sorry. I didn't mean to upset you. I understand everyone on earth has a doppelgänger somewhere." I smiled. She did not return the smile and pushed the children ahead of her into the tent.

"I'm sorry to have troubled you." I nodded to Mr. Rutherford and went on my way. I had reached the end of the line of tents and just entered a stand of Scotch pine trees when someone tapped me on the shoulder. I spun around.

"Mr. Rutherford!" I exclaimed.

He put a finger to his lips. "Listen," he said. "You were right. I am

Endicott. But Blanche doesn't know. She has no idea I have a wife back in New York. I've been coming out here for several years on business and a few years ago I met Blanche and she was so young and fresh and pretty . . . and she gave me a son. You've no idea what that meant to me. As you probably know we were childless, Mrs. Endicott and I."

His eyes were begging for understanding. "Ours was never what you'd call a happy marriage. More a marriage of convenience, I suppose. I had made up my mind never to return to New York, and now the quake has given me the perfect solution. Mr. Endicott died in the quake. His wife will be notified. And Edwin Rutherford will go on living happily."

"But your poor wife," I exclaimed. "She is worried about you."

"She will be relieved," he said. "And she will be well provided for. She'll inherit my businesses, for one thing."

"But what about you? How will you live?"

"Well enough, I expect." He smiled then. "I have been transferring assets to my new name for some time. I'll not starve. Neither will Mrs. Endicott. She has money of her own too, you know. And I—I have found out that money isn't everything."

His gaze swept over the tents. "Look at all these poor fools. Lost everything, but are they weeping? No, they are rejoicing at being alive, at being spared. And they are already talking about starting over."

He touched my arm. "Will you tell Rose that you met me and that I sent fond wishes the day before I perished in the quake?" His pressure on my arm increased. "Can I count on you not to tell her the truth? It would break her heart. It's so much better this way."

I couldn't think of what to say. "I'll have to give the matter some consideration," I said. "I will have to think about it."

His face hardened. "Is it money you want? I have money aplenty in East Coast bank accounts."

"That can hardly be accessed by a dead man," I reminded him.

"No, Mr. Endicott, I don't want your money. I want to do what is right."

"I'm never returning to New York, whatever you tell her. At least let her believe that I died thinking of her. I beg this favor of you."

I looked at him long and hard. "I will spare her any grief that I can," I said. And as I walked on I wasn't sure what I would tell her. But I can tell you that my heart was full of gratitude when I returned to my own husband and son. What a terrible thing to have believed all these years that your husband was away on business when all the time he had another wife, and children that he loved. A sad situation indeed.

I passed on information to Daniel about General Funston, wound the extra bandage around his head in spite of his protestations, and helped him rig up a primitive shelter under some big rhododendron bushes that were now in full flower. About my encounter with Mr. Endicott I kept silent.

✤ Thirty ✤

T hat evening I helped Daniel push the automobile out of the bushes to drive to the Presidio and find General Funston. We decided to leave before the light faded as the whole area was in darkness at night with no streetlamps, no lighted windows—not to mention roaming ruffians and soldiers, and streets still full of all kinds of hazards.

Daniel had wanted to go alone but I insisted on coming with him. "We've been split up enough recently. I'm not risking it happening again," I said. "What if more ruffians try to take the auto away from you and I'm not there to wield the crank handle? What if you're commandeered into a work party and I don't know what's happened to you? Besides, I have my own story to tell General Funston. I'd like him to see if there's still a body in the cellar of Bella Rodriguez's house."

"Very well," Daniel said with a sigh. "I suppose it makes sense not to lose each other again. And once I've told him what I know we're going across the Bay to Oakland to take our chances getting on a train. I can't wait to be safely away from here and heading home."

"Amen to that," I said. I climbed into my seat and settled Liam on my lap. He was clearly excited about going for a ride. As I watched his bright little face I thought how remarkable children are. He had been taken through an earthquake, watched his nursemaid killed, been rescued by strangers—Chinese people—and then stolen by a woman who called herself his mother. And yet now he was acting as if none of this had ever happened. I found myself vowing that I would never put him in jeopardy again. When we returned to New York I would make sure our lives were safe.

Daniel had never been to the Presidio and only knew vaguely where it lay. But we asked directions from soldiers at a roadblock and Daniel mentioned that he was on his way to a meeting with General Funston, just in case they decided that another vehicle would be more use to them at this moment. An avenue lined with more eucalyptus trees took us through a wooded area until we emerged, looking down onto a view of smooth, silvery water. The sky had cleared from its earlier promise of rain and a red sun was now sinking into a bank of white fog that lay just beyond the cliffs that guarded the entrance to the Bay. Down by the Bay was a collection of attractive buildings. The larger ones that surrounded the central open area were built in the colonial style and looked as if they would be more at home on the other coast. At the edge of the forest were white wooden houses with porches and red roofs. Apart from the central parade ground, I would not have taken it for an army base as it presented a most attractive aspect against the backdrop of forested hills, but there was no other sign of human habitation, and as we approached it down a winding road we were just in time to witness a color guard lowering the flag, then folding it and marching off.

Daniel stopped the auto in the trees.

"We're not going to walk from here?" I asked.

"Of course not. I just wanted to remove these ridiculous bandages," he said. "I'm not seeing the general pretending to be wounded when there is nothing wrong with me." He ripped them off and threw them into the backseat. Then he ran his hand over his hair to smooth it down before we set off again.

A sentry stopped us at the guard post and Daniel told him he had important information that could be given to nobody but General Funston.

"The general isn't here," the guard said flatly.

"When do you expect him to return?" Daniel asked.

"I couldn't say. He's needed everywhere at the moment so unless your information is of a vital nature I'd suggest you go away and come back later."

"I'm a senior police officer with serious charges to bring," Daniel said. "And I plan to leave this city tomorrow if the trains are running again."

"You could leave the general a note." He was still not impressed.

"Since this information involves two murder charges as well as high-level corruption, I hardly think it would be prudent to leave the general a note, as you put it." Daniel was sounding testy now. "Now if you'll let us in and direct us to the general's quarters, we'll be happy to wait for his return."

"You have no credentials. How do I know who or what you are?"

Daniel got out of the vehicle and stood face-to-face with the soldier. "Young man, in case you haven't noticed, there has been an earthquake. I am wearing a borrowed jacket. I saved nothing of my own, including my badge showing me to be a police captain from New York City. However if you care to send a wire across country, I'm sure they will be happy to verify who I am."

Daniel was a good four inches taller than the soldier and he had always had great presence. The soldier took a step backward.

"Very well, sir. I suppose I have to take you at your word. But as to the civilians with you . . ."

"Private, I am not leaving my wife and child unguarded in these circumstances. I am sure you can understand that."

The soldier didn't answer but stepped aside. "The general's house is at the top of the parade ground. One of those white houses. I just hope I don't get an earful for letting you on base."

"I'll take full responsibility," Daniel said. "And I'll commend you for doing your job so thoroughly."

He grinned at me as he got back into the automobile and we drove down into the Presidio. We crossed the parade ground where a platoon of soldiers were now marching toward one of the colonial-style buildings. Then we pulled up beside the row of houses. There seemed to have been relatively slight damage here, apart from red Mexican tiles that had fallen from roofs and the odd chimney lying beside a house as a pile of bricks. The sun had now sunk into the fog bank and the light was fading fast. Seagulls wheeled overhead and a parade of ships slipped silently out on the evening tide, toward the narrow entrance they called the Golden Gate. Tramp steamers, cargo ships, clippers in full sail—their prows cut through the silver water as they headed for the ocean beyond. They looked so small and frail from here and it was hard to picture them sailing to ports in the Orient or down to South America.

Then the light faded and we were left in darkness. A lamp glowed in one of the windows. Liam started fussing and I realized he hadn't eaten for quite a while. It was hard being dependent on others for our next meal, and even harder for a small child who hadn't had any milk for two days now. If only I had still been nursing him—that would have solved everything. My own stomach reminded me that I too had not eaten since lunchtime. I began to think it had been stupid of me to insist on coming with Daniel. What if the general didn't return until midnight? Daniel got out of the auto and took Liam for a walk, but there wasn't much to see in the darkness and he was becoming decidedly cranky.

"I don't think it was the wisest move to insist on coming with me," Daniel said. "What if we're stuck here for hours? The child needs to eat."

One thing I have never tolerated was someone else reminding me of failings I already knew about.

"Very well." I opened the door and got out. "I'll go and find the mess hall."

"Molly, you can't just walk around on an army base," Daniel said.

"You've just accused me of depriving my son of food. I'm going to rectify that."

And I strode off, ignoring his calls. When I reached the parade ground I encountered a couple of soldiers coming down the steps of one of those colonial buildings. I went right up to them and they reacted with surprise at being approached by a strange woman

"I'm sorry to trouble you," I said. "But my husband has a meeting with General Funston. However the general hasn't shown up yet. We've been waiting for hours and I've a baby boy with us who needs to eat something. I don't suppose you'd be kind enough to raid your mess hall and bring us something to eat? Anything would do—a crust of bread, a piece of fruit."

"Stay there," one of them said. "I'll see what I can do."

I waited and soon he came back with a plate containing a sausage, mashed potato, and boiled cabbage. "The best I could do," he said. "I don't know if your child can eat any of this but it's what they're serving in mess tonight. We're on short rations too as our supplies have gone to feed the city."

I thanked him kindly and returned triumphant. Liam ate the mashed potato and cabbage with relish while Daniel and I divided the sausage. With food in his stomach Liam fell asleep on my shoulder. The night turned chilly with a cold breeze blowing off the water. The fog crept in again. I don't know how long we waited, but it seemed like a long while. Eventually, though, a pair of auto headlights cut through the night and a vehicle came to a halt beside us. The driver got out, went around to open the passenger door, and General Funston himself stepped out. Daniel went to intercept him as he headed for one of the white houses. I only heard snatches of their exchange as the wind was now blowing strongly, but Daniel came back to me. For a dreadful moment I thought the general had refused to see him but Daniel opened my door.

"The general has invited us to come in," he said.

We went up the steps and were greeted by a woman.

"I'm Eda Funston," she said. "Do come in."

"Daniel Sullivan. My wife, Molly, and son, Liam."

She smiled at Liam, who was now stirring and looking around with interest. Then she led us through to a most interesting living room, its walls decorated with spears and ceremonial blankets and other primitive objects.

"From my husband's many campaigns," she said, waving a hand to the walls. "I can't tell you how relieved I was when he received this posting back to the good old U.S.A. and I didn't have to contend with snakes and insects and unbearable heat."

"It must be hard being an army wife," I said. "My own husband is a police officer and that's not easy either."

"I'm sure it's not." She looked at me with compassion. "And you were both injured in the quake, were you?"

"Only slightly," I said before Daniel could deny this.

"Was your home destroyed?"

"We are just visiting here from New York and I was able to rescue a few items of clothing so we're luckier than most . . ." I broke off as General Funston himself entered the room.

"Now then, what did you say your name was?" he asked. "And what is this matter of grave importance?"

"Captain Sullivan, New York police," Daniel said. "Currently on assignment for the president." He turned to me. "And this is my wife . . ."

"We have met, General," I said. "Although I believe I looked a little different at that meeting. At the party at the Crocker house?"

He frowned then recognition dawned. "Mrs. Sullivan. Of course. You look rather battle fatigued. Sit down. Can I offer you a drink?"

"I wouldn't say no to a whiskey, sir," Daniel said. Funston went over to a sideboard and poured from a decanter. It all seemed so incredibly civilized after what we had gone through, almost like stepping into another world.

"And for you, little lady? A brandy, maybe?"

I didn't like brandy but I thought it might be beneficial given the circumstances. I nodded my thanks.

"I won't keep you long, General," Daniel said. "I know you must be exhausted and wanting your dinner. But I have information that can only be given to you. Information of the gravest nature."

General Funston handed me the brandy glass with a generous amount in it. Liam eyed it with interest so I put it down on a side table, well out of his reach, and held him firmly on my lap. This was not the kind of room to let him wander in.

"Information?" the general asked Daniel.

"What I am telling you is strictly confidential, General, but since you have imposed martial law here, you are the only one empowered to act upon it. It concerns corruption charges against the mayor, the city attorney, and the chief of police. I was sent here purportedly on another matter but was also instructed to make contact with a federal investigator who had disappeared. I did make contact. I learned that evidence had been obtained and the parties were to be charged in federal court on April 18."

General Funston had to smile at the irony of this. "A lucky escape, wouldn't you say?"

He looked at Daniel, shaking his head. "I think that any such charges might have to be dropped, given the circumstances. For one thing all evidence has probably gone up in smoke. City Hall is a blackened ruin. The Hall of Justice is no more. And furthermore these men are currently being hailed as heroes. Mayor Schmitz has been working tirelessly, going from camp to camp, raising spirits, promising to get the city rebuilt as soon as possible. Police Chief Dinan's men have been instrumental in getting people safely evacuated ahead of the blaze and then in helping to stop looting. I don't have the authority to arrest them, and I suspect that in the minds of the country current heroism will outweigh former corruption."

"There's more that you should know," Daniel said. "The federal investigator I told you about was murdered, by Chief Dinan's men. I don't know whether the chief was present at the time but I'd like to wager he ordered the attack."

Funston's eyebrow shot up. "You have proof of this?"

"I was with him," Daniel said. "We had arranged a meeting at a remote cliff top, because he feared for his life. I met him there. He started to tell me what he had uncovered. Suddenly men emerged from the darkness and we were both hurled over the cliff. I was luckier. I managed to grab onto a bush that held me. He fell face forward to the rocks below. They thought they had killed us both."

"Good God," Funston said. I heard an intake of breath from his wife.

"I climbed down to him but he was beyond help," Daniel said. "Then an idea came to me. We were about the same size and build and this man's face was battered beyond recognition. I changed identities with him. Removed his wallet and left my New York police badge in his pocket. Then I went into hiding."

Funston was still scowling. "And you say Chief Dinan was part of this?"

"As the men walked away one of them laughed. An unpleasant laugh of triumph." Daniel was looking at him, his face expressionless. "I heard that laugh again yesterday. It came from either Chief Dinan or his henchman."

There was a long pause. Liam had snuggled against me and was falling asleep.

"I do have another piece of evidence," Daniel went on. "I rescued the key to the safe-deposit box from the dead man. I presume there is evidence to support the corruption charges in that box."

"If the bank is still standing," Funston said with a grim smile. "If the contents of the boxes are not ashes by now."

Daniel sighed and nodded. "You may be right."

"You say you were sent by the president himself," Funston said. "I suggest you write all of this in a report and let him decide how to proceed. As I just said to you we need these men at this moment to prevent anarchy and despair. But it will be up to President Roosevelt if he wishes to reopen this case in the future, and if you are prepared to testify."

"Of course," Daniel said. "I have been a police officer all my life. Justice is paramount to me."

"Brave man. I like that." Funston nodded. "But you do understand that my hands are tied at this moment?"

"Of course." Daniel stood up. "We should be going. We have detained you long enough."

"Where are you staying?" Mrs. Funston asked.

"We've been sleeping in a borrowed automobile in the park," I said. "I was staying with Mrs. Rodriguez, but she has fled and her house has burned."

"Then why don't you stay here? We've an extra bedroom and I'm sure Frederick wouldn't mind . . ." She looked toward her husband for affirmation.

"By all means." General Funston nodded curtly, leaving me feeling unsure whether he was really welcoming us or not.

"Oh, no, sir, really we couldn't impose when you are so busy," I said. "We're planning to leave the city tomorrow if the trains are running again."

"I understand the track has been repaired and the first train came in today with more supplies," General Funston said. "So stay the night here, by all means."

"And in the morning if you'll have someone drive us to the ferry terminal, you will have the use of an extra automobile," Daniel said. "I'm sure you could use one."

"Absolutely. You're leaving it for us?"

"It wasn't ours," I said. "Its driver was shot for looting and we had to borrow it to outrun the fire. But it didn't belong to the dead man in the first place."

Mrs. Funston stood up. "Frederick, come and eat. And Mr. and Mrs. Sullivan—let me show you to your room, and then please join us for dinner."

After so much terror and hardship it was almost too much to bear.

I found tears welling into my eyes. A clean bed. Water to wash in. I retrieved the belongings I had salvaged from Bella's house and was able to change Liam into clean clothes before we laid him to sleep. I couldn't brush my hair because of the bandages. How I was dying to get rid of those clumps and tangles but I suspected I'd have to wait until we were back in New York City. And how sweet it was to think that I was actually returning home. We went down to join the general and his wife at their table. Pork chops and wine had never tasted so good. I was glad I had only taken a sip of the brandy because that one glass of wine was making me feel light-headed. We listened to tales of the campaign in the Philippines and we were being served coffee by a smart young batman when I remembered I hadn't told the general my part in the story.

"How well did you know Mrs. Rodriguez, General?" I asked him.

"I attended social functions at her home occasionally," he said. "Apart from that, I knew nothing about her."

I took a deep breath. "I don't know how to tell you this, but I found a body at her house."

"After the quake, do you mean?"

"No, before the quake. A man had been killed and stuffed into a trunk in her cellar. It was the night before the earthquake. I planned to tell Daniel and let him decide what to do in the morning. Only I was shaken out of my bed and then the nursemaid ran off with my son, so the murder was never reported."

He looked grave. "You suspect that Mrs. Rodriguez was responsible for this man's death?"

"I don't know. It was her home and this was the man who had bought her ranch and was paying her a visit. But she didn't seem pleased to see him. In fact she was distinctly agitated." I toyed with my coffee spoon. "So I have to believe that either she killed him, or had him killed, or one of her employees thought they were doing her a good turn by killing him."

"She had that large cowboy type in attendance, didn't she?"

"She did. And also a Chinese man."

"The cowboy—he went everywhere with her, but there was something wild about him, wasn't there? Something not quite civilized, if you know what I mean."

"I know exactly what you mean," I said.

"This is a tricky one." General Funston sucked through his lips. "We have a city with maybe five thousand dead. Mrs. Rodriguez's home is in ashes. The body will have burned with the house and with it any proof of who the person was and how he died. I don't like anyone getting away with murder but on this occasion shall we say I've got better fish to fry. And we may need Bella Rodriguez's money to rebuild the city."

I swallowed back the bad taste in my mouth. "So she'll go free?"

"We're under martial law. I've ordered my men to shoot looters on sight and I'm pretty sure unjust deaths have resulted, but I have to keep the peace no matter what. I'm afraid a civilian murder is outside my jurisdiction. And Bella Rodriguez was a great benefactor of the city, so one understood."

I looked him straight in the face. "You're a soldier. Murder comes easily to you."

"I assure you it doesn't, Mrs. Sullivan," he said. "I've regretted every man I've had to kill. But I've always believed I've been working for the greater good. And at this moment the greater good is keeping order in a place of utter devastation. And this is the West Coast. Order is different here. You'll be back in New York, where there is law and order. In many ways this is still the Wild West. Life is cheap. Winner takes all. That's just the way of it."

"Then I'm really glad we're going home," I said. I stood up, nodded my thanks to Mrs. Funston, and excused myself.

❧ Thirty-one ❧

U p in our room I tried to swallow down my frustration. Of course everything the general said was right. And it wasn't anything to do with me in the first place. What did I know about the circumstances? Señor Garcia might have been an evil person who had somehow threatened Bella or wronged Bella. But my innate sense of justice whispered to me that murder is always murder.

As I paced I must have slipped my hand into the pocket of my skirt. My fingers closed around something smooth and sharp. I pulled it out and stared down at a small photograph. It was the snapshot of Douglas and Lizzy Hatcher I had rescued from Daniel's suitcase. I had completely forgotten that I had it. Not that it would do us any good now. If Douglas Hatcher had really been in San Francisco, he would have escaped and moved on. Or been killed by the quake.

I stared at the picture again, holding it up to the flame of the lamp. Douglas Hatcher's proud and self-satisfied smile. And his wife looking down, embarrassed at having her picture taken. I stared again, looking harder. There was something about her that I recognized. But surely I had never met her. Then suddenly I knew what it was. Her hands were clasped into tight fists, all of the tension in her body revealing itself in those hands. And I knew where I had seen them before.

I stared down at the photograph, my heart thumping. The table that held the water jug and basin was covered in a dark cloth. I went over to it and held the cloth next to that colorless face. At that moment the door opened and Daniel came in.

"Molly, you were rather rude to our hosts," he said. "You have to understand that General Funston has to act within the limits of his mandate and . . ."

"Daniel, stop." I held up my hand. "I've just made an important discovery."

"Well?"

I took a deep breath. "You were originally sent to locate Douglas Hatcher," I said. "What if we weren't looking for a man all this time but a woman?"

He looked amused. "You're telling me Douglas Hatcher was a woman?"

"No. I'm suggesting that Douglas Hatcher is probably dead and the person we are looking for is his wife." I held up the snapshot. "This was in your suitcase. I stuffed it into my pocket when I discovered the body and then forgot about it until now. Take a look at it. Douglas and Lizzy Hatcher."

He took the photograph, studied it, and then said, "Well?" again.

"We both stayed at Lizzy Hatcher's house."

He laughed now. "Are you trying to tell me that Bella Rodriguez is really Lizzy Hatcher?"

"I'd like to take a bet on it," I said.

"But they are nothing alike." He was still smiling.

"I agree at first glance they bear no resemblance. But remember that Bella wears a black wig. She wears lots of face paint and lip coloring. And—the crucial clue that gave this away. I noticed that Bella always stood with her hands clenched into tight fists, like this. It's a sign of hidden tension, isn't it? Now look at the photograph. See her hands?"

He peered at it. "Yes, but . . ."

I took the corner of black tablecloth again and held it up beside the woman's face. "Can you picture her now?"

"Maybe." He sounded unsure.

"Daniel, it all makes sense now. Douglas Thatcher makes a killing selling phony land grants. He disappears. Years later Bella Rodriguez arrives in San Francisco. I didn't tell you but one of the things I discovered in her cellar was a trunk full of money. Thousands and thousands of bills. And I've just thought of something else—" I paused, putting this thought into order. "She claimed her husband's ranch was in New Mexico. But Señor Garcia was from Mexico proper. And she told me he had bought her ranch after her husband died. So what if they had fled to old Mexico—a place of little law, where few questions would ever be asked. And Douglas was content to hide out there, but Lizzy was growing tired of his bullying ways. Perhaps they went beyond bullying. Perhaps he beat her."

I started to pace now, warming to my story, putting pieces together. "And Tiny was their ranch manager and she turned to him for sympathy and maybe more. Together they planned to kill Douglas. They buried him on the property, sold the ranch, took the money, and came here. And Elizabeth turned into Isabella, Lizzy into Bella, a flamboyant Hispanic woman who bore no resemblance to Lizzy Hatcher."

I had been staring out of the window into the darkness as I spoke, but now wheeled back to face Daniel. "But they didn't count on Señor Garcia digging up the body. He said he'd been making improvements, building new barns. So he discovered Douglas's body and I'd wager he started blackmailing her. So she and Tiny had to kill him."

Daniel was still looking at me quizzically. "Great story, Molly. How would you ever prove any of it?"

"Have the Mexican police find Douglas's body?"

He shook his head. "After all this time Bella could easily say he died of natural causes. He fell from his horse and broke his neck. In fact she could deny any connection to him and we'd have nothing to link her to that past."

"Maybe we could persuade Tiny to talk if he thought he was going to hang for a murder?"

Daniel sighed. "I'm afraid the general is right. There is nothing we can do for now. We can keep an eye on her if she returns to San Francisco, but my hunch would be she'd take this opportunity to move away, probably with that trunk of money you saw. I'm sure she knew that Mayor Schmitz and his cronies were in hot water and she was closely linked to them. So like so many people she'd take her chances and disappear."

"You're prepared to give up so easily on everything?" I asked.

"No, not give up. Bide my time. We've escaped an earthquake and fire, Molly. I have one task at this moment and that is to get you and Liam home safely. After that I'll hand the matter over to John Wilkie and he can decide how he wants to pursue it."

He put a hand on my shoulder. I sighed and turned away from him.

"Molly, you can't always make everything right," he said. "The world isn't fair or just. You know that." When I didn't answer he turned me toward him and took me into his arms. "You were very clever to figure all this out. I stayed in her house and it never crossed my mind that the person I was looking for was under my nose. I am married to a brilliant woman."

I gave him a slap, but I was smiling. "Stop trying to butter me up with your Irish blarney."

"Come on," he said. "Let's go to bed. It seems like ages since I slept in a real bed, and next to my wife."

I needed no more urging.

When we awoke in the morning I felt full of excitement and optimism. This was the day we were going home. The ordeal was over.

254

We had survived. We ate a good breakfast of eggs and ham, drank welcome cups of coffee, and then borrowed a valise to pack our meager possessions. I thought briefly about that pink silk dress, the like of which I should probably never own again. But when you have been as close to losing loved ones as I had been you realize how unimportant possessions are.

The general had left before we were awake but we thanked his wife profusely and invited her to our house if ever they were to find themselves in New York. A soldier was sent to accompany us to the ferry building, and to drive the auto back. We set off. It was a clear, bright morning with a sky like blue glass overhead. The Bay glittered and the green hills on the other side looked serene and inviting. But as we drove into the city the clear light only accentuated the utter devastation. From Van Ness Avenue all the way to the Bay there were only blackened ruins where once there had been homes and businesses and churches and concert halls. Soot covered everything and flew up in a cloud as we drove past. Gangs of men were already working heaving bricks out of the streets and piling them onto wagons. I said a silent prayer that Daniel had not been press-ganged into joining them or who knew how long we'd have had to wait before we could go home. As it was we were to catch the next ferry. . . .

We bade farewell to our driver and stood on the dock, waiting for the arrival of the boat. Other refugees joined us, clutching bundles of rescued possessions. A nun supervised a group of children who stood, huddled close together, looking around fearfully.

"These poor mites all lost their parents," she said. "Either killed or just got separated from them. I'm taking them out of harm's way, up to Oregon, where they've been offered a refuge. But who knows if any of them will be reunited with their families? It breaks the heart, doesn't it?"

I nodded, unable to speak, and thinking how close I came to losing Liam. Daniel was holding him, pointing out the ship that had docked on a nearby pier and was now unloading crates and bales of supplies. The ferry came and we piled aboard with the other refugees.

Oakland station was also crowded. We learned that a train would be arriving in an hour, but it was only normal carriages, no sleeping cars, and we'd have to change in Denver, to get to Chicago. Since all we wanted was to be away, we bought two tickets and were lucky enough to find seats, while others had to stand.

In such crowded conditions we pulled out of the station. Luckily quite a few people disembarked in Sacramento and we were able to enjoy the view as the train huffed and puffed its way up the mountains of the Sierra Nevada. The peaks were still snow-clad and the late afternoon sun painted the snow pink in scenes worthy of romantic painters. More people disembarked in Reno and we were met by reporters as we tried to buy food at that miserable shack at the station. The station was full of them, waiting their chance to take the next train to San Francisco, to report on the events. When I was questioned about my own exciting earthquake experiences, I told them about chasing the nursemaid into Chinatown and being hit on the head and losing my son. They seemed enthralled. Just the sort of story they wanted; full of drama and the human touch. And to my astonishment they handed me ten dollars for sharing my story, much to Daniel's disgust. But as I pointed out, I'd lost a whole wardrobe of clothes, for the second time in two years, and every penny counted.

We ate cold beef sandwiches. Daniel drank a beer, I a glass of sarsaparilla. Liam had a glass of milk and the rest of the muffin Mrs. Funston had packed for him. Darkness was falling as we set off again across the high desert. Eventually Liam fell asleep on Daniel. I was feeling restless and went for a walk. At the end of the last carriage I stood out on the little balcony, feeling the cold wind on my face and watching the moon rising over high desert and distant mountains. Snow still clung in hollows and there was no light, no sign of human habitation in any direction. The feeling of remoteness and loneliness swept over me as well as a great longing to be home and safe. How many years had my life been tinged with danger? Ever since I fled from Ireland and found myself on Ellis Island facing a handsome police captain who wanted to arrest me for murder.

I was tired of it. I wanted a normal family life. I wanted more children and to watch them grow up safely. At last the cold got the better of me. I returned to the warmth of the train car and started to make my way back to my seat. As the train lurched more violently than usual I had to grab onto the back of a seat. I was almost thrown onto the woman sitting there. I looked down at her to apologize. I started to walk on, but then I turned back and slid into the seat beside her. She was an older, grandmotherly type with gray hair and round spectacles. And she was knitting. She nodded and smiled to me.

"Lizzy Hatcher, I presume?" I said. "Or should I say Bella Rodriguez?"

❧ Thirty-two ❧

She gave me a puzzled smile. "I'm afraid I don't know what you're talking about. The name is Minnie Fenway."

I grinned. "Oh, that's right. They mentioned you originally came from New England. I'd forgotten that. You must be more creative with your choice of names, Mrs. Hatcher."

I saw her give a swift glance at our fellow travelers but they were either reading or settling down for a long night. There was nobody within hearing distance but she lowered her voice anyway. "I am Minnie Fenway, widow of Arthur Fenway of Massachusetts," she said. "And I defy you to prove differently."

"And what happened to Bella Rodriguez?"

"I understand that she died in the fire," she said smoothly, "like so many other poor souls. I'm glad to see you survived, my dear."

"And where is Tiny? Has he become a Bostonian too?"

"Tiny is no more, so I heard," she said. She was still speaking in that sweet, soft voice. "It would seem that Bella sent him back to the house to check on certain things for her, but soldiers saw him coming out of the house and he was shot for looting. Such a tragedy."

"And did Bella happen to tip off the soldiers that someone was looting her house?" I asked.

She sighed. "He was becoming a burden. A nuisance. He had outlived his usefulness."

"How conveniently you dispatch with people who are a nuisance to you," I said.

There was a swift flash of wariness on her face.

"I know all about Señor Garcia," I said. "I went down to the cellar. Such interesting things you kept in trunks there."

"Alas, all burned beyond recognition now." She was still looking at me with cool gray eyes, completely confident, almost as if she was enjoying this.

"And so you're reinventing yourself yet again?"

"I had grown tired of San Francisco and its lack of civilization. I think I'll be quite content to buy a small house somewhere in New England and return to the society of my birth."

"No more the grand dame of society? Won't you miss that?"

"Perhaps. We'll have to see. Maybe I'll marry again. A better choice this time. An honorable gentleman, a cultured man with no wild ideas."

"You were obviously attracted by Douglas Hatcher and his wild ideas once before," I said.

"I was young and foolish." She even smiled at this. "I'd grown up sheltered, raised by two maiden aunts. Can you wonder that I was swept off my feet when I met a man like Douglas during my last year at Radcliffe College? He always was a good talker, a complete showman. Here I was, the shy girl from Massachusetts. And he the flamboyant Texan. He told me about his ranch and his cattle and the prospects for oil. I ran off and married him. I had a small inheritance from my parents and Douglas got through that very quickly. That's when I found that the ranch and the cattle and the oil were all lies. He had nothing except big ideas."

She had been staring down at her hands. Now she looked up at me, expecting me to understand.

"I also found out quickly enough that he was a bully with a terrible temper. When he was crossed in any way he'd lash out. He thought nothing of knocking me clear across the room. He threw a knife at me more than once and pointed a gun at me."

"Why didn't you leave him?"

"I had nowhere to go," she said simply. "The aunts died. There was no one else, and no money. Douglas made sure I was completely subservient, and dependent." She sighed. "Then he came up with this grandiose scheme. A way to make ourselves rich beyond our wildest dreams, he said. I didn't really believe him but I was prepared to go along with it. If we were rich, I'd have a way to escape. And if he was caught by the police, I'd claim to know nothing about it."

"But it worked," I said. "He made a fortune and escaped with it."

She nodded. "And I thought, stupidly, I suppose, that we'd travel, lead the life I'd dreamed of. But instead we fled to Mexico and he bought the ranch he'd always wanted and was content. Can you imagine? Miles from anywhere in a country of peasants? I suppose I hoped we'd have children but it never happened. And I saw my life slipping away in misery. Then he hired Tiny."

"You finally had an ally."

"He wasn't the brightest lad," she said, "but willing. And I was kind to him. He came to worship me, following me around like a dog. I don't think anyone had ever spoken to him nicely in his life before. I think he was also attracted to me in a way, but there was never anything physical between us. One night Douglas got drunk and started to knock me around. Tiny came to my rescue and killed him. Shot him in the back. I was stunned. Horrified. Then I realized my luck. I was free. I could escape. Become a new person. We buried Douglas. I sold the ranch. Nobody asks too many questions in Mexico. So we escaped."

"You took Tiny with you."

She shrugged, as if she was trying to shrug me away like an annoying insect.

"I had to," she said at last. "He knew everything, didn't he? We went first to Mexico City and I admired the flamboyant women there—so fashionable and European-looking. So I became Bella Rodriguez. Black wig, face paint, lovely clothes. And when I was ready we moved to San Francisco. There was still plenty of Douglas's money to live the way I'd always dreamed. I invested it in thriving businesses and made even more. Everything was going exactly as I had planned."

"Until Señor Garcia showed up?" I suggested.

She frowned. "He bought the ranch and when he was making renovations he dug up Douglas's body. And enough evidence to realize he had been shot in the back. He searched me out. He found me in Mexico City and threatened to go to the police. I paid him off, but he traced me to San Francisco. I don't know how. I can't tell you what a shock that was."

"So Tiny took care of him too."

She nodded. "Tiny would do anything for me. Poor Tiny. Such a shame, but necessary."

"You're telling me all this so calmly," I said. "And yet you've been responsible for several deaths."

"Not me, my dear. I am not my brother's keeper. If my employee was a trifle impulsive and violent, then he met a just end, didn't he?"

"An end to which you sent him," I replied. "Are you not afraid that I'll go to the police myself?"

"With what? There is no proof that I was anyone other than Minnie Fenway. It will be assumed that Bella Rodriguez died in the quake or the fire. So many people did, after all."

She was still looking at me calmly, but I thought I detected a glint of satisfaction, almost triumph in her eyes.

"I'm sorry for you though, my dear," she said reaching across to pat my knee. "I liked your husband. It must be a great loss for you."

"And yet I suspect that you were the one who tipped off the police that Daniel was going to the cliff top at Lands End. Am I right? Ellen told me there was always a man waiting outside your house to follow him."

She looked away. "I said I'm truly sorry for your loss. I hope you'll marry again and have a happy life in New York City. Now if you'll excuse me, I'm rather tired of talking." She went back to her knitting. When she sensed that I hadn't left she said, "What are you waiting for? You've said your piece. You've been a clever girl, I'll grant you that. Now please leave or I'll have to summon the conductor and tell him that you're annoying me."

"I'd be careful about summoning anybody, if I were you," I said. "You see, you said I had no proof, but I do. I went down to your basement and found my husband's valise down there. And I wondered, why would you have claimed you turned it over to the police if you didn't have something to hide? And if you'd looked more carefully in that case you'd have found a photograph of Douglas Hatcher and his wife." I saw her blink but she said nothing. "I have that photograph," I went on. I was rather enjoying myself now. This woman calmly sent my husband to his death. She deserved no mercy. "And I have something else. One of Bella's wigs. I went back to the house and I found it, and rather naïvely I thought that you might be missing it and want it when I found you again." I actually smiled. "Oh dear, Bella. I bet you're rather annoyed that you invited me to stay, aren't you?"

Her eyes narrowed. "You stupid woman. No one will believe you. They'll think your mind snapped in the double tragedy of the earthquake and your husband's death. You'll be locked away in an insane asylum for your wild ideas."

"One more thing I failed to mention," I said, standing up now and looking down at her, my face an expressionless mask. "My husband isn't dead. He survived that fall down the cliff by a miracle. It was the man with him who died. In fact my husband is currently sitting a couple of cars further down this train and when we get back to civilization I think we'll find that his word carries a lot of weight."

I didn't wait for her reply. I simply went back down the train to our seats.

Daniel sat in silence after I recounted the conversation to him.

"So what will you do?" I asked. "Can you not simply walk down the train and arrest her?"

"I wish it were that simple," he said. "She is not in New York City, which is the extent of my jurisdiction. To arrest her I would have to present my case to a local magistrate, and I don't personally think it would be an easy case to prove. A small snapshot and a wig? Would they be enough to prove that she was once Lizzy Hatcher and then Bella Rodriguez? And when you give the facts, she was personally not responsible for the land fraud or the deaths of her husband and Señor Garcia. She could claim to be an innocent bystander to both."

"But, Daniel, she was living high on the hog from stolen money. She confessed to me that she was responsible for having Tiny shot. And she was partly responsible for your attempted murder and the murder of your federal agent colleague. She is a cold and calculating woman."

He held up his hand at my onslaught. "Calm down, Molly, please. Of course I shall make my report to Mr. Wilkie. It will be up to him whether he chooses to send out agents to apprehend her. I am more concerned that the bigger fish are going to walk away scot-free. Mayor Schmitz, Abe Ruef, and Chief Dinan. From what General Funston said it seems highly probable that they will never now face corruption charges. They will emerge as heroes and that sticks in my craw."

I wasn't exactly surprised to find that Minnie Fenway, also known as Bella Rodriguez, also known as Lizzy Hatcher, had left the train at one of the stops we must have made during the night. If she ever showed up in Massachusetts, the police would be waiting for her. But my betting was that she'd stay on in the lawless West, inventing yet another identity for herself.

❧ Thirty-three ❧

Smoky, dirty, noisy New York City had never looked so inviting as we drew into Grand Central. Daniel hailed a cab and soon we were clip-clopping down familiar streets. While we had been away spring had burst forth in full glory. The sycamore trees were in full leaf. There were flowers in those tiny squares of garden that appear miraculously tucked between buildings or outside churches. Store windows displayed summer bonnets. There was an air of gaiety as mothers pushed buggies and older ladies walked their dogs. "Summer is coming," everything seemed to be shouting. The harsh winter was over and forgotten. I felt tears come to my eyes when I realized how easily I could have returned home a widow, with no hope and no future. I glanced at Daniel, seated beside me with Liam on his lap. The nightmare was over.

At last we turned into our own dear Patchin Place. The cab came to a halt.

"You can walk the rest of the way, can't you, sir?" he asked Daniel. "You don't seem to have much in the way of bags."

"We lost everything in the earthquake and fire in San Francisco," I said as the cabby climbed down and then held out a hand to me.

"Did you really? Well, I'll be blowed. Of course we read about it in the newspapers. Was it really as bad as they tried to make out?"

"Utter devastation," I said. "A whole city in ruins and who knows how many lives lost."

"Do you think they'll ever recover?" he asked.

"They'll rebuild," Daniel said. "There is tremendous spirit out West. It's my betting that they'll build it up bigger and better."

The cabby passed Daniel our pathetic bundle of odds and ends. Daniel put Liam down and took his hand. Liam had been looking around with apprehension and suddenly gave a squeal of delight. He broke away from Daniel and set off down Patchin Place on his own. He too realized that we were now home and safe. I was about to put the key in our own front door when the door opposite opened and Bridie came out. She too gave a cry of joy and rushed up to us.

"You're safe," she said. "You came back." Tears started streaming down her face. "They said that San Francisco was all destroyed and so many people had died and we didn't get any news from you so we thought that you'd died too."

"We sent a letter, my darling, but it must have been held up," I said. "The wires were down so there was no way of sending a telegram to let you know." I hugged her to me and we stood there, locked in each other's arms, both of us crying. Liam tugged at our skirts wanting to be picked up. Bridie had just bent down to embrace him when Gus came to the front door.

"Who are you talking to, Bridie?" she asked, then her face lit up. "It's them, Sid. They're home. They're here!" she shouted. "Oh my darlings. You don't know how we've worried about you. Why didn't you write more often, you wicked girl? Here we were imagining all kinds of catastrophes and then we heard about the earthquake."

"There were all kinds of catastrophes," I said. "And we are really fortunate to make it out alive. But we'll tell you all about it when we've had a chance to change our clothes and have a bath. It feels as if I've been living in this dress for weeks and poor little Liam . . ."

Liam was now in Bridie's arms. Gus went over to give him a kiss. He resisted at first as if he couldn't quite remember her.

"What? You don't remember your Auntie Gus, who makes gingerbread and things for you?" she demanded.

Then his face broke into a smile and he allowed her to take him from Bridie. "Let's go and see Auntie Sid," she said.

"How is she?" I asked. "How is her leg?"

"What happened to Miss Goldfarb's leg?" Daniel asked. I realized that I had not had a chance to tell him. There had always been more pressing and immediate worries.

"Sid broke her leg skiing," I said. "She tried to go down the most difficult slope and took a tumble."

"Typical," Daniel said. "But I don't suppose she'll ever learn."

"I'm sure she won't," Gus said. "She's already planning our trip to India for when she is fully recovered. She does so yearn to ride an elephant."

She carried Liam into the house, calling, "Sid. Look who I have found."

And it was another happy reunion.

Later, when we were bathed and changed into clean clothes, we went across the street to their house for coffee and cake. They were agog to hear about the earthquake and fire, and we related all our experiences to them.

"Molly, you should write a book about this," Sid said. "The world would love to hear from a survivor."

"I'm not much of a writer. Not like you," I said.

She waved her hands excitedly. "Then we'll write it together. You will tell your story to me and we'll put it into words together. I have been feeling so trapped and frustrated with this broken leg. It will give me a challenge. Something exciting to do."

I glanced across at Daniel, who had said very little since we got home.

"Why not?" he said. "You have experienced more of the earth-quake and fire than many people. And it will help you to get back to your old life. You shouldn't be too active until you have allowed your head wound to heal properly. You've already had to do far too much."

"There you are. Your husband agrees," Sid said. "What a splendid time we shall have."

"We should invite my mother to come to stay and help with the work until you are fully recovered," Daniel said. "You are still clearly weak, aren't you? And dizzy, and headaches?"

"I'm fine, Daniel," I said quickly, thinking that having my mother-in-law in my house would cause more headaches than I was currently experiencing. In truth I didn't yet feel like my old self—definitely a little frail, but that was hardly surprising after all I had been through.

"And you, Captain Sullivan," Gus interjected. "We haven't yet heard your part of the story."

"My part?" I saw Daniel give a wary look in my direction.

"Why you were called to California in the first place and whether you really did summon Molly with that extraordinary letter."

Daniel shook his head, smiling. "I'm afraid I was on a mission that must remain secret, but I did indeed want Molly to join me, and very much regretted my rashness later. I would not have put her through such grief and torment for anything in the world."

"Then we are not to be privy to this enigma?" Gus asked.

"I regret no," Daniel said. He glanced at me again. Clearly I was not to divulge that Daniel had been pushed over a cliff and had to hide, disguised as an elderly professor. I would never be able to tell my friends of my utter anguish and despair for those two awful days I believed my husband to be dead. Nobody would ever know what that felt like. But then I realized that this was a good thing. Bridie sat on the rug at my feet, keeping Liam amused. I would not want her to hear that she had almost lost both of her guardians. She already worried enough about her missing father and brother. Let her at least feel secure here.

"But was the business successfully concluded? Was all put right in the end?" Sid asked.

"Let's just say that the earthquake put an end to my investigation and I doubt now that it will ever be satisfactorily concluded," Daniel said. He stood up. "We should be getting home," he said. "We have so much to do."

"You'll dine with us tonight?" Gus said. "You won't want to be rushing out to buy supplies and I have a fine chicken roasting in the oven."

"You're very kind, but I think . . ." Daniel began.

"We'd love to," I cut in. "You just said you don't want me running around too much and it's late in the day to go out to buy food."

"I'll go for you," Bridie said. "I've been running errands for the ladies. I'm turning into a good shopper, aren't I, Miss Walcott?"

"You certainly are, Bridie. And I must tell you, Molly, what a joy she has been to us. I've introduced her to *Jane Eyre* and Dickens and I started to teach her to paint. . . ."

Bridie gave me a shy smile.

"It sounds as if you won't want to come home to our boring house," I said, smiling back.

"Oh, yes," Bridie said. "I do want to come home."

❦ Thirty-four ❦

I can't tell you how wonderful it was to wake up in my own bed with the sun shining on the dear, familiar wallpaper and the sound of Liam babbling happily to himself in his crib in the back bedroom. Daniel lay still sleeping. I looked down at him, lying serene and peaceful, and my heart surged with love for him. As I brushed a dark curl from his forehead I thought how nearly I had lost him. I doubted I would ever fully get over it. Feeling my light touch Daniel opened his eyes and smiled at me.

"You look so beautiful," he said.

"So do you." I had to laugh.

"Kiss me," he said, and for a while we were too busy to talk.

Bridie had shopped for basic foodstuffs the afternoon before so I was able to make us scrambled eggs and coffee. I don't think either of those items had ever tasted better. When we had breakfasted Daniel announced his intention to go straight off to the telegraph office to wire Mr. Wilkie.

"I'll wait awhile to let the police department know I have returned," he said. "No sense in rushing things."

"Are you hoping that Mr. Wilkie might offer you a full-time job?" I asked, with a tinge of anxiety in my voice.

"We'll cross that bridge when we come to it," he said. "And, Molly, I'd like you to see a doctor today. You had a nasty blow to the head and I want to make sure you're healing well."

"I'm feeling much better now," I said. "A little dizzy occasionally but that's to be expected."

"And take it easy for these first few days." He wagged a finger at me.

"Daniel, I have been taking it easy on a train for five days now," I said. "I'm feeling fine. Honestly, I am."

"All the same, I'd like you to show that head wound to a doctor. Please do it today." He didn't wait for a reply, but left the house. Bridie went off to school and I had a pile of laundry to face. Only a small pile, I noted. The few items I had managed to rescue. Not my fine evening frock or Liam's sailor suit. It seemed that as soon as we took one step forward, it was then followed by two steps back. But at this moment, with all of us alive and well, I could not complain about the loss of a few possessions. I thought about those who had lost everything and were now camping in tents in chilly Golden Gate Park, wondering how they could possibly get on with their lives. I thought about Mr. Dennison, the man who had plunged to his death beside Daniel, and wondered if he had a wife and family, waiting to hear from him. And my thoughts went to Mrs. Endicott. I would have to steel myself to go and see her and tell her a lie. And Mr. Paxton— did he make it safely home to New York? I knew that Caruso and the stars of the opera had managed to escape on a ferry before the fire engulfed the whole of downtown San Francisco and would then presumably have taken a train back to New York. I only hoped he was with them. He had been very kind to me.

So after my morning chores I took Liam and we boarded the trolley going up Broadway. I remembered more or less where the Metropolitan Opera House stood. It had been pointed out to me once, in a most unlikely part of the city—on Broadway close to Macy's department store. And I had been surprised that the building was so ordinary. It was a square yellow brick edifice without adornment and would have passed for insurance offices had there not been a discreet marquee on Broadway, advertising the next performance. Liam enjoyed his trolley ride, pointing out things that attracted him—automobiles mainly. Clearly he was going to grow up like his father—fascinated by them.

As I watched his chubby face alight with joy I found it hard to believe how we had nearly lost him. How I had nearly lost my whole family. Our return to normality seemed like a miracle. I had almost gone past the opera house before I recognized it and had to walk back from the next stop. Then I paused outside, looking up at it. It was a building of many floors, many windows, but the only entrance I could see was into the theater itself, and clearly Mr. Paxton didn't work there. Nevertheless I went in through the glass doors. The box office was open and someone was in the process of buying tickets. I tiptoed past and stepped into the theater foyer. Then from beyond golden curtains I heard a wonderful sound—a sublime voice raised in song. I crossed the foyer, opened the curtain across the doorway, and stepped into a darkened auditorium. Oh, my. I had never seen anything this grand in my life before. The only lights were on the stage but even that small amount of light lit up tier after tier, balcony above balcony of gilded opulence. And in the ceiling an enormous chandelier. On the stage a male and female singer were now rehearsing, dressed in ordinary street garb. I could have stood and listened all day. I had no idea opera was so wonderful and could see now why the whole world adored Mr. Caruso.

But Liam didn't share my sentiments and wriggled in my arms. I retreated before he let out a wail only to encounter a stern woman in black.

"What are you doing here?" she demanded. "The theater is closed to the public."

"I'm sorry," I said. "I came to see Mr. Paxton and I couldn't seem to find the right way in to his office. And the singing was so glorious I had to just take a peek."

Her expression softened. *"Aida,"* she said. "Opens next week."

"And Mr. Paxton?"

"Will be up in administration. Go around the corner to Thirty-ninth Street and you'll find the entrance there."

I thanked her and left reluctantly, those glorious notes floating after me. Maybe my trip to California would make an opera fan of me! I was directed to Mr. Paxton's office and was delighted to find him sitting at his desk, safe and sound. His expression showed that he was equally delighted to see me.

"My dear Mrs. Sullivan." He rose from his seat and came around to me. "I can't tell you how glad I am to see you. I have to confess that I worried about you all the way home on the train. To have lost your husband and then to have had to endure that awful quake. And yet look at you—as fresh and healthy as if it had never happened."

"I was lucky, Mr. Paxton," I said. "We survived the quake and found my husband alive."

"Alive, after all?"

"Yes. It was a case of mistaken identity. A body found at the bottom of the cliffs was falsely identified as that of my husband." I did not elucidate any further.

"What a relief for you."

I nodded. "When I saw that awful destruction and what other poor souls had to endure I feel truly blessed. And you—you were able to escape with the rest of the company before the fire struck?"

He smiled. "I was given the task of transporting our stars to safety. I commandeered vehicles and whisked them away without a scratch, I'm glad to say. We were on a ferry to Oakland before there was any hint of fire. We had to wait until the train lines were repaired but we stood there across the Bay and watched the city burn. What a terrible tragedy, wasn't it?"

"And Caruso?"

"Is already on a ship heading back to Italy. He vows to come to America no more. Let us all hope he will change his mind."

I left him then, promising to invite him and his wife to dine with us as soon as we were settled. How lucky I was that he was assigned to share my compartment. There really are some good people in the world.

On the trolley back my thoughts turned to the other, less pleasant duty I had to fulfill. Mrs. Endicott. On the train ride home I had wrestled with what I should say to her. Should I let her think that her husband died in the earthquake and fire, or should I tell her the truth—that he had another family and would never be returning? Would I want to know that Daniel was alive and well, but with another woman, rather than mourning his death? Usually I am on the side of truth, but I wanted to spare that frail and delicate lady as much grief as possible. Let her think that her husband had died. Let her at least continue to live comfortably on the proceeds of his businesses. But when we approached Fourteenth Street I found myself hesitating. What could I say? That I knew he was dead? That I had been told he perished? In which case by whom? So I continued on the trolley to my own stop. Mrs. Endicott would have to wait until I had my story straight and I had thought out the kindest way to spare her pain.

When Bridie came home from school I did as Daniel had asked and went to the doctor's surgery, leaving her to look after Liam. I told him what had happened to me. He tut-tutted and examined the wound on the back of my head, which had now healed nicely.

"You're a lucky woman," he said. "That was quite a blow. Are you still experiencing unpleasant symptoms?"

"A little nausea and dizziness," I confessed. "The occasional headache."

"To be expected. I want you to take things easily and rest as much as possible."

"That's what my husband says."

"Sensible man. I like to hear of a man who has his wife's best interests at heart," he said.

I had to smile at this. I didn't tell him that my husband had summoned me across the continent into a scene of danger.

273

"While you're here, I'd better examine you," he said. "I don't think I've seen you since I delivered your child. What was that—two years ago now?" He listened to my heartbeat, poked and prodded, and then said, "The dizziness and nausea. Is it possible that you are expecting another child?"

I stared at him. "No. I don't think. . . ." Then it struck me. I hadn't exactly had the most regular monthly cycles since having Liam and I hadn't had an unwelcome visitor since . . . since before Daniel left for California. I had been too overwrought while I had been in San Francisco to have noticed such trivialities. And I remembered the queasiness on the train.

"Do you think I'm expecting?" I asked.

"Let's just say I'd like to examine you more thoroughly. Then we'll know."

Half an hour later I walked out of there with a big smile on my face. Not only were my husband and son safe but I had been given an added gift!

Daniel was gone all day. I waited impatiently for him to arrive home that evening. When he did I dragged him into the front parlor and had just shared the news with him when there was a knock at our front door. Daniel went to answer it and I heard him say, "Good heavens, sir. You got up here in a hurry."

"Caught the next train," said a voice that I recognized and I came out to see Mr. Wilkie standing in our hallway. "I can't tell you how relieved I was to get the news that you were still alive and had escaped from that hellhole. I was blaming myself for sending you there."

He came over to me and took my hands. "I must apologize to you, my dear Mrs. Sullivan, for putting your husband in such a precarious situation. Presumably you had no idea he was even in San Francisco, let alone trapped in the middle of an earthquake."

"Oh, but . . ." I began when Daniel cut in.

"Actually she did know because I sent her a postcard," he said firmly and deliberately, giving me a warning look. "So naturally she was extremely worried until I could send her a wire."

"It seemed like an eternity," I said. "I was so worried I couldn't even concentrate on my embroidery."

I watched Daniel trying to keep a straight face at this.

"You must lead a charmed life, Sullivan," Mr. Wilkie said as Daniel ushered him through to the back parlor.

"It certainly feels that way at the moment," Daniel said. He closed the door behind them, leaving me standing in the hallway fighting off frustration again. I went back to the kitchen and got on with preparing our evening meal. I had bought Daniel a steak to celebrate. I waited impatiently but it was a good half hour later that the door opened again and Daniel emerged with Mr. Wilkie.

"Regrettable, but inevitable, I suppose," Mr. Wilkie was saying. "But don't worry. We have the evidence. We'll try to retrieve that safe-deposit box. We'll get them when the time is right, you'll see."

"I hope so," Daniel said.

"And that other matter. You'll think about it then?" Mr. Wilkie asked as they shook hands.

"I'll think about it," Daniel replied.

It was as if I was watching a scene replayed. My heartbeat quickened. *Was Daniel being sent off on another dangerous assignment?*

"Good-bye, Mrs. Sullivan," Mr. Wilkie said. "And if you are ever interested, I am sure that I could make good use of your skills as well."

"Oh, no, thank you," Daniel said quickly. "She'll be too busy looking after the children."

And he opened the front door, reacting with surprise when he saw two people standing outside. One of them was Sid, now walking with the aid of crutches, and the other I recognized after a moment as Mr. Graves, who had insisted on interviewing me for his magazine.

"Molly, guess what?" Sid called to me before Daniel could say anything. "Mr. Graves published your interview and received such a positive response from so many people. You are deemed to be a champion of the women's movement. And when I met him today and he heard about your adventures in California he is determined to get the scoop on that story too." She looked up and appeared to notice Daniel and Mr. Wilkie. "Oh, I'm sorry, Captain Sullivan. Have I just interrupted something?"

"It's fine, Miss Goldfarb," Daniel replied. "Mr. Wilkie was just leaving. Let me find you a cab, sir."

And he bundled him off down the street before he could ask any more questions.

"You published my interview?" I asked. "Without telling me?"

Mr. Graves looked sheepish. "You were gone for an indeterminate amount of time and the material was good. Miss Goldfarb said you wouldn't mind . . ."

He broke off as Daniel returned to me. "What is this all about, Molly? Interview? Magazine?" he asked.

I smiled sweetly. "I can have my little secrets just as you do, Daniel Sullivan. And I'll be happy to recount my adventures in San Francisco, Mr. Graves. Just not right now. I'm about to cook my husband's dinner."

We parted company. Daniel followed me into the kitchen.

"So what did Mr. Wilkie want this time?" I asked. "He wants to send you off on another dangerous escapade?"

"No, he wants to offer me a job," he said.

"A permanent job? With him?"

"Yes."

"And it would mean moving away from here to Washington?"

"Yes."

"Leaving my friends and going to a new city?"

"Yes."

"And spending your life in constant danger?"

"Molly," he said, "I didn't say I'd take the job. I said I'd think about it. Discuss it with you. But if I'm going to be forced out of the police department here . . . well, it's good to have some alternatives, isn't it?"

"But Washington, and danger . . . you've a family to think of, Daniel Sullivan."

"I know. I'm quite aware of that."

I had a sudden idea. "It might not be so bad," I said. "After all, Mr. Wilkie did offer me a job too, didn't he? I'd rather like to get into the spy business. It could be fun . . ."

And I enjoyed watching Daniel's face.